THE HOUSE OF BROKEN BACKS

ACBT Books
LONDON

Copyright © 2014 Amy Cross

This book is a work of fiction. Names, characters, places and incidents are either the product of the author's imagination or are used fictitiously, and any resemblance to actual persons, living or dead, events or locales is entirely coincidental.

All rights reserved. No part of this book may be used or reproduced in any manner whatsoever without prior written permission.

First published: June 2014

Published by ACBT Books

ALSO BY AMY CROSS

The Joanna Mason Series

The Dead and the Dying
The House of Broken Backs
The Company of Angels *(coming soon)*

Thrillers

Ophelia
The Girl Who Never Came Back
Other People's Bodies

Horror

Asylum
Ward Z
The Night Girl
Devil's Briar
The Devil's Photographer
Darper Danver series 1
The Vampire's Grave

Dystopia / Science-Fiction

The Shades
Finality series 1
Mass Extinction Event series 1, 2 & 3

Fantasy / Paranormal

Dark Season series 1, 2 & 3
The Hollow Church (Abby Hart #1)
Vampire Asylum (Abby Hart #2)
Lupine Howl series 1, 2, 3 & 4
The Ghosts of London
The Werewolf's Curse
Grave Girl
Ghosts
The Library
Journey to the Library

Erotica

Broken Blue
Broken White

Contents

Part One: The Family Man
page 1

Part Two: Flames
page 61

Part Three: Burned
page 115

Part Four: Ashes
page 181

Part Five: The Paper Man
page 231

Part Six: Hunted
page 287

Part Seven: A Face in the Crowd
part 341

Part Eight: The Man Who Disappeared
page 389

THE HOUSE OF BROKEN BACKS

A JOANNA MASON NOVEL

AMY CROSS

Part One

The Family Man

Prologue

"What was that?" she asks suddenly, looking over at the window. "Joe, did you hear something?"

Keeping his eyes fixed on the TV screen, Joe tries to ignore his wife's question. It's getting late, and he's used to the woman's constant paranoia. Ever since they moved to the new house, at the end of a dirt road in the middle of nowhere, he's had to endure her constant requests to 'go check it out' every time Kath hears even the slightest sound. It's nothing. It's always nothing. He's got more important things to do, like watch the news or pick his nose or just stare at the screen.

"Joe," she says after a moment. "I heard something. I think there's someone out there. I mean it this time."

"There's no-one out there," he says glumly, taking a sip of stale beer but still not looking away from the TV.

"I heard someone," Kath continues, her voice filled with concern. "This isn't like last night, Joe. I definitely *heard* someone. Go check it out."

"You always hear someone," he replies. "There's never anyone out there."

"This time I *heard* someone," she says, glaring at him with barely-concealed annoyance. "Joe Wash, are you gonna go and check or do I have to do it myself?"

"Door's right over there," Joe mutters, although he immediately realizes that he probably should have been less sarcastic. Grunts normally do the job, and the last thing he wants is a conversation.

"My God," Kath says, wheezing as she lifts herself up from the armchair and starts limping across the room. "There was a time when men were only too willing to grab the shotgun and go check the view from the porch. Not today, though. Not in this house, anyway. The only time you're ever gonna notice anything is if it happens on that goddamn TV. I thought I married a real man."

"Moved you out to a farm, didn't I?"

"And for what? It's not like you use the land."

"Huh," Joe replies, barely even listening.

"What if it's a murderer?" Kath says as she gets to the door. "Or a coyote?"

"Could be," Joe says quietly.

Sighing, Kath peers out the small glass panel at the top of the door. "Why'd you have to get frosted glass, anyway?" she asks after a moment. "Can't see a damn thing. We need a peephole, Joe. Why can't you get us a peephole? Go down the store some time and buy a goddamn peephole!"

"I'll do it Saturday," he mutters.

Sighing again, Kath limps over to the window, pulls the curtain back and takes a look outside. "I can't see anything," she says eventually. "Just the porch light and the porch and then darkness."

"That's 'cause there's nothing to see," Joe replies, watching as the weather report starts. "Nothing to see and no-one around for miles." His lips continue to move as the hot young weather-girl comes onscreen, but this time he keeps his thoughts to himself.

"There could be a gang of mass murderers out there for all you know," Kath says, turning the latch to unlock the door. "I don't know why I let you persuade me to move out here. It's not like this land's any good for anything; hell, if it was, your family would've made a go of it by now instead of letting you rent it for a couple of peanuts a month." She pulls the door open. "I'm not cut out for -" she starts to say before stopping suddenly and letting out a scream.

"What the hell is wrong with you now?" Joe shouts, hauling himself to his feet so fast that he's momentarily a little light-headed.

"Oh my God!" Kath shouts, taking a step back as a bloodied, painfully thin young woman slumps through the doorway and lands on the welcome mat, groaning with pain.

"Where the fuck did she come from?" Joe asks as he stumbles around the sofa and makes his way over to the door, pushing Kath out of the way before crouching down next to the woman and immediately checking her pulse. "She's alive, alright," he says, glancing out at the darkness that surrounds the house. "Who the hell is she?"

"Check for coyote scratches," Kath says urgently.

"There's no coyotes for miles," Joe replies. "Stop with all the crap about goddamn coyotes!"

"Who is she?" Kath asks, taking another step back. "Joe, she's bleeding. Call an ambulance! Jesus Christ, look, she's hurt!"

Grabbing the girl's shoulders, Joe drags her inside and then kicks the door shut before kneeling next to her and brushing the matted hair from across her semi-conscious face. There are a couple of large gashes on her cheek, and a series of sore red lines run around her neck.

"Can you hear me?" Joe shouts, leaning down toward her ear. "Can you tell me your name?"

The girl whispers something.

"What was that?" Joe shouts. "I need to know your name!"

Again, the girl whispers something, but it's too quiet to make out.

"This blood's dry," Joe says, gently tapping the side of the girl's face before reaching up and turning the latch to lock the door. "Kath, call for help. Tell 'em we've got an injured girl out here. Tell 'em there's no sign of any major injury, but..." He stops as he notices thick, worn wounds around the woman's wrists and ankles, and for a moment he struggles to comprehend what he's seeing. Finally, he turns back to his wife. "Are you calling or not?" he shouts. "Jesus Christ, woman, this is an *actual* emergency! For once in your life, can you move your ass?"

"I told you I heard something," Kath replies, her hands trembling as she grabs the phone and dials 911. "I told you, but you wouldn't listen. I told you there was a noise, but you were more interested in that goddamn television."

"Yeah yeah," Joe says, looking down the girl's body, which is barely covered by scraps of a thin, faded beige cloth dress. Wiping his brow, Joe pauses for a moment, trying to think of the best thing to do. "You got through to someone yet?" he asks eventually.

"I'm on hold," Kath hisses.

"Did you dial the right number?" he asks. "They don't put people on hold when you need an ambulance."

"Well they are right now!" she shouts.

"She's got a fever," Joe replies, running his hand over the girl's brow before checking her pulse again. "Her heart's weak," he adds. "She's in a bad way. Look at her skin, she's so pale." He pauses. "Where the hell did she come from? There's nothing for miles. Nearest building's that gas station on the interstate, but there's no way she could've walked ten miles in this condition."

"I need an ambulance!" Kath shouts into the phone. "818 Sycamore, out on Dewey Farm! It's a young woman! I don't know what's wrong with her, but she's hurt!"

While Kath explains the situation, Joe looks down and sees that the woman's bare feet are covered in scratches and cuts, as if she's been walking for miles and miles. There are gashes around her ankles and lower legs as well; in fact, her whole body seems to have been through the wringer, and as Kath puts the phone down, Joe looks up at her with a sense of disbelief in his heart.

"They said twenty minutes," Kath tells him. "That's as fast as they can get out herE."

"You need to get a cold towel or something," Joe says, checking the woman's fever once again. "She's burning up. And get some water too." He runs a hand across her wrist. "My God, I've never seen anyone so thin. She's -"

Before he can finish, there's a faint banging noise out on the porch.

Joe and Kath look at one another, neither of them daring to say anything.

Seconds later, there's another knock, fainter this time, less certain.

"Who's that?" Kath mouths silently.

Another knock.

"It's okay," Joe says quietly, getting to his feet and grabbing a rifle from the closet. Hurrying to the window, he looks out at the darkness. "I can't see a damn thing," he mutters.

"You should've got a peephole," Kath says. "I told you, you should have -"

"It's okay," Joe replies testily, interrupting her. "Whatever it is, it's nothing I can't handle. Maybe it's just someone come to help."

"Someone come to help?" Kath replies, watching as Joe makes his way to the door and turns the latch. "What the hell are you doing?" she asks, her voice filled with panic. "You can't seriously be planning to open that thing! You have no idea who's out there!"

"Ain't nobody who can take me down while I've got this," Joe replies, checking his grip on the rifle before grabbing the door handle. "This is my property, and I'm not letting anyone act like they can have the run of the place." Pausing for a moment, he suddenly pulls the door open and aims outside, his finger poised on the trigger. At first, he doesn't see anyone standing in the doorway, but just as he's about to relax, he spots a frail, weak arm reaching up to the porch from the lawn.

"What is it?" Kath whispers. "Be careful!"

Joe nods cautiously as he steps through the door. Looking down at the edge of the porch, he sees to his surprise that there's a second girl on the grass, trying desperately to pull herself up onto the decking. Unable to quite process what he's seeing for a moment, Joe stares in stunned horror as the girl painfully attempts to haul herself up; finally, snapping out of his daze, Joe reaches down and grabs her arm, pulling her up the rest of the way.

"Oh my God!" Kath shouts from inside. "Another one?"

"Another one," Joe says, getting ready to drag the second woman inside before glancing across the lawn and freezing in his tracks.

"Joe!" Kath shouts. "Get back inside! Now! It's not safe out there!"

"Holy shit," Joe whispers, letting go of the second woman and walking to the edge of the porch, with his rifle raised as if he expects trouble at any moment.

"Joe!" Kath shouts. "What is it? What the hell's going on out there?"

Unable to draw his gaze from the horror unfolding in front of him, Joe finally manages to step down off the porch. His wife is still calling out to him from inside, but Joe no longer has any interest in listening to her. He's too focused on the sight before him: the entire lawn, and much of the scrub-land further off, is covered in weak, crawling women, all of them groaning as they try to pull themselves toward the little house. There must be at least twenty of them, maybe even more, and they all look to have more or less the same clothing and the same injuries as the first girl.

"Jesus Christ," Joe says, as the women crawl past him, as if they've barely even noticed his presence. All he can do is stand and stare as more and more reach the house, their groans conspiring to fill the night air with an anguished cry.

Joanna Mason

"Joanna Mason," I say, annoyed that the dumb pharmacist doesn't recognize me after all the weeks I've been coming to his stupid store. "Joanna, not Joanne."

"Do you have a middle name?" the pharmacist asks, staring at the computer screen.

I wait for him to give me my pills.

"Do you have a middle name, M'am?"

"Yes," I say with a sigh.

"To confirm your identity," the pharmacist replies, his droning voice making clear that he doesn't really care, "I need to see government-issued identification and I need you to verbally confirm your middle name for me."

"Seriously?" I ask.

"Seriously."

I check over my shoulder to make sure that no-one's close enough to hear, before turning back to him. "Marilyn," I say quietly.

"I'm sorry?" he replies. "Can you repeat that?"

"Marilyn," I say, more firmly this time. "Joanna... Marilyn Mason."

"Joanna Marilyn Mason," he repeats as he types something into the computer, and I swear to God there's a faint smile on his lips. "And your identification?"

I hold up my old police card, hoping that he doesn't notice it expired a month ago.

"That's great," he replies, barely even paying attention to the card as he types some more details into the computer. Reaching over to the far counter, he grabs a large paper bag containing my seven separate prescription medications. "The first drug I'm going to be giving you this morning is -"

"I know," I say, snatching the bag from him. "I've been taking this stuff for three months now. Believe me, I know what pill to take when, and how many, and what color it'll turn me pee."

"I'm obliged by state law to list the dosage requirements," he says blankly.

"And I'm obliged to get going," I reply, turning and heading to the door. Ignoring the pharmacist's call for me to return to the counter, I push the door open and emerge onto a bright, busy New York street. Heading back toward the subway station, I stop by a trash can and dump the entire bag of pills. Nearby, a homeless guy is watching with keen interest.

"Help yourself," I tell him, before turning and walking away. I have no doubt that he'll be dumpster-diving for my pills by the time I reach the next corner, and I'm sure he'll get quite a high from the mixture of pain medication, cancer-fighting drugs and nausea-relief pills that Dr. Gibbs has been prescribing for the past few months. Of course, if he's smart he'll skip the drugs and sell them instead; I paid almost ninety dollars for this latest prescription, and I'm sure the pills are worth at least twice that on the street. Then again, if the guy was smart he probably wouldn't be going through street trash in the first place.

As I head around the next corner, I feel a buzzing sensation in my jacket pocket. Fishing my phone out from the detritus of candy and old tissues, I look at the screen and see that it's just Dr. Gibbs, doubtlessly calling to make sure that I'm following his instructions to the letter.

"I just picked them up," I say wearily as I answer the call. "You don't need to check up on me."

"I know you picked them up," he replies, his voice sounding a little faint over the line. "Believe it or not, Jo, I have the system set up so I get an email whenever you pick up any prescription that I write for you. Clever, huh? The wonders of modern technology."

"What's wrong?" I ask, glancing back around the corner and watching as the homeless guy lifts my bag from the trash. "Don't you trust me?"

"I prefer to keep tabs on you," he replies, "just in case the pills cause any memory issues." He pauses. "Has anything like that been happening, Jo? To be honest, I'm a little surprised you haven't got in touch to report any side effects."

"What can I say?" I reply. "I've got a strong gut and I'm not much of a moaner. I guess all the years of chemo and radiotherapy have toughened me up."

"Just make sure you stick to the regimen," he says. "Those pills are going to help you, Jo, but you need to take them at set intervals during the day. The instructions on the side of the boxes are there for a reason. Every time you skip a pill, you reduce the overall efficacy of the whole treatment. You have to keep the faith."

"That's why I never skip them," I lie, glancing across the street to make doubly certain that he isn't loitering nearby. It's been three months since I last took one of his goddamn pills, and I'm damn well not going to start now; the side effects were too strong and they made me feel like I wasn't myself, and I figure that if I'm gonna die anyway, I might as well keep my head clear during the time I've got left. "I appreciate the very personal and attentive care you're providing," I continue, "but I've gotta run. Police business, you know?"

"I thought you were still off duty?" he replies.

"I'm consulting on a case by case basis," I say, lying again. "Sorry, someone's waiting for me. Gotta go. Thanks for the call, though!" With that, I end the call and start scrolling through my list of received calls, finally finding the most recent call from Dawson.

Five weeks ago.
Five weeks.

What the hell's going on here? There's no way he hasn't needed my help, or at least my advice, in five whole stinking weeks, so why hasn't he called? I know for a fact that the department's swamped with cases, and I also know that they're gonna be missing my input like crazy. I don't want to get big-headed here, but the fact is, I'm pretty much indispensable to them. So what's going on? Why am I being completely ignored by the people who need me the most?

John

"Hey, honey!" I call out as I swing the front door shut. "I'm home!"

"Hey!" Sharon calls out from the kitchen. "The family man returns from his travels! Right on time, too! You hungry?"

"You have no idea," I reply with a smile as I place my briefcase on the chair and then proceed to hang my coat up. "Something smells delicious. What's cooking?"

"It's probably the pecan pie you can smell," she replies. "That's for dessert, though. First we've got lasagna to get through. It should be ready in about twenty minutes, and everything's under control, so you just need to put your fet up and relax. Do you want a glass of wine while we wait?"

"Sure," I say calmly as I head through to the kitchen. As usual, Sharon is slaving away in there, working like a trooper as she keeps her eye on five or six different things at once. It's always something of a miracle to see the way that she can keep so many plates spinning in the air at one time without dropping any; she might not be a real beauty, and she's certainly not been blessed with great intelligence, but Sharon certainly has her areas of expertise. She's one of the few women who really *do* belong in a kitchen.

"Hard time at work?" she asks as she pours us each a glass of wine.

"Tell me about it," I say with a weary sigh.

She wraps her arms around me and gives me a big hug. "We missed you," she says after a moment. "Two weeks is a long time for you to be gone, but I guess those insurance packages won't sell themselves."

"I have to give it the personal touch," I remind her. "Until the robots take all our jobs, anyway."

"I hope you're going to give me the personal touch later," she says, stepping back with a glint in her eye. "I still have a few wifely needs, you know."

"Of course," I reply with a smile.

"The kids are upstairs," she replies, handing me a glass and then raising her own toward me. "Cheers."

We clink glasses, before each taking a sip.

"Actually," I add, checking my watch, "I think I need to make a quick phone call to Barry in the accounts department. I'm sorry, honey, I know it's late, but those guys really need someone to crack the whip."

"It's fine," she replies, stepping closer and kissing my cheek. "I know you're a busy guy, John. Do what you need to do, but try to be done in twenty minutes, okay? You can always keep working after dinner. I know they can't manage without you sometimes." She kisses the side of my neck. "My big, important husband."

"And *I* can't manage without *you*," I reply, grabbing her by the waist and pulling her closer. "I hope the kids get to bed nice and early tonight," I add quietly. "I could really use some time to unwind. Just the two of us, you know?"

She smiles, and it's clear that she knows exactly what I've got in mind.

"I'd better go make that phone call," I add, carrying my glass of wine to the door before glancing back over at Sharon. For a moment, she almost looks appealing, although the thought of making love to her tonight is, at best, tolerable. "Back soon," I say, before heading out of the kitchen and along the corridor to my office. Once I've stepped inside and pushed the door shut, I walk over to the desk, take another sip of wine, and remove the latest burner phone from my pocket.

"Fucking assholes," I mutter as I manually type in Albert's number and then wait as the ringtone starts.

"It's me," he says as soon as he answers. "Who's this?"

"Who the fuck do you think it is?" I whisper, keeping my voice low just in case Sharon or the kids might overhear. "You'd better have good news for me, cocksucker, or I swear to God I'll rip your body into so many shreds, a light breeze'll be enough to blow you away."

"It's the Staten building," he replies, sounding stressed. "It's like I told you, there was a huge fuck-up. You remember that guy Manuel we hired to watch the girls? He completely flipped his shit and shot out from under us."

"Tell me what happened," I say, forcing myself to stay calm even though I want to vent my fury. My hand is almost shaking as I take a sip of wine.

"He gave a key to one of the girls -"

"Jesus Christ," I splutter, "I thought you'd checked him out!"

"I did!" Albert replies defensively. "I did! I swear, I did! It's like this fucking pang of conscience just came out of nowhere. Right? So he gave a key to one of the girls and then he shot through. Fortunately, I had a tracer on his truck, so I was able to get after him pretty damn fast." He pauses. "I caught up with him a few miles away and made sure he won't be a problem again."

"Where'd you put the body?" I ask.

"Usual place."

"And the girls?"

I wait for an answer.

"Albert," I say firmly, feeling a rising sense of panic in my chest. "Are the girls secure?"

"That's where it gets tricky."

I take a deep breath, followed by another sip of wine. "Go on," I say eventually.

"The job with Manuel took a little time," he continues, "and by the time I got back to the Staten building, the girls, well, most of them, were gone."

"Gone?" I spit. "What do you mean *gone*? Thirty-five girls can't just fucking disappear in the blink of an eye!"

"Seven were still there," he explains. "Just the ones who were too sick or scared to move. I dealt with them. Back of the head, like we agreed. They're totally out of the picture, but the other twenty-eight had already managed to get away. It wasn't easy to work out which way they'd gone -"

"Jesus Christ," I whisper, realizing that this fuck-up is several magnitudes greater than I'd feared.

"So it turns out," he continues, "they'd already reached this fucking farmhouse. Remember the one I told you about? The one that was abandoned a few miles away, and then some fucking hick asshole moved in with his wife? Well the girls went there. I guess they saw a light on or something. Pretty much all of them, together, and by the time I was in a position to do anything about it, the hicks had called the cops and the place was crawling."

"Oh," I say quietly, "you incompetent fuck."

"I torched the Staten building," he says. "That's the important thing, right? There's absolutely nothing to link any of this with us, or to any of the other sites. It's a clean cut." He waits for me to say something. "I mean, I know it's a big loss, but it's not the end of the world, right? We just have to accept that mistakes were made and see what we can do differently with the other buildings. We always knew that something like this might happen one day if we continued to expand."

"A mistake?" I reply, barely able to spit the words out. "Is that what you call this? Thirty million dollars worth of human capital escapes from one of our buildings and you think the word 'mistake' is enough to cover it?" I take a deep breath, trying to stay calm. "Not to mention the investment we put in. No, scratch that... The investment *I* put in. Some of those girls were in their late teens and early twenties, for God's sake. They were beyond ripe!"

"They won't talk," he continues. "They've got nothing to say. Hell, they can't even string together more than a few words, most of 'em, and it's not like they can describe us. They're just empty slabs of meat, dribbling along."

"I should never have given you so much responsibility," I reply. "There. That's the fucking *mistake* at the heart of all this. I thought you could fucking handle a few extra parts of the job."

"Hey," he replies, "it's Manuel who had the little moral moment and gave them a key -"

"And who hired Manuel?" I hiss. "Jesus Christ, Albert, you fucking moron!"

"Dinner!" Sharon shouts from the kitchen.

"Christ," I whisper, taking another swig of wine.

"What do you think we should do next?" Albert asks.

"Do?" I pause as a thousand ideas race through my mind. "First," I continue, trying to sound a little calmer, "we focus on cleaning up after ourselves. We have to double check that there are no loose ends that could tie us to this fuck-up, and then we have to look at our forward strategy and see what we need to change. We just lost a third of our production base, and call me old-fashioned, but I prefer to keep that base as high as possible. And then..." I pause as I hear the clinking of cutlery elsewhere in the house; I guess the table is being set for dinner. "Meet me at the drop house," I add eventually, before checking my watch. "I'll be there at midnight, sharp. Don't be late."

"Are you sure it's a good idea to meet right now?" he asks.

"Oh yes," I say firmly. "It's a very fucking good idea."

"I'm really sorry about this situation," he replies, "but you talked to Manuel, right? He seemed like a good guy."

"Maybe that's the problem," I mutter. "Good guys are the last thing we need. They tend to have consciences. Just... Midnight. Be there."

As soon as I've finished the call, I open the back of the phone and remove the battery, before swigging the last of the wine and trying to regather my composure. I always knew that delegating responsibility would lead to fuck-ups, but I never thought things would get quite this bad. I guess I made the mistake of trusting Albert, and now I can see that my original instincts were right all along: the only person I can trust is myself, and I need to view everyone else as expendable. This is, at heart, a one-man operation.

"Honey!" Sharon calls from the kitchen, as I hear the sound of the children running down from their rooms. "Dinner's up! Come and get it!"

Joanna Mason

"Hello," says a familiar, bitchy voice on the other end of the line. "Elaine Dawson speaking."

I open my mouth to say something, but the words catch in my throat. To be honest, it had never occurred to me that when I called Dawson's phone, Elaine might answer instead. Still, I can't exactly hang up; she'd inevitably realize it was me, and then there'd be a whole mess and she'd totally get the wrong idea. Taking another sip of beer, I pause for a moment and try to think of something polite to say to her. It's not easy.

"Hello?" she says again. "Joanna? Is that you?"

"Hi," I reply, signaling to the barman for another drink. "Yeah, it's Joanna Mason. I'm sorry, I thought this was Mike's phone."

"He's in the shower," she says with a confident, slightly mocking tone to her voice. "He left his phone by the bed. I don't normally answer his calls, but... Is there something in particular that you wanted, Joanna?"

"No," I reply, my mind racing as I try to work out how to cover my ass here. "I guess I was just calling to... check up on some... cases we were discussing a while back."

"Cases?" she says. "I was under the impression that you were still off work sick?"

"That's right," I say, counting out some notes for the barman as he places a beer in front of me. "The thing is, I've been off work for so long, I've actually started to think about some of the old cases that we never quite tied up, and I was just calling to see if Mike might be able to send me some documents by email." I pause, relieved that I've finally stumbled upon a reasonable explanation. Even the psychotically jealous Elaine should believe this one. "It's nothing urgent, really. I just thought it'd be a good way for me to pass the time and maybe contribute something. You know, my sick pay is building up, and I feel kinda guilty not doing anything to earn it."

"I'll be sure to let him know," she replies, with the very faintest edge of grit to her voice. "And how are you doing, Joanna? I heard you'd taken time off for health reasons."

"It's nothing important," I say quickly. "Trivial shit, you know?"

"It can't be *that* trivial," she replies, "not if you've been off for three whole months."

"I'm just gaming the system," I add, trying to sound like I'm making a joke. "You know, dragging my heels a little, coughing a few extra times, generally making myself seem sicker than I actually am. I mean, why go back to work when I can just sit around pulling sick pay, right?" I pause for a moment, keenly aware that I just contradicted myself; the truth is, I'm desperate to get back to work, but I need Dr. Gibson to sign off on the decision, and then I need Schumacher to make the first move. There's no way I can just go marching back into the office and ask if they need some extra help. I don't want to seem so goddamn desperate.

"Well as long as you're okay," Elaine says after a moment, sounding a little concerned. "Obviously, when Mike told me that you were off sick, I was concerned that..."

I wait for her to finish the sentence, but she seems to be leaving it hanging on purpose.

"You thought my cancer had come back?" I ask, keen to push her into uncomfortable territory.

"Well..."

"It hasn't," I lie. "I'm fine. It was a totally unrelated and completely non-life-threatening thing that just knocked me off my perch for a few months." I pause for a moment, feeling a little disturbed by the fact that for the first time in years, maybe even the first time ever, I'm talking to Elaine is if she's a normal human being rather than the spawn of Satan. "Don't worry," I add, "there's no need to start planning what to wear to my funeral. Not just yet, anyway. The worst thing is that I really miss working with Mike. We have a lot of fun together. I miss his smile."

"I'm sure he misses you too," she replies icily.

"I guess I just wanted to hear his voice," I add, layering on some extra charm. Elaine has always been worried about the closeness between Mike and me, and sometimes it's fun to play with her jealousy. "Mike's a good guy," I continue, "but I guess you know that already. Don't worry, though. I'll call back some time and arrange to meet him for a drink. I know this little bar, real out of the way, where they've got great booths and -"

"I don't think Mike really likes going to bars much these days," she says. "That's more of a single person's lifestyle."

"Really?" I reply with a smile. "That's news to me."

"Joanna," she says suddenly, interrupting me, "I'm so sorry, but I'm gonna have to get off the phone. I think I hear the oven timer beeping, and Mike's still in the bathroom, so I'd better get going."

"Cooking up a storm, huh?" I reply, glad that I've managed to piss her off.

"Actually, it's my..." She pauses.

"Birthday?" I ask. "How old?"

"It's not my birthday," she replies. "We're just having some friends over for a little celebration. I thought Mike would have told you, but I guess you can't have talked to him for a while. I'm actually pregnant, Joanna. I've just entered my second trimester, so we're going to have a spring baby."

I look down at my beer, and for a fraction of a second I feel as if my entire mind has been derailed. I should say something smart and witty, perhaps even a little cutting, but all I can do is replay those last few sentences over and over, as if they're cutting through me. Even though I know that this is an irrational response, I can't shake it. I was winning this conversation right up until that last little bit about a baby, and now I'm floundering.

"I really have to go," she continues, "but I'll tell Mike you called, and maybe we should all get together some time. At a restaurant, perhaps? I hope you're feeling a lot better soon."

"Yeah," I say, keenly aware that I've kind of hit the buffers. "Yeah, you too. Good luck."

Once the call is over, I'm left sitting alone at the bar, staring at my beer and trying to get my shit together. Since I stopped taking the cancer drugs, my mind has been pretty clear, but suddenly it's as if all my thoughts are rushing in different directions, colliding and spinning off into the ether. For a moment, I'm convinced that somehow the drugs have found a way to strike back at me, but finally I realize that this is something else entirely.

A baby.

Mike and Elaine are having a baby.

After taking a swig of beer, I hold the glass up to the light and watch the bubbles. There's absolutely no reason why this news should have affected me at all, and yet I've got this empty, aching feeling in my gut. All I want right now is to just rewind time and go back to a moment *before* I called Mike's number. Damn it, that was a real moment of weakness. I'm sure Elaine'll tell him I tried to get in touch, and he'll realize that I cracked first. Taking another swig, I check my watch and see that it's just after 5pm. I'd only planned to come in for a quick drink, but suddenly I feel as if I might stay until closing time.

I take another swig of beer.

Damn it, why the hell would Mike want to have a baby with that shrill, manipulative bitch? It was bad enough when he married her, but now he's letting her get her hooks even deeper into his flesh. I really thought he was smarter. I guess *that's* the real reason the news has affected me so badly: I just hate to see a friend getting sucked deeper into a bad relationship, but I guess you just can't save some people from their own bad decisions.

"Send me a whiskey," I say to the barman. "Make it a double."

John

"So we were talking," Sharon says, smiling at me in that way she does whenever she and the kids have come up with a plan, "and we thought that maybe you'd like to head off on vacation after Christmas. Maybe somewhere abroad?"

"Abroad, huh?" I reply, struggling to focus on the dinner conversation when all I really want to do is race to the Staten building and find out what the hell kind of mess Albert has caused. "Whatever, um... Whatever made you think of something like that?"

"I want to go to London," Kieran says excitedly.

"You do, do you?" I say, keeping things purposefully vague. "And why's that?"

"I want to see where Harry Potter lives!"

I glance over at Sharon and see the look of happiness in her eyes. She clearly agrees with Kieran and thinks our family should go away together; she knows we have enough money to afford an ambitious trip, and I guess she feels that after the past few tumultuous years, we deserve some time to relax. It must be hard for her, being stuck here with the kids for weeks on end when I'm away on 'business'; by rights, she's owed a good time.

"Daddy," Kieran continues, "can we go? Please?"

"I tried to keep him from getting too excited," Sharon says with a smile, "but one of his friends went to England recently and told him all about it. His head's been filled with all sorts of ideas, and he's been looking at photos online."

"England," I mutter, before taking another sip of wine. I check my watch and see that it's a little after 8pm, which means I have just a few hours left before I need to go and meet Albert. I think maybe I'll have to fuck Sharon when I get back, instead of before I go. "That's quite a long journey," I say, turning to Kieran. "We'll have to fly for five or six hours just to get there."

"I want to fly in a plane," Kieran replies.

"Aren't you scared?" I ask.

He shakes his head.

"You've got to admit," Sharon adds, "this family deserves a vacation. We've barely been to the end of the block recently."

"I can't argue with you there," I tell her, eating a mouthful of lasagna. The truth is, although I instantly bristled at the idea of going abroad, I can't deny the appeal of spending some time with Sharon and the kids. Looking over at our daughter Eliza, I see the smile on her face and realize that although she's a little too young to really understand what we're talking about, she too would undoubtedly enjoy a trip to Europe. There's really no reason for me to refuse, although I feel that a full-on family vacation would represent quite a commitment on my part. I'm not sure I'm ready.

"Maybe we should talk about it some other time," Sharon says, clearly keen to keep expectations in check.

"No," I reply, turning to her, "why not do something a little exciting and spontaneous once in a while?" I turn to Kieran. "You've never had a proper vacation, have you?"

He shakes his head.

"Then I guess it's settled," I continue. "We're going to England. Big Ben, red-top buses, the Tower of London.... The whole damn package!"

"Are you *sure* we can afford it?" Sharon asks, trying to strike a cautious and realistic note even though she can't wipe the grin off her face. She's been wanting a vacation for so long, and although I managed to dissuade her for a while, the kids have finally won me over. For now, anyway. I guess I can always back out of the whole thing later, if I decide it'd be a bad idea.

"Of course," I say, reaching out and squeezing her hand. "Anything for the family."

"Wow," she replies, clearly shocked that I was so easily persuaded. "There are so many fun things we can do in London. We can go shopping, and see Buckingham Palace, and Trafalgar Square, and -"

"Harry Potter!" Kieran shouts.

"Absolutely," I reply, before looking down at my lasagna and feeling a faint pang of sadness. I check my watch again and see that only a couple of minutes have elapsed since the last time I looked; the meeting with Albert is playing on my mind, and I'm still not entirely sure that our entire operation is on course. Everything with Sharon and the kids seems so perfect right now, but it could all be derailed if Albert has particularly bad news. Still, I have to keep a smile on my face for now. After all, there's still a chance that everything might be okay. A slim chance, but a chance.

"I want to go ice-skating!" Kieran says.

"In London?" Sharon says. "I think maybe that can be arranged."

"Excuse me," I say quietly, getting up from the table.

"Are you okay, John?" Sharon asks, with concern in her voice.

"Of course," I reply, stepping over to her and kissing the top of her head. "I'm sorry, work's very difficult at the moment. I just need to check something. I'll be back in two minutes."

"But -"

"Two minutes," I say again. "I promise."

Without waiting for a reply, I head back through to my office, where I immediately hurry to the desk and pull open the middle drawer. Reaching inside, I carefully unfasten the false bottom and lift it up, before pulling out the six passports I've been keeping in there for the past few years. Flicking through them, I feel myself starting to relax. There's really no need to be worried. All I have to do is make a few arrangements regarding my other commitments, and then enjoy a nice family vacation in England.

It's what a good family man would do.

Still, everything depends on what Albert has to tell me later. There's still a chance that my whole operation, my whole world, is about to go to hell. If that's the case, a trip to London might still be in order, except that I might only need a one-way ticket.

Joanna Mason

It's the sound of the TV that wakes me. Somewhere in the distance, a man is droning on and on with that peculiar cadence that people only ever use when they're talking to a camera.

I blink a couple of times, wondering why my eyes feel so sore.

"This is the house where the women first appeared," the TV voice is saying. "Several miles from the nearest town, at the end of a dirt road, it's certainly isolated from civilization. Who would ever have thought, though, that such an innocuous looking location could have played host to such horror?"

Sitting up, I realize that somehow I managed to get home after my evening in the bar, although I don't remember the journey at all and I'm completely naked under the bedsheets. Looking down, I feel a shiver pass through my body as I see the two faint, raggedy scars running horizontally on either side of my chest, where I used to have breasts. It's been three months since the operation, and I still haven't got used to the way my body looks these days. Still,

I'm not the kind of person to dwell on morbid thoughts, so I figure I just need to -

"Damn it!" splutters a male voice from somewhere else in the apartment.

I freeze.

Who the hell was that?

Keeping the sheets pulled up to cover my naked body, I lean across the bed and look down on the floor. Sure enough, not only are my clothes scattered around as if they were taken off in a hurry, but there's also a torn-open pack of rubbers. I lean a little further, straining to look under the bed, and finally I spot my sneakers. It's been many, many years since I had a random one-night-stand (or one-evening-stand, in this case) with a guy, but I still remember the tell-tale signs. Taking a deep breath, I feel an unassailable sense of embarrassment - maybe even humiliation - start to rise through my body.

What the hell happened?

"Stupid bitch," I mutter as I spot my reflection in the bedside mirror.

I glance at the clock by my bed and see that it's still only 10pm. Christ, I'm completely out of sync with the world.

Getting out of bed, I keep the sheets over my body as I gather my clothes and then I quickly get dressed. My shirt smells of beer, and sure enough there's a partially-dry stain on one sleeve, but I figure I don't have time to change right now. I check the drawer of my bedside table and find that my gun is still where I left it, so I figure I'm not in any immediate danger. Whoever this guy is, however, I need to get him the hell out of my apartment as fast as possible.

As soon as I get out into the corridor, I realize that there's a distant hum coming from the kitchen, as if someone's singing. I make my way slowly to the door, tensing with every step and already trying to think of an excuse to kick the guy out as fast as possible. When I reach the door and look through, however, I'm immediately both relieved and horrified as I see that my unexpected guest has a familiar face and, as he stands with his back to me, a familiar ass.

"What the hell are you doing here?" I ask.

Standing stark naked by the sink, Jason turns to me. "Good evening to you too. You know, I really like your apartment. It's great to finally see where you live"

"What are you *doing* here?" I ask again, shuddering at the realization that I invited him back here.

"My job," he replies, drinking a glass of water before walking over to the kitchen table, his dick swinging with every step. "*You* called *me*, remember?"

I stare at him blankly.

"Oh Jason," he continues, clearly mocking my tone of voice, "I know it's a bit last-minute but I really need to get fucked right now. I can't be bothered with a motel, just meet me at my place.

Please, Jason, just come and fuck my brains out with your big hard cock! I'll pay double!"

"I didn't say anything like that," I reply cautiously, even though I know it sounds a lot like me. When I'm drunk, anyway. Which I guess I was.

"Do you wanna hear the voicemails you left while I was on the subway?" he asks with a raised eyebrow. "You were in a hell of a hurry to -"

"Okay," I reply, interrupting him as I double-check that the sheet is firmly tied around my chest. "I get it. So I called you." I pause for a moment, trying not to stare at his fat, flaccid penis. "Did I at least pay you already?"

"A hundred and fifty plus travel costs," he replies. "You know, you're starting to become one of my regular customers. I could almost quit the rest of my clients and just use the money I make from you to get myself through chef school."

"Don't get too comfortable," I tell him, heading over to the coffee machine just as my head starts to pound. I have no idea how much I drank this evening, but it's starting to catch up to me. Damn it, I'm pretty sure this hangover's gonna feel worse than my last session of chemotherapy. "Hang on," I add, turning to him. "Chef school?"

"You think I wanna be a male escort all my life?" he asks.

I look down at his penis for a moment. "Cover yourself up," I mutter, before turning away and starting to fill the machine.

"So I was right, I see," he says.

"About what?" I ask, even though I'm pretty sure I know what he's talking about. For the past few months, I've always kept my top on during sessions with Jason. Based on how I woke up this morning, however, I'm pretty sure that in my drunken stupor I stripped completely naked and let him see, for the first time, the full extent of my scarred chest.

"You could have just told me," he continues. "I'm not superficial."

"There was nothing to tell you," I reply, wishing the ground would open and swallow me up.

"Don't think I didn't notice," he says. "About two, maybe three months ago, you suddenly got real defensive about keeping your shirt on when we were going at it. I suspected something was up, but I wasn't sure whether..." He pauses. "So was it a preventative mastectomy, or..."

I set the coffee machine running before turning to him.

"None of your business," I say firmly.

"Well, if -"

"Why are you still here?" I add.

"You told me to stay around for as long as I want," he replies. "You said you were worried about sending me back home so late."

"It's 10pm," I point out.

"You said you were concerned for my welfare."

"*I* said that?" I reply, genuinely shocked.

He nods.

"I guess I really must have been out of my mind," I continue, blinking a couple of times as my headache gets worse and worse. Looking over at the TV, I see that a news report is still running at low volume, with a journalist standing outside some kind of rundown old house in the middle of nowhere.

"You hear about that?" Jason asks. "A bunch of tortured girls just turned up on this couple's doorstep with, like, injuries and broken backs and stuff. No-one knows where they came from or who they are. They just appeared out of nowhere."

"No-one appears out of nowhere," I mutter.

"You know what I mean."

I stare at the screen.

"It's a sick world, huh?" Jason continues. "The thought that people could do that kind of thing to others... And it's always women, isn't it? Almost always, anyway. Men doing fucked-up things to women. Those poor girls are probably gonna be scarred for life now."

"You can live with scars," I say darkly, before turning to him. "Scars mean you survived. Now get your clothes on. I've got things to do tonight."

"Aren't you gonna offer me a coffee?" he asks with a smile.

"No," I say firmly.

As he gets dressed in the bedroom, I try to focus on the job of making a big pot of coffee and sorting out some food. Hell, I don't think I've eaten a proper meal at home for five years, but right now I need to distract myself. My refrigerator is pretty bare and I don't want to contemplate the ancient packages that are lurking in the cupboards, so I figure I'm limited to some old bread and maybe some cereal. There's an old bag of popcorn somewhere, too, but I really don't want to lower my standards so far that I end up eating something like *that* for dinner.

"So are you feeling better now?" Jason asks as he comes back into the kitchen, still buttoning his shirt.

"I'm absolutely fine," I mutter. "As long as I paid you already, I figure we're done here, right?"

"Oh yeah," he says with a smile, heading to the door. "You insisted on slipping the wad of notes between my butt-cheeks. Using your mouth."

I can't help but shudder at the thought of how drunk I must have been. Looking up at the ceiling, I realize that the room is still slightly spinning.

"You seemed angry," he continues. "Something seemed to have pissed you off. I don't mean the usual level of being pissed off that's normal for you. This was something extra. You were sad, too. You kept making jokes about getting pregnant and -"

"Okay," I reply, smiling forcefully as I interrupt him, "it was great to see you again. Unfortunately, this'll be our last session, but good luck with your life. Don't let the door-knob hit you in the ass on the way out."

"But -"

"Leave!" I say firmly, feeling as if I'm on the verge of physically ejecting him.

"See you soon," he replies, opening the door and stepping out into the corridor. "You know, every time we hook up, you always say it'll be the last time, but then you always - "

Before he can finish, I kick the door shut in his face, and finally I have some damn peace. Filled with piss and vinegar, I make my way to the counter and pull a loaf of bread out of a paper bag, only to find that the damn thing is covered in blue mold. Sighing, I look over at the TV and watch as the reporter continues to talk outside the remote house. This looks like exactly the kind of case that I used to love, and I have no doubt that Dawson's probably been assigned. If he doesn't call for my help soon, I guess he never will.

John

"Okay," Albert says, "here's the thing. I think I've worked out where we went wrong with Manuel and the Staten building, and I'm one hundred per cent certain I know how we can guarantee that nothing like that ever happens again."

It's a little after midnight and we're sitting in the squalid little drop house we've been renting, in cash, on the far side of town. The place is a goddamn dive, complete with cockroaches and rats, but at least there's no chance of us being recognized here. It's a hell of a lot more secure than talking by phone; even burner phones give me the sweats, and I prefer to meet Albert face to face so that I can be absolutely certain we're not being watched or recorded. I don't like leaving anything to chance: everything has to be pre-planned to the nth degree.

Sometimes, I feel as if Albert doesn't share my dedication.

"Go on," I say after a moment, taking a deep breath. "Tell me your great idea."

"The problem with Manuel," he continues, "is that he couldn't stomach the job. I mean, the guy had a pretty rich past. His hands weren't clean, if you know what I mean. Still, it's one thing to go around enforcing matters against a bunch of cheap dime-store hoods, but it's another to watch over a bunch of our girls. I mean..." He pauses, and I can see that he's worried. "Even *I* sometimes feel a little shifty, you know?" He waits for me to say something. "Don't you?"

I stare at him. "No," I say eventually.

"But sometimes you must wonder," he replies. "You know, about whether they're feeling pain? Whether they understand what's happening to them?"

"No," I say again.

He clears his throat. "The point is," he continues, "it's one thing to feel a little sorry for the poor bitches, but it's something else entirely to act on those impulses, but the key difference is that the Staten building was purely populated by women."

"So?" I ask.

"So women and men are different," he replies. "Women tend to look more pitiful when they're in pain, don't they? I'm thinking, if Manuel had been at one of the other buildings, with just men to watch over, none of this shit would have happened. He'd have just ignored their moans. It's because he had women, John. That's the problem, right there. He started feeling sorry for them."

"You think he went soft?" I ask.

"Totally. Some men, they just get all protective when a girl's in pain." He pauses again. "Maybe you don't feel the same way, but it's human nature for most of us, we start feeling sorry for them. Now, I can deal with that and get over it with a bottle of rum and some smokes, but other guys..." He pauses yet again, as if for some damn reason he's having trouble getting the words out. "So here's the deal," he adds eventually. "I think we need to shift our staffing patterns. Hired help watches the *men*, and *only* the men. As for the women, we'll make sure that only you and I ever go near them. I mean, we both know we're not gonna flip and do a Manuel, right?"

I stare at him.

"We can trust each other," he adds. "You and me. No-one else."

"Maybe we should reduce the number of women we hold," I reply. "Women don't sell as well as men, not in our line of business. We probably have twice as much demand for men."

"Exactly," he continues. "We cut the women down to maybe half a dozen, maximum. Keep them all together, and you and I can watch over them while we hire people in to watch the buildings with the men. I know it'll mean more work for us, but it's not like we got into this line of business because we're lazy, right?" He grins nervously. "And then, when we reach the bail-out point, we just do what we always planned. Torch the places and walk away."

"And that's your great idea?" I ask.

"Maybe this was a good thing," he continues as he starts rolling himself a cigarette. "Maybe it was the wake-up call we needed. We were getting ahead of ourselves."

"And the girls," I reply. "The ones who got away. The many, *many* who got away. Where are they now?"

"They've got 'em somewhere in the city," he replies. "The story's only just starting to break on the news channels, but I'm pretty sure it's gonna be huge by morning. Still, we both know, there's no way they can trace this back to us. Hell, there's no way they can even work out why we were keeping those women. They'll probably just assume it was some dumb-ass slavery or sex thing, you know? They'll be so busy getting all lathered up about prostitution rackets or some other kind of shit, they'll never work out the truth. It's not like the cops are that smart, right?" He pauses. "We're in the clear, John. We've taken a financial hit, but we're in the clear."

"As long as Manuel didn't leave any other nasty little surprises," I point out.

"Like what?"

"How do we know that he didn't call the authorities before you caught up to him?"

"I had his phones and email bugged," he replies, grinning as he taps the side of his nose, "and the guy was in a hell of a panic. It was a split-second decision. I really don't think there's any reason to worry."

Sighing, I realize that the situation is untenable. Sure, it's unlikely that Manuel planned his little revolt in advance, but the possibility exists, and I always pride myself on reacting to *every* possibility, no matter how remote. The one thing I hate more than anything else is uncertainty.

"This is going to be okay," Albert says after a moment. "I've taken care of Manuel, I've taken care of the Staten building, and now we've gotta move on to consolidating the *other* two buildings. Hell, I don't even see why we need to necessarily replace what we've lost. Maybe we were getting too big. I mean, once we cash out on our existing stock, we're made for life, right?"

I stare at him.

"Right?" he continues.

"I suppose that's one way of looking at it," I reply eventually.

"So let's just move forward like I described," he says. "Slim down the operation a bit, focus on what we've got and forget about trying to expand too much. There's no need to keep adding more and more buildings. Everything that happened today was like a sign from God -"

"Don't bring God into this," I say darkly.

"Let's just at least *try* my way," he continues. "Please, John, just agree to try it and see how it fits. I think you'll be surprised. It'll be a little slower-paced, a little less frenetic, but it might be just what we need, I mean... haven't you felt a little overwhelmed lately? Like things have been getting out of hand?"

I stare at him for a moment, utterly shocked by his lack of ambition. It's as if he's slowly creeping back into his shell, hiding from the possibilities.

How the hell did I end up associating with such a mundane mind?

"Fine," I mutter. "We'll try it your way."

"Good," he says, checking his watch. "It's getting late, so I guess one of us should check on the other buildings. I can do it if you like, I mean, I'm sure you've got someone waiting for you at home."

"I'm sure I do," I reply.

Getting to his feet, he grabs his coat and gets ready to leave. "This is just a blip," he continues. "One day, we'll look back on this moment and, well, maybe we won't laugh, but I think we'll see it as a turning point."

"Maybe you're right," I say, getting to my feet. I pause for a moment, watching as Albert zips up his jacket and takes some cigarettes from his pocket.

"You want a ride?" he asks absent-mindedly as he lights up. "I'm headed east."

"Actually..." I reach into my pocket and feel the butt of the gun I brought this evening. The past sixty seconds or so, since I agreed to try Albert's approach, have felt appalling, as if suddenly our operation has lost all its ambition and all its appeal. "I think I've got a better idea," I say, pulling the gun from my pocket and aiming it at the back of his head. "I think the best thing would be to take the entire operation in-house from this point."

"What do -" he asks calmly, starting to turn toward me.

Without hesitation, I fire a single shot into the side of his face, felling him immediately. The silencer keeps the sound of the gun to a minimum, and the only real noise is the thump of his body as it hits the floor. I turn to walk to the door, but blind rage overtakes me and I step back over to his body; leaning down, I empty the remaining five shots directly into his face at point-blank range, until his head is cracked straight down the middle.

I close my eyes.

Finally, the cold anger seems to crystallize and fade.

I take a deep breath.

"No more mistakes," I mutter, putting the gun back into my pocket as my mind races with ideas about how to dispose of Albert's remains. The truth is, I always knew that a day like this would come, and I already have the rough outline of a plan worked out. It won't be pleasant, but it's the only way to ensure that the operation remains on-track.

Joanna Mason

"Police are said to have called in a team of psychotherapists from Boston, Chicago and Washington to help them work with the victims," the reporter says, staring straight at the camera, "but sources say that most of the girls have little or no capability with the English language, and in some cases it's believed that their level of education is low or even non-existant."

"Huh," I mutter, eating another mouthful of the popcorn I found in the back of a cupboard. I'm sitting on the sofa, watching a news channel on my laptop, and this particular case is unfolding in just the kind of way that hits all my buttons. Glancing at my phone, I see that there's still no call from Dawson. Damn it, I'm really starting to get all itchy and scratchy here, but I already tried to call him once today. It's his turn.

"One potentially significant new development in recent hours," the reporter continues, "is the discovery of a burned-out building several miles away from the rural home where the women were first spotted. Sources have told this channel that the building consists of little more than a metal frame, but it's believed to have had wood panels before being deliberately torched by a person or persons unknown. A search of local planning databases reveals no information on such a building, raising the possibility that it was constructed without permission and in secret."

"No way," I say as I take another mouthful of popcorn, while engrossed in the story. I've had some meaty cases over the years, but this one is coming together perfectly. There's a bunch of random, unknown women in various states of distress, all of them forced to crawl to freedom 'cause their backs were broken; there's a remote house with a pair of halfwits who found the women; there's a mysterious burned-out building in the middle of nowhere; and there's a faint hint of some kind of cult or slavery ring about the whole thing. In other words, this might well be the juiciest story to hit this area in years, and I guess it's just my luck that I'm off sick from work when it strikes.

Then again, I've never let that kind of thing stop me before.

"Come on, asshole," I mutter, checking my phone for the thousandth time tonight. I know damn well that Dawson's going to need my help on this case. The guy's smart and he's a good detective, but when it comes to wild, out-of-whack incidents, he tends to think too slowly and laterally. What he needs is my talent for making intuitive leaps, and I know for certain that if he's been assigned to this case, he'll be desperately in need of my input.

Normally, he'd have called me immediately, but this time he seems to be holding off. He's probably trying to play it cool.

Finally, figuring that I'm going to develop an ulcer if I just sit here like this all night, I push the bag of popcorn aside and make my way through to the bathroom. As I pee, I find myself still obsessing over the details of the case and, more specifically, over the fact that Dawson hasn't called. Even the fact that there's a small amount of blood in my urine doesn't really distract me from thinking about -

Suddenly I hear it.

Somewhere else in the apartment, my phone is ringing.

Barely even taking time to wipe, I race back through to the sofa and grab the phone. Sure enough, it's Dawson trying to get hold of me. I take a moment to gather my composure; standing in the darkened front room with my pants around my ankles, bathed in the flickering light from my laptop screen, I close my eyes for a moment and remind myself that it's vital to make sure that I don't sound too eager.

"Hello," I say calmly as I answer the phone. "Joanna Mason speaking."

"Hey, Jo," he replies, sounding as if he's outside somewhere in some pretty foul weather. "It's me. Have you seen the news?"

"No," I lie. "Why? Anything interesting going on?"

"There's this case," he replies, having to raise his voice to be heard over the wind. "Look, I'm really sorry to disturb you, and I know you're supposed to be off sick and this has kinda come out of the blue, but I was wondering if maybe I could persuade you to come and meet me? I need to pick your brains."

I look down at my pants and realize that as well as being down around my ankles, they're dangling in the remains of the takeaway I ate for lunch. Frankly, I'm a complete mess right now.

"I'm kinda busy," I say after a moment, lying again, "but I guess I could spare a few minutes." I can't help but smile as I pause to let him sweat a little longer. "So," I continue, "where do you want to meet?"

John

"Hey, honey," Sharon whispers in the darkness as soon as I step through the bedroom door. "Sorry, I went to bed without you. What time is it?"

"Almost midnight," I reply calmly.

"The kids are in bed."

"I know."

As I walk across the room, I hear the rustle of the sheets as Sharon sits up.

"Is everything okay?" she asks. "You sound tense?"

"I'm fine," I reply, fumbling a little in the darkness but determined to keep the light off.

"Are you sure?"

"Yes!" I say firmly, a little annoyed by her constant questions and, also, by the thought that she - or anyone - might be able to tell that I have something on my mind. I've always prided myself on my ability to keep my emotions hidden, and there's no way Sharon should be able to pick up on even the slightest hint of concern in my voice. Not even after five years of marriage.

"I'll turn the light on," she says.

"No," I reply. "Please. It's okay."

She doesn't say anything, and as I climb fully-clothed into bed, I can tell that I've done an unusually poor job of concealing my true intentions. I'd hoped that she wouldn't wake up when I came back, although I know that she likes to wait up for me on nights when I come home late. There's always been something very kind and caring about Sharon, as if she dotes on me; I'm sure that, in different circumstances, I would have been happy to spend the rest of my life with her, accepting her plain looks and mediocre intelligence as a sacrifice that had to be made in order to acquire such a loyal and capable wife.

"Are you still wearing your clothes?" she asks, reaching out and running a hand along the inside of my trouser leg. "Honey, why haven't you got undressed? I only changed the sheets yesterday, you'll track all sorts of dirt into the bed."

"Sorry," I mutter, placing a hand on her bare belly before reaching up to cup one of her small, pert breasts.

"John?" she says, with concern in her voice. "Your hand's wet. And... warm."

"Sorry," I say again, trying to fight the tears that are welling up in my eyes. The truth is, although I'd planned to be as steely and calm as possible, I'm finding at the last minute that my feelings for Sharon are much stronger than I could ever have imagined. It's not that I love her, particularly; it's more that I feel desperately, achingly sorry for her, and I want to get this over with as quickly as possible. I don't want her to suffer, or to realize what's happening; I just want her to slip away in an instant, which means that I have to find the precise moment when I can do this cleanly. I've imagined this moment so many times over the years, but I never expected to have this kind of emotional reaction.

What the hell is wrong with me?

Reaching into my jacket, I slowly pull out the gun.

"It's sticky," she says, reaching up and lifting my hand away from her breast. "John, what *is* this? Oil?"

I pause for a moment, wondering whether I should tell her the truth.

"I've changed my mind," I say eventually, aware that my voice sounds weak and frail. If I'm not careful, she'll guess that there are tears in my eyes. "Honey, can you lean over and turn the bedside lamp on? I... need to be able to see properly."

The sheets rustle as she rolls away from me. I wait in the darkness, with the gun poised and ready to fire, and I listen to the sound of her hand fumbling on the bedside table.

I take a deep breath.

As soon as the light comes on, I'll do it.

I wait.

Suddenly there's a click and the bulb flickers on. For a fraction of a second, I stare at the back of Sharon's head, before she starts to turn back to face me.

I have to do it now, before she sees.

I raise the gun and fire once, straight into her temple.

Her body jerks and slumps down onto the pillow as blood sprays against the headboard. I quickly fire a second shot into the side of her head, just to make sure that she's dead, and finally I sit back and stare at her body.

That was much, much harder than I expected.

Harder than it *should* have been.

I look down at my hands, covered in hot, sticky blood that hasn't quite dried yet. I accidentally smeared some on Sharon's left breast; I didn't really think much of it at the time, but now the blood seems horrifyingly symbolic.

"Onward," I mutter, hoping to strengthen my resolve as I get out of bed and walk back over to the door, with the gun still in my hand. Stopping in the doorway, I turn and look back at the bed, where Sharon's body remains slumped against the pillow with a slow bloodstain seeping through the fabric. It's a tragic sight, and one that I'd always hoped to avoid, even if in the back of my mind I suppose I was aware of the inevitability of this moment. It wasn't her fault, of course. It was all mine.

"Sweet dreams," I whisper.

Realizing that there's no point being sentimental, I turn and head along the corridor, before stopping at the door to the room our two children share. We have a four-year-old son named Kieran and a two-year-old girl named Eliza, and over the course of their lives I've watched them grow to become fine young people with promising futures of their own. Reaching down to the handle, I pause for a moment, unsure as to whether I can ever summon the strength to go inside. Finally, after reminding myself that I need to remain calm, I turn the handle and push it open.

Inside, on their beds, the two little dead bodies rest in pools of their own blood. I had to kill them before I killed Sharon. It was the only way. At least the silencer ensured that Sharon and Kieran didn't wake up after I started with Eliza.

Pulling the door shut, I make my way quietly through to the kitchen. Everything is so neat; as usual, Sharon tidied away the remains of dinner and set the dishwasher going before heading to bed. She was always a very neat, very ordered woman who took her homely responsibilities extremely seriously. She did almost everything right, and yet she made one awful, fatal mistake: she met, and fell for, a man with no heart, no conscience, no soul; a man who never really existed. She looked into my eyes and thought she saw love, when in fact there's nothing inside me but emptiness. I guess she saw what she wanted to see, and once she'd made that mistake, her days began to count down to this inevitable moment. I tried to hold back the pain for as long as possible, but there was only so much I could do.

Still, the alternative would have been worse. If she'd ever learned the truth about me, she'd have been horrified and distraught. By killing her and the children, I've saved them from lasting torment. At least I was able to do that for them. And before all of this, I gave them a decent life.

I check my watch.

Time to get moving.

Part Two

Flames

Joanna Mason

It takes me almost three hours to drive out to the house, and without any kind of GPS system I'm forced to park up several times and consult an old paper map that's been badly folded a few too many times. Sometimes I think I should just surrender and join the twenty-first century, but then I wouldn't be able to mock all those goddamn technophiles with quite so much assurance. The map's far from ideal, but with regular glances and only a couple profanities I'm eventually able to work out the route.

Kind of, anyway.

For a while, I start to worry that maybe I'm lost; finally, however, just after midnight, I spot lights up ahead, and soon I'm reaching the end of a long dirt road, surrounded by flashing blue lights.

"Joanna Mason," I say, leaning out the window and flashing my old badge at the cop manning a small roadblock. I make sure to keep the badge moving, but he reaches out and grabs it, holding it still for a moment.

"This badge is out of date," he says humorlessly.

"Is it?" I reply, feigning surprise as I pretend to look at the badge. "Huh. I hadn't noticed."

"I'm sorry," he continues, "but you're not allowed to pass this point unless you have an up-to-date badge."

"It's out by, like, a few weeks," I point out, hoping that I might be able to get him to change his mind. "That's nothing!"

"I'm sorry," the cop says sternly. "I can't -"

"It's okay!" a familiar voice calls out from the darkness, and seconds later Dawson hurries over, fighting his way through the high wind. "She's with me," he adds, before leaning down toward me and flashing a faint but tense smile. "It's good to see you again, Jo."

"Where do I park?" I ask, unable to resist a faint smile of my own.

A few minutes later, once I've pulled up a little further on, Dawson comes to meet me. It's not exactly a grand, emotional reunion, but then I guess that's not how either of us likes to do things. As he takes me toward the house where the women apparently just showed up earlier today, he fills me in on the basic details, and it's almost as if we've picked up right where we left off. It's difficult to get to the front door, since several parts of the garden and porch have been marked off with police tape. Although he comes up with a few pleasantries, Dawson doesn't really tell me anything I hadn't already worked out from media reports, and as we reach the house I can't help but notice a reporter - the same one I was watching a few hours ago - loitering nearby with his cameraman, watching like jackals.

"So how are things going?" I ask, figuring I should try some small-talk, even though it's not exactly my strong-point.

"Could be better," he mutters. "Schumacher's already getting onto me for answers about this mess and threatening to pull me off the case and give it to this new guy, Jordan Carver. I swear to God, Schumacher's getting more and more paranoid about media coverage since he started getting feedback from the precinct's public relations department."

"The precinct has a public relations department?" I reply.

"Oh yeah. And they're *much* happier now you're not around so much."

"What about *you*?" I continue. "How's life?"

"Fine," he replies, clearly keen not to get involved in a detailed conversation. "You?"

"Fine," I say, figuring that maybe Elaine didn't tell him that I spoke to her earlier. Either that, or Dawson really doesn't want to get drawn into a personal discussion right now.

"Okay," he says, leading me up onto the porch. "So the first girl knocked on the bottom of the door." He steps into the house, before turning to me. "Mr. Wash opened the door and found the girl, a Caucasian in her early to mid twenties, down on the decking with injuries to her face, neck, torso, arms and legs. He then became aware of other women crawling toward the house with similar marks.

Twenty-eight of them in all, each with a broken or fractured back."

"You got names for any of them yet?" I ask, turning and looking out across the dark garden and at the vast wilderness beyond.

"Nothing so far," Dawson replies. "We've tried everything we can think of, but it's as if these girls just landed here from nowhere. No DNA matches, no distinguishing marks, not even any dental records to go on."

"Nothing at all?"

"It's like they're non-people," he continues. "How does that happen? Hell, you sneeze these days, it gets recorded in some database somewhere. How do twenty-eight people manage to completely avoid ending up in the system?"

"They don't," I mutter. "Not unless someone goes to great lengths to keep them hidden."

"Two of them have died since they showed up," he replies, handing me a set of photos showing some of the girls. "Respiratory failure, although autopsies are being carried out as we speak to determine the underlying causes. Wherever these women were being held, they were being fed very little, although they weren't completely malnourished. Someone wanted to keep them alive, even if there was no need to keep them in prime health."

"Any sign of sexual abuse?" I ask.

"Nothing. That was one of the first things we looked for, but almost all the girls appear to be virgins. Whatever was going on here, it wasn't anything to do with sex, although..." He pauses. "I guess it's possible that they were being sold for sexual purposes. I'm sure a genuine virgin might fetch a decent price on the darker parts of the internet. I guess I'm gonna have to do some heavy wading in the digital black markets."

I look down at the photos. Without exception, the girls look more confused than pained, as if they have no idea what's happening to them. Judging by their expressions, it's almost as if they've never had any real contact with the real world before, which I guess might be possible. When I first heard about this case, I assumed that they were probably kidnap victims, but now I'm not so sure; I'm starting to wonder if they've been kept like this since birth.

"No," I say eventually. "This isn't about sex."

"But maybe virginity would -"

"It's not about sex," I say again. "Sure, there are markets for that sort of thing, but not enough to justify this kind of major operation. Look at them. These girls all seem to be in their late teens or early twenties. Without wanting to sound too cynical, I don't think they'd be kept back this long if their sole purpose was to get fucked." I flick through some more of the photos. "How old did you say they were again?"

"It's hard to say for sure," he replies. "They don't seem to know themselves, and it's not like we can cut them open and count the rings. Some were pretty young, though. The youngest appears to be six or seven."

"But none older than early twenties?" I ask.

"As far as we can tell so far."

Still staring at the photos, I wait for a moment of inspiration to strike. I guess it's natural, in a situation like this, to assume that sex is somehow involved in the mix, but I can't shake the feeling that something else has been happening to these women, something more cold and clinical.

"You want to come inside and speak to the home-owners?" Dawson asks eventually. "They're -"

"No need," I reply, interrupting him. "I doubt they can tell us anything. They're just the unlucky ones who happened to have this explode on their doorstep." Turning to look out into the darkness surrounding this remote little house, I pause for a moment as a cool wind continues to blow. "Whatever's been going on here, the answer isn't in the house. It's out there somewhere."

"What makes you say that?" Dawson asks.

"Because if *I* was going to keep a load of women chained up somewhere, I'd want to do it out in the middle of nowhere so that there'd be no chance of getting overheard by the neighbors." I turn to him. "This place is a total bust, and I'm not in the mood to waste time. Take me to the burned-out building you found."

"Let me take you inside first -"

"There's no time," I say firmly.

"Why not?"

"Because I think these girls are just the tip of the iceberg," I tell him. "I think there are probably more of them out there somewhere."

John

"Mr. Noone?" a familiar voice calls out. "What are you doing out here so late?"

Freezing in place, I look down at the can of gasoline in my hands. My mind seems to have gone completely blank, and for a moment I have no idea what to say. Slowly, I turn to find my neighbor, Patricia Nolan, standing nearby, wearing her nursing uniform. I guess it's just my luck that she's coming home from a late shift in the small hours of the morning, but I need to think fast. The last thing I can deal with is a last-minute complication, not after the hellish day I've had so far.

"I was just..." I start to say, before carefully placing the can on the ground and glancing over at the street to make sure that there's no-one around. "I was trying to kill some weeds," I continue, even though I know that the explanation is painfully thin. "You know how it is," I add. "The damn things just keep growing through. They won't take a hint."

"I guess," she replies with a frown, before checking her watch.

"I know it's a weird time to be gardening," I continue, trying to walk a careful line between being too talkative on the one hand and too quiet on the other, "but I've just been so busy lately, and as you know, I have to be on the road for weeks at a time with my job, so sometimes I have to grab spare moments whenever I can get them. I tried going to bed but I couldn't sleep, so I figured that rather than toss and turn and risk waking Sharon and the kids, I'd come out here and..."

My voice trails off.

She stares at me.

I wait for her to go into her house.

She sniffs, almost as if she can smell the gasoline.

"And how have you been?" I continue, forcing a smile.

"Good," she says, still looking skeptical. "Working hard, you know?" She glances past me, as if she's convinced that something's wrong.

"Huh," I reply. "Yeah. Sure." I pause, trying to work out whether this is going to be a problem. She's clearly having trouble believing my story, and given what's about to happen, I really don't need to have interfering neighbors telling stories to the police. She might not have worked out what's really in the can just yet, but once the house goes up in flames, it won't take a rocket scientist to ignite her suspicions.

"Well," she adds after a moment, "I'm exhausted, Mr. Noone. I think I really need to just get inside, grab something to eat and get some sleep." She pauses, and it's noticeable that her gaze moves down to the gasoline can next to my feet.

"Good luck with your gardening," she continues. "See you around."

"See you around, Patricia," I reply.

She turns to walk over to her door.

After checking one more time that there's no-one nearby, I reach into my pocket and pull out the gun that I thankfully kept when I left the house. Raising it, I take a moment to aim before firing a single shot that goes straight into the back of Patricia's head, dropping her down onto the garden path before she even has time to gasp. I hurry over and check her pulse, and sure enough she's dead, with blood having sprayed across the path.

"Great," I mutter, putting the gun away before grabbing Patricia's arms and starting to drag her toward my back door. I keep looking up to make sure that no-one else happens to be out at such a ridiculous hour, but fortunately the rest of my neighbors all seem to be tucked up in bed. As soon as I get Patricia to the door, I pause for a moment as I try to work out what to do with her body. I had everything worked out before this little interruption, but Patricia's a real thorn in my side and I'm not sure how her body can be explained.

For a few seconds, my mind feels completely blank. Why can't people just mind their own business?

"Think," I whisper, trying to get myself back into gear. "Come on, you fucking idiot, come up with something!"

Finally, I realize that there's only one solution.

"Fuck it," I mutter, pushing the door open and dragging Patricia into the house. At least this way, there's no chance of anyone finding her until the fire's over, by which point she should be nice and crispy. Sure, the police might think it's strange that one of the neighbors was in the house when it burned down, but I'll let them worry about coming up with an explanation. As long as they don't suspect my involvement in any way, nothing else really matters.

Hurrying back out of the house, I make my way to the front and quickly finish my work: I empty the rest of the gasoline can all over the front door and then once it's empty, I toss the can to the ground and take a step back, staring up at the bedroom window and imagining Sharon's dead body still slumped on the bed. Looking at the next window, I think of the children; I wish there'd been a way to avoid all of this, but in a way I've known for a long time that the moment was coming. I gave them some good years, but it was always bound to end like this. Reaching into my pocket, I pull out a matchbook and strike one, before staring for a moment at the flickering flame.

This is it.

Another one down.

"Fuck you, Albert," I whisper. "This is all your fucking fault. Manuel too. If you morons had been able to do your jobs properly..." I pause for a moment, consumed with rage, until finally I take a deep breath and force myself to face the truth: those two assholes are dead, and there's nothing else I can do except make sure that this situation is dealt with.

I pause.

Slowly, I walk to the sidewalk and then turn to look back at the dark house. Near my feet, there's the beginning of the thick gasoline trail I laid earlier, ready for this moment. Leaning down, I hold the burning match just above the surface before finally dropping it. I turn and start to run, and although I don't look back, I can hear the whoosh of the flames. When I get to the end of the street, I glance over my shoulder just in time to see that the entire house has become an inferno. Soon there'll be screams from the neighbors; soon there'll be the sirens of fire trucks; soon there'll be shouts as people try to stop the blaze.

But by then, I'll be long gone.

Joanna Mason

"There's no way we can be absolutely certain that this is linked," Dawson says as he parks close to the dark remains of the burned building, a few miles from the house where the women were found. "It might just be a coincidence."

Staring out the window, I watch as police officers and forensic examiners continue to sift through the debris. Strong portable lights are illuminating the scene, and when I check my watch I see that it's almost 5am. My head's pounding, and I'm starting to think that instead of being hungover, I might actually still be a little drunk. Still, I've worked like this before, and I can damn well do it again. All that really matters is that I have that moment of inspiration that always used to hit me during a big case; if that moment doesn't come, I'm not sure I'm even 'me' anymore.

"So are you okay?" Dawson adds.

"I'm fine," I reply a little defensively, opening the car door and stepping out.

"You'd tell me if something was wrong, wouldn't you?" he continues, getting out the other side and coming around to join me.

"Of course," I say, staring at the ruins of the building. "I'm totally fine. I've got absolutely nothing to tell you." I turn to him. "Why? You got anything to tell me? Any news?"

He pauses, looking a little uncomfortable. "No," he says eventually.

"So tell me about this place," I reply, starting to walk toward what's left of what appears to have been quite a large structure, perhaps an old barn. Twisted metal girders are poking up from the ground, but the place looks to have been mostly made of wood: there's ash and charred panels all over the place, and when I get to the edge of the police cordon I realize that while a cold wind is still blowing, there's actually a noticeable heat haze rising from the wreckage. "This was linked to the girls," I continue, watching as a forensic examiner works nearby. "There's no way something like this could be a coincidence."

"Hang on," Dawson replies cautiously. "Just because two things happened on one night, you can't assume they're linked."

"I know," I mutter. "But they *are*."

"And you know that... how?"

"Common sense," I reply with a faint smile. "Think about it. The women were being held here, like cattle in a barn. God knows why, but we'll work that part out later. They were held here, probably chained and with their backs broken to keep them from escaping, and then suddenly, all at once and completely *en masse*, they got free and crawled to freedom. It would've taken them, what five or six hours to get to the Wash family house from here?" I pause for a moment. "That's pretty much impossible," I add. "Maybe one could get free. Maybe. But all of them? Someone must have intervened, which means someone intentionally set them free, probably someone who had a key." I turn to Dawson. "A crisis of conscience, maybe? Or just someone who didn't need the women anymore and saw no reason to kill them?"

"We're thinking that maybe some kind of cult -"

"This wasn't a cult," I say firmly.

"It might have been."

"Have you ever actually been to a cult's compound?" I ask. "This doesn't have the same sting. Anyway, it sounds like the women were completely uneducated."

"Some of them don't even have basic language skills," he replies.

"Exactly," I continue, "and how do you persuade someone to join a cult if you can't even talk to them properly? How do you get them to worship you and follow you if they blatantly don't understand what's happening?" I pause for a moment as I feel a tremor of excitement; the moment of inspiration is coming, and I figure I just need to keep working a little longer before it hits. I live for these moments, when the doubts vanish and crystal clear truth suddenly arrives fully-formed in my mind. I don't claim to understand it; I just know that my brain works on things subconsciously and then, when it's done, the answer seems to pop into my head from nowhere. The best part is, I'm always right. Always.

It's been months since I was on the verge of something like this. I feel alive again.

"Over here!" a voice calls out.

Turning, I see that one of the forensic examiners is waving at Dawson.

"I'm not dismissing the idea of a cult," Dawson mutters as he hurries past me, slipping under the cordon and making his way across the wreckage.

"Of course you're not," I reply with a smile as I follow him. "It's okay, though. I'll come up with the real explanation and you can thank me later, once you've caught up."

"Human remains," the medical examiner says as we reach him. He points at a tell-tale glint in the ash, and it's clear that there are several sections of charred bone scattered across the ground. "Impossible to be certain, but I'd say there are at least two victims here, maybe more."

"Not everyone got out alive," Dawson mutters.

"Most did, though," I point out. "You've got twenty-eight, including the two who died after they were picked up. There can't be more than a few left here, so most made it away. I guess the ones who stayed were too sick, or too scared to rebel against their masters."

"Still think this wasn't a cult?" Dawson asks, clearly believing that his theory is gathering support.

"Absolutely," I reply, feeling as if I'm closer than ever to a breakthrough. Any second now, I'm going to come up with an idea, something that makes this whole mess make sense, and I'm damn certain it's not going to have anything to do with a cult. Frankly, a cult is the kind of dumb suggestion that your average plodding detective would usually come up with, so it's a good job I'm here to keep things on track.

"We're beginning to get a picture of how the fire started and spread," the forensic examiner continues. "There was an accelerant, so someone *wanted* to burn this place to the ground. The whole building was doused in gasoline."

"Maybe it was part of some kind of ritual," Dawson suggests.

I can't help but smile at his continued insistence that a cult was involved in all of this.

"There are also several sets of tire marks in the area," the examiner continues. "We're working on them now, but they're going to be of limited use unless we can get a sample and try to make a match. It's definitely three different vehicles, with one set of tracks being much fresher than the others."

"People were coming and going," Dawson continues. "Makes sense. A cult would need -"

"It wasn't a cult," I say firmly, my amusement starting to give way to annoyance that Dawson won't listen to me. "I'm telling you now," I continue, turning to him. "This has none of the hallmarks of a cult, and even if it did, it still *wasn't* a cult."

"You can just pick that up from the air, can you?" he asks.

"Can't you?"

"Then what was it?" he asks after a moment.

"Give me a minute," I reply testily, before looking over at the forensic examiner and realizing that he's staring at me. "What are you looking at?" I ask, suddenly feeling a little paranoid that maybe he can tell that I'm ill.

"Nothing," he mutters, looking back down at his work.

"Jo," Dawson says after a moment, "are you sure you're okay? Maybe we should go back to -"

"I'm fine," I say, pushing him away as he reaches out a hand. "Just stop talking about cults. It's a dumb, off-the-shelf answer and it doesn't fit. Something else was happening out here." Feeling a little dizzy, I walk away, making my way around the edge of the cordon until I'm on the far side. Turning and looking back across the wreckage, I try to empty my mind as I wait for that moment of inspiration to strike. I know it's coming, and I'm certain that there's no cult involved. Still, I won't be able to persuade Dawson until I've come up with an alternative explanation.

"Come on!" Dawson calls out, heading to the car. "There's no point staring at a load of burned rubble. We should get back to the house and speak to the only witnesses we've got so far!"

"You go," I say, staring at the wreckage. "I'll come later."

"Jo -"

"There's no point talking to them!" I shout, turning to him. "Just because they saw the women first, there's no reason to think that they've got any special insight. They're just -" I pause as I feel the moment of inspiration arrive, but suddenly I feel weak, as if I might collapse. Instinctively, I reach out to steady myself on one of the posts that's being used to mark the cordon, but it's not strong enough and I almost fall over before finally managing to keep myself upright.

"Jo?" Dawson says, clearly concerned as he hurries over to me. "What's wrong?"

Suddenly, I realize I can taste blood.

"Jo?"

"Nothing," I say firmly, determined to ignore my physical shortcomings and focus on waiting for the moment of inspiration. "I..." Pausing, I try to organize my thoughts before taking a step forward and realizing that the whole world seems to be pivoting around my mind. "Just be..." I stammer, before suddenly feeling as if my head's so heavy, I can't keep it up. I slump to the ground, and as I pass out, the last thing I hear is Dawson shouting my name, and the last thing I feel is his arms reaching under my body.

John

"It's me," I say calmly, staring at the gate ahead. "Let me in."

With the engine still running, I sit and wait for the automatic gate to swing open. It must be three or four in the morning by now, maybe even later, and I'm exhausted, but there's no time to waste. The failings of other people have forced me to take action, and if that means pushing myself to the limit, then so be it. I've spent too long building this business up to let it fall apart just because a couple of hired hands couldn't do their goddamn jobs.

Speaking of which...

"Are you listening?" I say after a moment, before double-checking that the phone is still lit up. "It's me. Open the fucking gate, Leonard."

Silence.

Just as I'm starting to get worried, there's a nearby whirring sound and the large metal gate starts to swing open. Tossing the phone onto the passenger seat, I ease the car forward and into the yard, where I quickly park up next to the little tin shack that serves as our office. The last thing I need tonight is to have to deal with morons and halfwits, but it seems that I've surrounded myself with them. Lately, it's as if my whole world has come crashing down, culminating in the unfortunate but entirely necessary execution of Sharon and the children. I still can't help thinking about their bodies burning in the house, but the alternative would have been far worse.

For them, anyway.

"Hey!" a voice calls out, and I turn to see Leonard traipsing over from one of the far sheds, fastening his trousers along the way. He looks disheveled, as usual, and I can't help but sigh as I realize that in constructing my little empire, I've surrounded myself with men who lack my sense of purpose and rigor. It's hard to believe that Leonard - with his week-old stubble and his scrappy clothes - is my best employee.

"Any problems tonight?" I ask with a sigh as I get out of the car.

"Nothing," he replies with a faint smile. "Didn't think we'd be seeing you tonight, though, boss. It's not Tuesday already, is it?"

"No," I mutter, glancing across the yard. "It's not Tuesday, and this isn't a normal inspection. Have there been any visitors at all? Any lights nearby, maybe? Any helicopters?"

"Nothing."

"Not a single thing that seemed out of the ordinary?"

"You okay?" he asks. "You seem skittish."

"I'm wary," I reply, "and I'm cautious. I'm also tired. I need coffee."

"Come on in," he says, turning and slouching his way toward the office door. "Coffee's one thing I've got plenty of, so long as you don't mind it black. I forgot to buy milk."

"Black's fine," I mutter, following him to the door before stopping to glance back at the barn on the other side of the yard. Given the events that took place at the Staten building over the past twenty-four hours, I can't help but feel worried about this second facility. Then again, Leonard's much more reliable than Albert or Manuel ever were, and as I duck through the doorway and head into the office, I force myself to remember that it's important not to become paranoid. Fortunately, I'm not the kind of person who gets easily overcome by emotion.

"So were you just passing or something?" Leonard asks as he starts to boil some water. "I mean, if you don't mind me saying, it's not like you to just drop in unannounced. I thought you prefer things to run like clockwork."

"I wanted to surprise you," I mutter, walking over to the window and parting the blinds to look out at the yard. "I have some bad news," I continue. "The Staten site is no longer in operation. In fact, you might be seeing something about it on the news in the next few hours. I'm afraid the staff there proved to be inadequate to the task they were given." After a moment, I turn and see the shocked look on his face. "Relax," I add, "there's no need to worry. I've always kept the different sites completely separate from one another. There's not a scrap of evidence linking that place to this facility or to any of us."

"But -"

"Not a scrap," I say firmly. "Believe me, I took extra precautions." For a fraction of a second, I can't help but think back to the moment when I pulled the trigger and killed the children, and then the moment when I killed Sharon. Leonard has no idea of the sacrifices I make in order to keep this business running. "In fact," I continue after a moment, "I took more precautions than were strictly necessary."

"So what happened?" he asks, clearly agitated. "Did the cops just stumble onto the place?"

I shake my head. "Albert hired some local idiot named Manuel, but unfortunately Manuel had a pang of conscience and freed the women."

"You're not serious," Leonard replies, his eyes as wide as dinner-plates.

"Fortunately," I continue, "Albert was able to intercept Manuel before he could cause any more damage. Manuel is very much out of the picture." I pause for a moment. "So's Albert, actually," I add. "I couldn't tolerate his continued involvement in the project, and it's not as if I could just fire him and write a reference note."

"So..." He pauses. "You slugged him?"

"I had no choice," I reply, trying to sound calm. "I'm sorry, Leonard. I know you and Albert had built up something of a rapport, but there was no way I could let a weak link remain in the system. Please try to understand."

"Oh, I understand just fine," he replies, pouring hot water into two mugs before adding some instant coffee. "I think it's a damn shame, but I understand." He stirs the mugs. "I never thought Albert was the type to fuck up like that, though. He seemed like he had a good head on his shoulders."

For a moment, he seems lost in thought as he continues to stir the coffee.

"I need to know that this isn't going to cause us any problems," I say eventually.

"Us?" He smiles as he hands me a mug of coffee. "Hell, boss, you know you can rely on me. I don't hire anyone to help me, for precisely that reason. As long as you keep me around, you've got nothing to worry about. Not with *this* facility, anyway."

"I'm sure," I reply, before taking a sip of coffee. "This is foul," I mutter. "Are you sure it's coffee?"

"Cheapest in the store," he says with a smile, as if he's proud of the fact.

I pause for a moment. "I need to see them," I say finally.

"Who?"

"The boys," I continue. "The men. Whatever you want to call them. The assets. I need to see them."

He stares at me. "You *never* want to see them," he says after a moment. "You make a thing of -"

"I want to see them right now," I reply, interrupting him. "After all the crap that's gone down, I want to see them with my own eyes and make sure there are no problems." I wait for him to answer. "Is this going to be difficult to arrange?" I ask eventually. "I'm sorry if I'm intruding, Leonard, but I'm sure you'll understand that I'd like to double-check our arrangements."

"Well... sure," he says, setting his cup of coffee down before reaching into his pocket and pulling out a set of keys. "I should warn you, though. They stink. I mean, they really *stink*. I wash 'em down when they're going out usually, but when they're just in the barn, I let 'em live in their own filth. They don't know any better, so it's not like it's cruel or nothing."

"I want to see them," I say again, forcing myself to go through with this even though the thought makes my stomach churn. "I want to see for myself that everything's running smoothly. We can't afford any more mistakes, not after what happened at the Staten building tonight. The situation's under control, but any more knocks and we might have to start looking over our shoulders."

Joanna Mason

"So is this a new hobby?" Dawson asks. "Fainting?"

When I open my eyes, it takes me a moment to realize that I'm on a trolley in the back of an ambulance. I try to sit up, but I still feel a little dizzy; pausing for a moment, I wait for everything to settle, and finally - even though I've still got a pounding headache - I'm able to see that there's a drip running into my arm, connected to some kind of clear fluid in a bag hanging above the trolley. For a moment, I can't work out whether or not I'm back at the hospital having more of that dreaded chemotherapy.

"I'm not really the kind of person who needs a hobby," I tell him.

"Still," he replies, "it might help."

"What would you suggest? Stamp collecting?"

"You were pretty badly dehydrated," he continues. "Your blood alcohol level was kinda high too. Definitely over the limit for driving." He pauses. "Jesus, Jo, you could have just told me you were drunk. I'd have understood if you didn't want to come out until the morning."

"I'm not drunk," I say firmly, starting to panic as I realize that the paramedic might have given the game away and inadvertently told Dawson about my illness. "I'm fine," I continue, even though I feel like crap. "I didn't faint. I just... passed out a little. It's a different thing."

"Sure."

"It is!" I insist, although I immediately realize that I'm being way too defensive. "Where's the paramedic?" I ask after a moment.

"I told her I needed to talk to you alone," he replies.

I stare at him for a moment. "So why did it take you so long to call me?" I ask.

He frowns.

"As soon as I saw this case on the news," I continue, hoping to distract him, "I knew you'd be here, and I knew you'd need my help. I could almost see you in my mind's eye, fumbling around and trying to work out what the hell's going on. You've always needed me for this kind of case, but it took you hours to get in touch. So what gives?"

A faint smile crosses his lips. "Believe it or not," he says after a moment, "my first instinct isn't *always* to turn to you for help."

"It should be," I snap back. "You can't do these big cases without me."

"I can't do them *with* you, either," he replies. "Not if you're drunk or..." He pauses again. "People don't just faint like that if they're healthy, Jo. Even if they've been getting wasted. I saw the look in your eyes just before you collapsed. Sure, you've been drinking, but you can hold your liquor, so this was something else."

"I'm fine," I say firmly.

"Come on," he continues. "It's me. You can tell me -"

"Congratulations on the baby," I reply quickly, determined to get him off my case. "I spoke to Elaine earlier and she gave me the happy news. You must be so happy. I know you've always wanted to be a father."

He stares at me, and it's clear that I've finally managed to turn the tables. He looks shocked, as if this is the last thing he wants to talk about. Dawson knows my feelings about Elaine, and he's probably braced for a barrage of insults and ridicule.

"I can't believe you didn't tell me sooner," I continue with a smile, hoping to twist the knife a little deeper into his soul. "I hope I'm going to be invited to the baby shower. Of course, I'll have to find out what a baby shower actually involves first, 'cause the name along sounds kinda crazy."

"Jo -"

"It's great news," I add, determined not to let him get a word in. Not yet, anyway. "How long have you two been married now? Four years? Five? It's about time she started popping out little Dawsons. I mean, between us, I think if you'd waited any longer, people would have started wondering whether maybe there was a problem. Weak sperm, maybe, or knotted ovaries." I smile, keenly aware that I'm making him feel desperately uncomfortable. "This is gonna make me sound mean," I continue, leaning over to him and lowering my voice to a conspiratorial whisper, "but Elaine's got the kind of face that makes you think of knotted ovaries. It's hard picturing her as a mother, but I guess -"

"Jo -"

"Maybe it'll be the making of her?"

"Jo, please -"

"I wonder if she'll get a radiant glow -"

"Stop!" he says firmly.

Leaning back, I can't help but smile.

"Yes," he adds after a moment, "Elaine and I are having a baby. We've been trying to start a family for a while now, and eventually we went to see a fertility specialist. Everything went well and now it's all on course. She had her latest scan last week and it's all looking good, but you and I both know that we're not here to talk about my personal life."

"A fertility specialist?" I reply with a smile. "Does that mean you didn't actually have to put your -"

"Will you just shut the fuck up?" he adds, interrupting me. "Please? For one fucking minute, will you stop talking and just listen to me?"

I pause, forcing myself to keep smiling even though I'm a little surprised by his outburst.

"You're not fooling anyone," he continues. "You're sick, Jo. I can see it in your eyes. You've been off work for three months, and the only thing that could ever keep you at home would be..." He pauses, almost as if he doesn't want to say the words. "I know you," he adds. "I know you better than anyone else. I've been there before with you, remember? I've seen you when you're fighting this thing, and I know those little telltale signs of fear in your eyes, and in your voice. You think you can hide them, but you can't."

"You don't know what you're -"

"Cancer," he says suddenly.

I stare at him.

"It's back, isn't it?"

I sigh. The truth is, I was confident I could keep this whole mess from Dawson, but he seems to have surprised me and become a little more observant. Damn it, when did he decide to start noticing things?

"The same as before?" he asks.

We sit in silence for a moment.

"More or less," I say eventually, shifting uncomfortably on the awkward, creaky metal trolley. Looking up at the drip-bag, I see that I should be almost done soon, which is a relief; this is by far the most excruciating conversation I've ever had in my life, and I desperately want to get the hell out of this ambulance. After all, it's hard persuading someone that you're healthy when you're literally sitting in front of them with a drip running into your veins, even if the two situations are completely - *completely* - unconnected.

"And you're getting treatment?" he asks.

I nod.

"Chemo? Radiation? Pills?"

"All of the above."

"So how's it going?"

"Absolutely splendidly," I reply, forcing myself to meet his gaze even though eye contact is the last thing I want right now. "It's all, you know... super duper, that kind of thing. The treatment options have really come on leaps and bounds since the last time I was sick, and the doctor says I'm a real model patient. Get that, huh? I always thought I should be a model something."

"Are you in remission?"

"Sort of. I guess."

He sighs.

"What do you want me to say?" I continue, starting to feel a little exasperated.

"I want you to tell me if you're in remission," he replies.

"I'm in remission," I tell him, which isn't strictly true.

"Well that's one good thing," he mutters.

"I know what you're really asking," I reply. "You're asking if I'm gonna die." I pause, realizing that I still need to keep the truth from him. "No," I add. "I'm not gonna die. Not from cancer, anyway. Not this time. I have it, but I'm fighting it and it's almost gone. Another month, maybe two, and I'll be completely clear, and then I'll be back at work and I'll be putting you in the shade again." I pause, waiting for him to say something. "So watch out," I add with a smile.

"When did you find out?"

"A little while before all the recent stuff with Sam Gazade."

"Why didn't you tell me sooner?" he asks.

"Why didn't you tell me about the impending baby?"

"They're two very different things, Jo," he replies.

"Not really," I point out. "I have tumors growing in me, Elaine has a baby growing in her. It's just that the thing growing in me is evil and has to be killed, and the thing growing in Elaine is a wonderful little bundle of joy." I pause for a moment, unable to miss the irony. "She and I are pretty similar, really, when you think about it."

"Jo -"

"It's kinda funny, actually."

"Jo..." He pauses.

"What?" I ask, worried that he might somehow have figured out that I'm dying.

He shakes his head. "Forget it," he says quietly.

"Come on," I continue. "Out with it."

"It doesn't matter."

"What's wrong?" I ask. "Embarrassed?"

We sit in silence for a moment.

"This is a really awkward thing for me to ask," he continues eventually, "and I wouldn't say anything if it wasn't important, but I want to know the truth. When they carried you into the ambulance, I couldn't help noticing that you seem very..." He pauses again. "You seem very, *very*..." Another pause. "I couldn't help but notice a physical change. Like, something that you considered a few years ago, and now maybe you had it done..."

As soon as he says those words, I feel a wave of nausea pass through my body like a shiver.

"I know you swore not to have that kind of procedure last time," he continues, "but -"

"Typical," I say, interrupting him. "I'm being carted into an ambulance, and you're trying to sneak a peak."

"Jo -"

"You want me to look more like Jane Mansfield?" I ask with a smile. "You're a married man, Mike, with a kid on the way. You probably shouldn't be thinking about my boobs so much. Or if you have to, at least keep it to yourself."

"You had it done," he replies. "Didn't you?"

"Yeah," I say cautiously, keen to avoid the actual words. "Sorry, Mike. Those good old fun-bags are gone. Still, they had a pretty good ride, huh? I guess the only way was down, anyway; better for them to go out while they were on top, so to speak, than to watch gravity slowly drag 'em all the way to my belly. Just think of it as a more extreme, very localized form of liposuction." I pause, seeing the look of extreme discomfort in his eyes. "They were pretty damn good, though," I add, hoping to lighten the mood. "You remember, don't you?"

"I should get the paramedic," he replies wearily, standing up and climbing down from the back of the ambulance.

"Are you *angry*?" I ask incredulously.

"I'm tired," he replies. "I just wish you'd talked to me sooner."

"About my boobs?"

He doesn't reply.

"Congratulations about the baby," I call after him.

He turns to me.

"I mean it," I add, trying to strike a conciliatory tone. "It's a good thing. I'm sure..." I take a deep breath as I realize I'm going to have to say words I never, ever thought I'd say. "I'm sure you and Elaine will be wonderful parents."

"Your drip's done," he replies calmly. "I'll get the paramedic to unhook you."

Once he's gone, I sit alone in the back of the ambulance. I swear to God, I feel like I just want to crawl under a blanket and never let anyone see me again. I'd been hoping that somehow I could hide my condition from Dawson forever, and I'd been taking comfort from the fact that he didn't know the truth about what was happening to me. Still, he doesn't know *everything*, and that's good. He doesn't know I'm dying, and I always like to keep at least one lie between us.

John

"Jesus Christ," I mutter as Leonard unlocks the padlock and pulls the wooden door open, immediately releasing a cloud of the most foul-smelling stench I've ever encountered in my life. For a moment, I turn my back to the door and cover my face with the sleeve of my jacket. "What the hell's going on in there?" I splutter. "It smells like a farmyard!"

"Piss," he says, sounding bored. "Shit. Vomit. Sweat. God knows what else. I try not to think about it too much."

"I need them to stay alive," I reply, trying not to retch.

"I give 'em the antibiotics," he continues, "just like you wanted. I've got this friend who runs a pig farm, so I buy some of the drugs he uses."

"Still..." I pause as I try to get used to the smell. It's a thousand times worse than I ever imagined.

"I warned you," he replies matter-of-factly. "It's a waste of water to go dousing 'em down every day, so I just let 'em wallow in their own filth. It was good enough for the pigs on my friend's farm, so I reckon it's good enough for these fucking idiots. When you need to take one to get his photo taken, I can easily give him a quick swill and a haircut. I've become quite good at cutting hair, you know. Hell, maybe I should switch careers some time."

After taking a moment to calm myself, I switch on the flashlight and turn back to look through the door. It's dark in the shed, but I can hear a kind of general moan, as if some of the assets are already reacting to my arrival.

"Aren't they supposed to be asleep?" I ask.

"It's hard to get 'em in a real routine," Leonard replies. "They don't really do anything during the day, so they're mostly not tired at night. They kinda just stay like this most of the time. Not asleep and not awake. Just... twitching."

"Goddamn animals," I mutter, stepping through the door and shining the flashlight straight ahead. Sure enough, everything looks exactly the same as it looked the last time I was here: rows and rows of twisted, writhing men are chained to concrete blocks, with their curved, broken backs sticking up in the air. Although they're all wearing ragged clothing, it's quite clear just from looking at these people that they're developmentally sub-human. It's hard to believe that they could ever survive if we let them out of this place. What we're doing for them here is, in a way, far more humane than any treatment they'd receive in the real world.

"There are no changes, really," Leonard explains as he steps through the door and joins me in the raised platform at the head of the room. "Same old story, really. They're just waiting for when you need one of them."

"Good," I reply, shining the flashlight across the hunched, huddled figures. Most of them are curled up on the floor, either sleeping or pretending not to notice my arrival; as the light flickers across rows and rows or arched backs, however, I spot one or two assets who have dared to raise their heads and look directly at me. It gives me no pleasure to see the look of fear in their eyes, but it doesn't distress me either; the fear is simply part of the process, and it would benefit none of us to develop even the most basic of relationships. Besides, none of these fools can communicate with anything more than grunts and moans. I'm not even convinced that they can feel pain, since they lack the language skills necessary to form such complex ideas in their minds.

"See?" Leonard says, standing next to me. "They're all completely fine. There's nothing to worry about."

"That's what I thought about the Staten facility," I mutter, before stepping back out and waiting while Leonard re-locks the door. "We're down from three buildings to two," I continue after a moment. "That's a theoretical one third capacity reduction, although the loss is somewhat mitigated by the fact that the assets at the Staten location were all female. We can take the hit, but we can't afford any more losses. This has really pushed our backs against the wall."

"Are you gonna replace the lost assets?" he asks, putting the key in his pocket as he leads me back across the yard.

"There seems to be little point," I reply. "Besides, some of those women were reaching their twenty-second and twenty-third years. I should have cashed out on the older ones earlier. The simple truth is, there's not as much demand for women as there is for men." Pausing by the gate, I glance back at the barn, and suddenly I realize that Albert might have been right when he said that this mess was a blessing in disguise. After all, the operation has been running for years without an end in sight, and now I'm starting to contemplate the possibility of winding it all down. I could cash out over the next few months and finally go and do something respectable.

"It's okay, boss," Leonard says after a moment. "You can trust me. Come rain or shine, I'll keep this place ticking over."

"I know," I reply, turning to him. "Just hold the fort and wait for my next visit. I might stay low and skip Tuesday this week, but don't worry about anything. I've prepared for a moment like this, and soon we'll be back to normal. Just trust me when I say that the loss of one facility can in no way be linked to any of our other operations."

"You don't have to persuade me," he says, pulling a lever that activates the gate. "I've been working here long enough to know that you're in charge of things. If Albert fucked things up at the Staten facility, then that was his mistake. Shame, I liked the guy, but still, it was nothing to do with you. Maybe I misjudged him. The last thing we need around here is a fool."

"I hired him," I reply as I walk to my car. "I have to accept at least some of the responsibility."

As I drive away, I can't help but glance in my rear-view mirror and watch as Leonard secures the gate. He's a good man, and he's the only person apart from myself who can be trusted to keep this operation running smoothly. Still, it might be time to look to the future and start thinking about winding things down. I'm in my forties now, and one day I'd like to retire and actually enjoy the fruits of my labors. First, though, I need to get some rest. After the drama of the past twenty-four hours, I feel as if I'm about to collapse, and for some reason that I can't quite fathom, the sight of Sharon's dead body keeps playing on my mind.

Joanna Mason

Somehow, with everything that has been happening tonight, I've managed to lose track of time. I'm kind of surprised, therefore, when I climb out of the back of the ambulance, rubbing the sore spot on my arm where the needle went in, and see that the first rays of morning sun are starting to show in the distance. It's actually kind of a beautiful sight, and for a moment I just stand and stare at the wonders of nature.

"Fuck," I mutter finally, turning and looking over at the wreckage of the burned-out building. Forensic examiners are still crawling all over the place, and I guess they'll be continuing their microscopic analysis of the scene for days. As I wander over to the police cordon, trying to spot Dawson, I can't help but worry about what happened to me tonight. I was on the verge of a moment of inspiration, but then finally, just as it was about to strike, I passed out like a goddamn pussy. Is that how it's going to be from now on? Am I permanently fucked in the head?

"Detective Mason?" asks a voice nearby.

Turning, I find a cop standing next to me.

"Detective Dawson asked me to tell you that he was called back to the station," the cop continues, sounding a little unsure of himself. "He said to thank you for coming out, and he'll be in touch soon."

"He's gone?" I ask, somewhat stunned to realize that Dawson didn't wait around for me. Glancing over my shoulder, I realize that his car is gone.

"He asked me to arrange a ride for you back to the Wash house so you can get a lift home. He also gave me orders to arrest you if you try to drive your own vehicle while you're under the influence of alcohol." He pauses. "I'm sorry, that's just what he told me I had to do."

"Huh," I mutter. Dawson's been pissed off at me before, and annoyed, and sad, and a hundred other things, but he always sticks around for the duration. Feeling a cold chill pass through my body, I try to think back to our earlier conversation in the ambulance and work out where I might have said anything to upset or offend him. After a moment, I realize that I didn't say anything bad at all, so he's obviously just got some kind of bee under his bonnet and it's blatantly not my fault. Damn it, what the hell is wrong with him?

"Are you ready?" the cop asks.

"Just give me a minute," I reply, walking past the cordon until I reach the forensic examiner we spoke to earlier. He's still working at the same spot, except this time he's managed to fully uncover a number of bones. I stare at them for a moment:

charred and in some cases splintered, they look like the remains of people who died hundreds of years ago, and it's hard to accept that just a day or two ago, they were living, breathing women. "How's it going?" I ask after a moment. "Those look very human to me."

"There were at least five women here when the place burned," he replies. "Possibly as many as eight, but I'm going to have to get back to the lab before I can give a definitive answer. The fire caused a lot of damage, and I think some pieces are still missing."

"And they were all in this one spot?" I ask.

"It seems that way."

"Like they were huddled together," I continue, trying to imagine what it must have been like for them as the entire building burned around them.

"Or piled up," he points out. "If I had to guess, based on the arrangement of the bones, I'd err on the side of them having been dead before the fire started, and then someone gathered their bodies together like this." He pauses, before turning to me. "Detective Dawson still thinks this is the result of cult activity, but I've been to that kind of crime scene and -"

"I know," I say, interrupting him. "Dawson just likes to have a theory. Any theory'll do, even if it's wrong. He hates admitting that he doesn't know, so he usually just grabs the first thought that pops into his head and runs with it until I turn up and point out that he's being an idiot." I glance over at the spot where Dawson's car was parked earlier, and for a fraction of a second it occurs to me that maybe I could have been a little nicer to him; these thoughts quickly evaporate, however, as I remind myself that if he's offended or annoyed, it's entirely his own fault. If anything, I was *too* nice and *too* polite to him back in that ambulance. Whatever's up with him, I'm sure he'll be over it by the next time I see him.

"You got any ideas?" the examiner asks. "So far, this site isn't making much sense to me. We've got plenty of pieces, but the overall picture just hasn't come together."

"It will," I reply, turning and making my way across the wreckage until, finally, I'm standing in what appears to have been the center of the building. I look at the metal girders and realize that this place was basically one large enclosed structure with a high roof. It's exactly the kind of facility where someone would store animals; in fact, it reminds me of those barns where chickens are kept in little cages. The most obvious explanation, then, is that someone was farming those women and keeping them here because they wanted to use their bodies, but at the same time I'm getting the feeling that this was a commercial operation. Sure, there might be a few cannibals knocking around, but not enough to justify a human meat farm.

I stand in silence for a moment.

That moment of inspiration is still inside my mind, waiting to come out. It's almost as if my brain already knows the answer, and I just need to tease it out, but it's so much harder than it ever was before. Sometimes, I worry that those cancer drugs have caused permanent damage to the way my thoughts work, and that even though I've been off them for three months now, I'll never get back to my old brilliance.

"Come on," I whisper, hoping against hope that I don't faint again. "Just one more time. I swear, just once more and I'll be happy. Give me this one."

Closing my eyes, I wait.

And that's when it comes.

"Identities," I whisper, opening my eyes as I imagine all those women being chained up in this place, kept away from the outside world. Suddenly the whole goddamn thing seems so simple and so obvious, I can't believe I didn't see it sooner. Whoever was keeping these women captive wasn't doing it for their bodies or as part of some kind of sexual game, and it sure as hell wasn't a cult: it was an identity farm, where people could be raised until they reached a certain age, at which point their whole identities could be sold off to the highest bidders.

It sounds crazy, but it make sense in a twisted kind of way.

Reaching into my pocket, I pull out my phone and bring up Dawson's number, but at the last moment I pause as I realize that maybe he doesn't want to hear from me right now. Hell, after the way he treated me, I'm not even certain I *should* drop the answer in his lap so easily. Still, I'm absolutely goddamn certain that I'm right. Turning, I look across the wreckage and watch for a moment as the forensic examiner lifts a set of human bones onto a small black sheet.

I'm right.

I *know* I'm right.

This was an identity farm, and if I had to put money on it, I'd bet there's at least one more out there. After all, the victims here were all female. Somewhere, there have to be men too.

John

This is crazy. I shouldn't be reacting like this, but I can't help it.

It's almost 8am and I'm sitting in my car, watching as sunrise slowly transforms the street from a dark and foreboding place to a pretty little suburban thoroughfare, lined with trees and neat, well-maintained houses. The horrors of last night seem to have fallen away completely, like the last remembered ashes of a nightmare. In many ways, this street is the American Dream writ large, with picket fences and lawn sprinklers as far as the eye can see. I can still remember when I was a kid and I used to walk the long way home from school just so that I could pass by houses like this; I knew from an early age that I wanted a quiet, normal life, but it took me a while to work out how to get what I desired.

And now I'm sitting here, quietly sobbing.

The truth is, I feel desperately sad about Sharon's death, and about the death of our two children. They were good people and they deserved nothing but happiness, yet they had the misfortune to have me as a husband and father. Sniffing back more tears, I think back to the moment when I pulled the trigger and ended Sharon's life, and I can't help but wonder whether, in that split second, she knew what was happening. Did she realize that I was killing her? Did she feel pain? Did she suspect that she was married to a monster and that he was finally showing his true colors?

And what about the children? I tried to make their deaths quick and painless, and I *think* I succeeded, but there are always a few doubts. Might they, too, have had some inkling of what their father was about to do to them? Eliza was perhaps too young to really understand, but did Kieran have a moment of realization before the bullet split his head open? At least the silencer meant that each of them could be killed in order, without the next waking up. I hate it when people have time to scream.

Still, I did the right thing. If they'd lived, they might have found out the truth about me. Sharon thought I was on the road all the time, selling insurance in distant cities. She used to ask why I couldn't just use the internet to do my work, but I always told her that I specialized in the personal touch, and eventually she came to understand that I'd be away for weeks on end, but also that I'd make the most of our time together whenever I managed to get home. She was happy with her life, and I could never have let her endure its collapse. She would have suffered far more, and for far longer, if she'd lived and the truth about my facilities had become known.

Realizing that the tears have stopped, I take one final look at my eyes in the rear-view mirror and then I get out of the car, pushing the door shut and taking a step back before brushing my suit down and making sure that I'm neat and tidy. Walking around to the rear of the car, I open the trunk and take out one of my three briefcases, before slamming the trunk closed and starting the short trip along the sidewalk and then, finally, up the driveway that leads to one of the nearby houses.

I slip my key into the lock as quietly as possible.

Once I'm inside, I set the briefcase down quietly and remove my coat. The house seems so still and quiet, yet at the same time it's full of potential: potential for noise, and for joy, and for happiness. I can never understand how anyone could live alone, when surely the whole point of life is that one must live with other people and share their lives? All that really matters in the world is family. With a heavy heart but a faint smile on my lips, I loosen my shirt collar while heading upstairs. It feels good to be here. I've missed this place, and I need to relax for a few days.

"John?" a weary voice calls out from one of the bedrooms. "Is that you?"

As soon as I get to the door, I push it open and see Barbara sitting up in bed, rubbing her eyes.

"Hey honey," I say, keeping my voice down so that the kids don't hear. "I'm home."

"I thought you weren't due back until next week," she says. "Is everything okay?"

"Everything's absolutely fine," I reply, my heart gladdened by the sight of her beautiful eyes. Stepping over to the bed, I lean down and kiss the side of her face. "I just shuffled a few appointments around and realized I had a small window to come back home."

"You should have called ahead," she replies. "I'd have made breakfast."

"No need," I say, sitting on the side of the bed. "You look as beautiful as ever, my darling. Have the children been behaving?"

"Just about," she says with a smile, "although Claire's been something of a little madam. I guess she's just been missing you, like the rest of us, and her back's been giving her a little trouble. I was thinking of taking her to get the screws checked."

"Well," I reply, kissing the end of her nose, "I'm home now, and that's what matters. I'm sorry, Barbara, but I think I might have to get some rest. I drove through the night, which probably wasn't entirely wise, and I just need to crash out. Do you think it might be possible to keep Claire from disturbing me until at least lunchtime?"

"Of course," she says, kissing my cheek again. "I'm so pleased you managed to surprise us, John. I hope you're not neglecting your work."

"Never," I reply with a smile.

"I guess this is what I get for marrying such a romantic guy, huh?" she replies, slipping out of bed and grabbing her dressing gown. "Go on, in you get. I'll sort everything out."

Once she's left the room, I start to undress. Sharon's death is still playing on my mind, but at least I can take comfort here with Barbara and Claire. I suppose most men would be cut up and distraught by the events of the past day, but I think I'm starting to cope quite well, despite the tears I cried earlier. I did the right thing by Sharon and the other children, and I must simply work hard to ensure that the same fate doesn't befall Barbara and Claire. My life would be so much easier if I didn't complicate it with all these entanglements, but I have no choice.

At heart, I guess I'm just a family man.

Epilogue

She stays where she is, not daring to move. Even breathing seems like a terrible risk, so she restricts herself to shallow intakes of air, trying to keep her chest completely still. She has to blink, of course, but she only allows herself this luxury once every thirty seconds. Other than these few small indiscretions, she stays completely motionless, terrified to move a muscle.

But still the visitor comes.

Every hour or so, the door opens and a woman enters the room. She has a kind face and she's wearing some kind of neat, clean gray tunic. She tries to talk to the girl, to get her to respond, but she uses words that the girl doesn't understand. At first, the girl was scared that the woman was going to hurt her, but now she's convinced that it's a trap. The man must have sent the woman to trick her into moving when she hasn't been given permission, but the girl is too smart to fall for such a ruse.

So she ignores the woman completely.

Eventually, the woman leaves, although the girl knows she'll be back eventually. For now, though, the girl simply focuses on remaining still and hoping that - if he's watching - the man will be able to see that she's being obedient. As far as the girl is concerned, the only thing that matters is that she's able to please the man, because she knows from first-hand experience that his anger can be terrifying. She's felt his kicks and punches in the past, and she's witnessed the way he treated some of the others back in the barn. More than anything in the whole world, the girl just wants to avoid pain.

He's in her mind, though.

Whenever she allows her thoughts to wander, she can see his image, coming closer and closer. She doesn't entirely understand what's happening, and although she wants to be certain that the image is just part of her dreams, she can't entirely dismiss the possibility that in some way he might really be watching her, waiting for her to make a mistake so that he can strike. She can see the look in his eyes; he's ready to punish her, to beat her down again, to make her pay for daring to run away.

After what feels like an eternity, the girl can handle the strain no longer. Looking up at the ceiling of the little white room, she feels tears pour down her face as the broken bones in her back click together. Finally, she opens her mouth and lets out a wild, animalistic wail of misery.

Part Three

Burned

Prologue

22 years ago

He picks his way through the darkened building, keeping one hand in his jacket pocket so that he can pull out the gun if it's needed. This isn't his usual territory, but he bent the rules tonight because he desperately needs to make another purchase. There are risks involved, but he's thought them through and decided that he's willing to let his pulse quick just a little: he wants to get the hell out of this place, but first he needs to conclude the deal.

"It's me!" he calls out, his voice echoing across the vast, open shell of the old cannery. Checking his watch, he sees that it's precisely 9pm, which means she should be here by now. He hates it when people are late, but he knows he shouldn't expect too much from this woman; when he spoke to her a couple of weeks ago, she seemed to be high on some kind of drug and barely able to form whole sentences.

Just another piece of human trash.

"Are you here?" he shouts.

No reply.

"Bitch," he mutters, before turning to walk away.

"Wait!" she calls out, her voice sounding half-frozen.

Stopping, he looks back and sees a small figure shuffling out of the shadows, carrying a bundle of rags in her arms. She makes her way hesitantly across the broken glass that litters the floor, but finally she gets close enough for him to see her tired, pained face and her large, heavily ringed eyes. Whatever drug she's on, it seems to have aged her terribly. She could be any age from late teens to early fifties.

"I thought you weren't coming," he says firmly.

"I just..." She pauses. "You know, I wasn't sure..."

"I'm not here for a conversation," he replies, reaching into his pocket and taking out first the gun, then the envelope of money. "I assume you're still going to go through with this," he continues, eying the suspiciously motionless bundle in her arms. "Please, tell me you're not going to waste my time."

She nods.

"One thousand dollars," he continues, holding the envelope up for her to see. He's practiced this moment so many times in front of the bathroom mirror, testing out different ways to make himself seem imposing. "That's a lot of money, isn't it? A thousand dollars could buy you a whole lot of stuff. Hell, it could get you a new start in life. Move away, see if you can get yourself back on track." He pauses, and as he stares at the woman's terrified face, he realizes that the thousand dollars won't be spent on anything meaningful; she'll just blow it on drugs, and then she'll be right back where she started. "So is that it?" he adds, looking at the bundle.

"His name's Tommy," she replies, her voice faltering a little.

"Did you bring his papers?"

She nods.

"And you're alone?"

She nods again.

"Then give him to me. Quick."

She pauses, before stepping forward and passing the child to him and then snatching the envelope of cash. There's something hesitant and alert about her, almost as if she's a wild animal.

"Is he healthy?" the man asks, looking down at the child's sleeping face.

"He's fine," the woman replies as her trembling fingers open the envelope to check the cash. "It's all in his papers. They're in there, in his blanket, just like you wanted."

"That's fine," he says calmly.

"What are you gonna do with him?" she asks. "I mean, are you gonna raise him? Like, are you and your wife gonna raise him as your own or something like that?"

He nods, even though it's a lie.

"You promise?"

"Apple pie, picket fences and all the trimmings," he tells her.

"And he'll have a good life, right? I mean, I'm only giving him away because I want him to have a future. If he stays with me, he's just gonna end up..." Her voice trails off. "Well, you know..."

"You don't want him to end up like you," the man says after a moment.

"No."

"Of course he won't," he says darkly. "He'll be fine."

"Just look after him, yeah? Make sure he has a good life."

"Go on," he replies. "Get out of here. You've got your money, so what are you waiting for? There's no need to stand around and pretend that you care. We both know you just want to get off and buy more drugs."

"That's not fair!" she says.

"Then give me the money back," he suggests. "If this is really about giving little Tommy a better life, then why are you selling him to the highest bidder? You don't know a damn thing about me. For all you know, I could be a goddamn monster."

"You look kind," she replies cautiously.

He smiles. "You don't strike me as someone who has a history of good judgment."

"Please..." she whispers.

"You're an idiot," he continues, "but at least your son will never have to grow up and come face to face with the complete mess that his mother has become. Don't worry; even if he asks, I'll never tell him anything about you. As far as he's concerned, you'll just be an idea, a concept... I'll give him a real home, and a real mother. He won't even miss you. Hell, he won't even know you existed."

The woman opens her mouth to say something, but finally she just turns and starts hurrying away.

"Bitch'll be dead in a few months anyway," the man mutters, before looking down at the child. "Sorry, kid, but you were born to a woman who's in no way equipped to be a mother. If you'd stayed with her, you'd have ended up freezing to death or starving. At least with me..." He pauses. "Well, you won't starve, and you'll have a roof over your head. And then one day, in many years' time, you'll make me a whole heap of money. Until then, you won't have too much of a hard time."

With that, he turns and carries the child toward the exit. He's got what he came for, and he has no intention of hanging around any longer in such a rough neighborhood. Besides, he doesn't really care about the child *or* its mother; all he cares about is the fact that one day, not soon but one day far off in the future, he'll be able to sell the child's identity for a hell of a lot more than the thousand dollars he paid out today. To him, the child is just another asset to be broken, reshaped and then eventually sold.

As they reach the car parked outside the deserted cannery, little Tommy Symonds finally starts to cry.

Joanna Mason

Today

"Hey," says Mezki with a shocked look on his face, "I thought you were off sick?"

"I am," I reply, barely even stopping to smile as I hurry into the office. "I just came in to use the facilities." Pulling Dawson's empty chair out from the desk in the corner, I take a seat and start typing a password into the computer. I was hoping there'd be no-one around this morning, but if someone *has* to be here, Mezki's one of my more tolerable colleagues. The guy might as well have 'harmless' tattooed on his forehead.

"Does your log-in still work while you're sick?" he asks, coming over to stand next to the desk. "I thought -"

"It's not *my* log-in," I reply, just as an error message comes up on the screen. Figuring I must have mis-typed Dawson's password, I try again, but the same error message appears.

"Huh," I mutter, staring at the screen.

"Told you," Mezki replies with a self-satisfied smile. "When an officer is off sick for more than three days, his or her log-in credentials are restricted until -"

"I know," I mutter, trying for a third time, and once again striking out. "Like I said," I continue, "this isn't my log-in. Dawson must have changed his password."

"Why would he do that?" Mezki asks.

"God knows," I reply. "He knows I use it sometimes, so why the hell..." I pause as, suddenly, it all starts to make sense. "That slippery bastard," I continue, genuinely shocked that he'd make such a passive aggressive move. "He knew full well that I'd come in and try to get onto the system," I continue, thinking out loud, "so he changed his password purely to piss me off."

"Or to comply with the rules," Mezki points out.

"I need your password," I reply, turning to him.

He raises an eyebrow.

"Come on," I continue, "I just need to check up a few details about two cases. I'm looking for something, and I can't wait until I'm back on duty. This is actual police work here, okay?"

"There's no way in hell I'm giving you my password again," he replies firmly. "Not after last time. Do you realize how embarrassing it was when I was called into Schumacher's office and asked to explain all the porn that my account had accessed?"

"You're such a prude," I reply with a smile. "The stuff I was looking at would be perfectly acceptable in a country like Sweden or France." I wait for him to capitulate, but he seems to have learned from his past mistakes. "Fine," I mutter. "If Dawson changed his password, it'll still be something pretty obvious." I type the name Elaine into the password field, but all I get is an error message; next, I try Juha, which is the name of his dog, but I strike out again; just for a laugh, I try a few variations of my own name, but of course nothing works. Sitting back, I stare at the screen, trying to work out what the hell he could have chosen. Although Mike Dawson is a smart guy, he's also *totally* the kind of person who'd write his password down on a note next to his keyboard; glancing around the desk, I spot various files and print-outs, but nothing that screams 'password'.

"What's so important, anyway?" Mezki asks. "Are you coming back to work soon?"

"Sure," I mutter, focused on the urgent need to crack Dawson's password. Finally, realizing that I need to get out of here before Schumacher sees me, I try to work out what a guy like Dawson would opt for if he was in a hell of a hurry. He'd pick a complex password, something that he hoped no-one else would guess, but it'd have to be something easy to remember. Finally, I try the pin-code for his ATM, then the pin-code for his mobile phone and the code for the security system at his house, and finally his phone number itself. When all of these come up short, I try my own phone number, and then out of sheer desperation, I try Elaine's.

Bingo.

"His wife's phone number," I mutter, smiling at the thought of Dawson's naive belief that something so simple would ever keep me out. "The guy's got ambition, I'll give him that."

"So now that you've illegally accessed his account," Mezki says, "what's your plan? You know, just in case I ever need to recount these events in front of some kind of disciplinary panel."

"I need the files related to two cases," I reply as I plug a USB drive in the computer. Opening various folders on Dawson's desktop, I start looking through for file names related to the women who turned up out at that farm the other day, as well as anything covering the fire at the nearby building. I'm not certain how Dawson would have titled any relevant reports, so I just start going through everything I can find and copying it to my drive.

"You realize this is grossly unethical, right?" Mezki says after a moment.

"Don't you have work to do?" I ask, focusing on getting the files copied as quickly as possible.

"I *should* be stopping you," he replies. "The only reason I'm not is that I'd rather stand back and watch the resulting storm from afar. Dawson's gonna know you've done this, Jo."

"How?" I ask.

"Because you'll tell him. You'll decide to show off by bragging about how easily you guessed his new password and got into his files."

"I -" I start to say, before realizing that he's right. "Not for ages," I reply bitterly. "I'll wait until it doesn't matter anymore, and anyway, I'll put it in context and he'll totally understand. He'll be fine with it. Hell, he's always fine with it eventually." Searching through the last set of files, I realize that there's nothing relating to the two cases I'm interested in. Opening up the main database, I start searching for the cases, but pretty quickly I come up against another password-protected folder.

"Problem?" Mezki asks.

"The IT system's all fucked up again," I reply. "Dawson's working these cases so he should have full access to the relevant files."

"Not anymore," Mezki replies. "He requested to be taken off both those cases this morning. He's been transferred to a suspicious house-fire out in the suburbs instead. Jordan Carver's taken over the case about those girls."

"Jordan who?" I ask, frowning as I stare at the screen.

"Some new hot-shot guy who's been parachuted in to give us a kick up the ass and get better results. So far he's done a hell of a lot of kicking, and... well, I guess the results are supposed to come through any time now." He pauses to take a sip of coffee. "The guy's got crazy eyes. He's intense, Jo, and he's got the whole department running scared."

Still trying to get the files I want from the network, I can't help but wonder why the hell

Dawson would ask to be taken off an investigation. He's covered dozens of cases exactly like this in the past, and even though the pieces didn't seem to be coming together so far, he must have known that I'd come riding to the rescue eventually. With a new boss to impress, I'd have thought he'd be keen to get some early glory.

"You're the medical examiner," I say suddenly, turning to Mezki as I realize I could try a different approach. "You have access to *all* the files -"

"No way!" he replies. "I told you, Jo, I'm not letting you onto my account."

"I promise I won't download any more porn," I reply, trying to reassure him, before realizing that I've probably burned this particular bridge. "Not even so much as *one* photo of a horse."

He shakes his head.

"Fine," I add, taking the USB drive out of the computer and passing it to him. "Copy the files yourself. Everything relating to those girls, and the fire at that building out in the middle of nowhere... and while you're at it, give me the details on whatever cases Dawson's work on these days. I'd like to keep up to date."

"And what do I get in return?" he asks with a skeptical frown.

"Do this for me," I reply with a smile, "and I'll tell you how to remove the virus I installed on your computer last time I used it."

He narrows his eyes.

"Keylogger," I whisper.

"You're bluffing."

"Am I?"

He pauses, clearly undecided.

"All I have to do is check the logs. Don't worry, though. If you've been doing anything embarrassing, I won't go to Schumacher about it. I'll just -"

"Okay!" he says hurriedly, snatching the USB drive from my hand. "But this is the last time, okay? I'm not your goddamn performing monkey. That's Dawson's job."

"He seems to have resigned," I mutter as Mezki heads over to his desk and plugs the USB drive into his computer. As I turn back to look at Dawson's screen, I find myself trying to work out why the hell he'd get himself reassigned to different cases. He seemed off-color the other night, but although I've always been able to predict his moods, this particular development has taken me by surprise. Something about Michael Dawson has changed, something deep down and far-reaching, and I need to find out what, and why.

And then I need to solve all his cases for him.

John

"So can I have some money?" Claire asks, standing in the doorway and watching as I pour myself some coffee. "It's really important, Dad. This camp could be totally make or break for me."

"I know the feeling," I mutter, staring at my phone as it sits silently on the table.

"It's only three hundred dollars," she continues, "and it's not like I'm gonna be spending it on parties or anything like that. Two-fifty's for the camp fees, forty's for travel, and the other ten's just so that I'm not completely socially ridiculed. I mean, I kinda became a recluse while I was having my back surgery, so don't you think it's only fair if I try to catch up with my peers?"

I turn to her, and suddenly I realize I have no idea what she's talking about. "Camp?" I ask. "What camp?"

"No-one ever listens to me!" she replies, stamping her foot in frustration.

"Talk to your mother," I reply, aware that I'm being rather vague but unable to stop thinking about the phone call I'm expecting. "If she -"

Before I can finish, my phone rings and I grab it. Sure enough, the number calling me is unlisted.

"I have to take this," I tell Claire as I hurry though to my office.

"Dad!"

"Talk to your mother!" I call back to her, before heading through to the next room and walking over to my desk. "It's me," I say as I answer the phone. "You're two minutes late. I was expecting you to be bang on time. You're lucky I didn't burn this number already."

"I'm sorry," says the voice on the other end of the line, sounding frazzled and stressed. "It's not that easy right now." There's a roaring sound behind him for a moment.

"Where the hell are you?" I ask.

"Gas station."

"Jesus," I mutter. "Okay, so I assume my colleague explained all the details."

"Sure," he replies, "I've got the money. I just need to know that you've got what I need."

"There's no need to worry about that," I reply, walking over to the window and looking out at the garden. Barbara's down by the herb garden, pottering about in her usual way; she looks very happy and peaceful, which is always nice to see; I like to provide a good home for my family, even if my methods are somewhat unusual. "I want to be very clear," I continue, "that there are to be no re-negotiations at any stage. If the asking price is not met, even if the shortfall is just a solitary cent, the deal will be off. I offer reliable, bullet-proof solutions to big problems, and I expect to be compensated in return."

"The money's not a fucking problem," the guy hisses. "What worries me is whether I look anything like the guy!"

"That's not going to be a problem," I reply with a smile. "We have a unique system set up to ensure that all our customers are matched to an identity that closely resembles their original appearance. I think you'll be very pleasantly surprised when you see what we have to offer." I wait for a reply, but all I can hear is background noise from the gas station. "I understand why you're feeling nervous," I continue, determined to keep him on the hook, "but when you see the facilities we operate, you'll understand the scale of our operation." I glance over at the door, just to make sure that no-one can overhear me. "Words are empty, though," I add. "I need to show you. How soon can you be at the location my colleague told you about?"

"Tomorrow," he says quickly.

"Shall we say... midday?"

"If you try to pull anything on me -"

"There's no danger of that," I reply calmly.

"Don't bullshit me!" he continues. "I won't have the money with me, if that's what you're thinking. I'll have a deposit, but the rest'll be delivered once the whole thing is done. I'm not defenseless, okay? If you think you can get a drop on me, I'll fucking make you pay. I didn't get this far by being an easy target."

"I don't see why we need to draw this out," I continue. "The whole 'thing', as you describe it, can easily be completed tomorrow. You can walk away from our facility with a new life and a new future."

"I just..." He pauses. "I just need this second chance, yeah?"

"I understand completely," I reply. "My associates and I specialize in helping people like you. At the same time, I have no need or desire to get into the details of your background. None of that is important or relevant to me in the slightest. In fact, I think it would be better if we refrain from developing any kind of personal relationship. I don't need to know anything about your past life and transgressions, and I certainly have no intention of telling you any details about myself."

"That's fine by me," he says, clearly in a state of panic. "I'll be there at noon. You'd better show up, though. I don't want to be messed around. I don't fucking have time to be stood up by a bunch of assholes! This is life and death!"

"Don't worry," I say with a smile. "I'll be there. I want your money, remember? Just think of me as a businessman. I have a product to sell, and you wish to make a purchase. It's as simple as that." I wait for a reply, but suddenly the background noise from the gas station is cut off dead as he puts the phone down. Smiling, I remove the back of my cellphone and take out the card, which I quickly fold in half before dropping it into the trashcan next to my desk.

"Who was that?" asks Claire.

Turning, I see that she's standing in the doorway.

"Just a colleague," I say, taken aback by the fact that she was able to sneak up on me so easily. I'm usually very careful, and it pains me to realize that I let my guard down. "I was discussing a business deal," I add, trying to work out how much I should smile in order to put her at ease. Although she's only fifteen years old, Claire's a very smart and precocious girl, and she's eying me with a look of great suspicion. "You know," I continue, "I was also thinking about your request for money for that... what was it, again? A camp of some sort?"

"It's a summer sports camp."

"And your back won't be a problem?"

"I'm not an invalid," she points out.

"Right," I say, hurrying to my desk and pulling open the drawer where I keep some of my spare cash. Opening an envelope, I count out three hundred dollars and then, just to give her an extra little boost, another two hundred. "Here's five hundred," I continue, hurrying over to her and pressing the money into her hand. "We don't want you being caught short while you're making new friends, do we? Kids these days are so shallow and fixated on material gain. They'll probably judge you based purely on how much money you've got."

"I don't need five hundred," she replies darkly. "I just need three hundred."

"But five hundred would give you some leeway," I point out with a smile. "You know, to have a little extra fun. Maybe buy some new clothes, impress your friends, that sort of thing. I mean, Jesus Christ, it's a dark day when a father has to help his teenage daughter think of ways to spend a few extra bucks." I wait for her to reply. "Am I right?"

She stares at me.

"What about a thousand?" I add, although I immediately realize that I've gone too far. Damn it, I'm not good under pressure; I prefer to plan ahead and have some kind of plan worked out in my mind before I deal with difficult situations. When I'm forced to improvise, I usually go way too far.

"I just need three," she says, counting out three hundred dollars before passing the remaining two hundred back to me. "You keep the rest. You can't go splashing all this cash about. After all, you're only an insurance salesman."

"Are you sure?" I ask, forcing a smile. "I've been doing very well at work lately, and I don't see why the whole family shouldn't benefit. I mean, money isn't supposed to be hoarded, is it? We should all be able to do the things that interest us, even if..." I pause as I realize that I'm starting to press home the point a little too far. "Well," I add finally, "I'm sure you get the idea."

"You've sold a lot of insurance, huh?"

"Lots and lots."

"But still, it's... *just* insurance."

There's a part of me that wants to tell her the truth, to make her understand that I'm not some loser in a dead-end job. It's an outrage that my own daughter has no idea of her father's brilliance, but for now at least, I guess I have to keep pretending that I'm nothing more than a lowly insurance salesman.

A faint smile crosses her lips. "You must be very good at what you do."

"Does it surprise you to realize that your father happens to be one of the best insurance salesmen in the whole goddamn country?" I ask, although once again I recognize that I've gone way too far and, besides, the boast sounds pathetic. "If you change your mind," I add, putting the rejected two hundred dollars in my pocket, "just let me know. The offer will remain on the table for the duration, so keep it in mind. Seriously, Claire, money's no object. Two hundred dollars? I could wipe my ass on two hundred dollars!"

She glances at my desk for a moment. "Nice to know," she replies, before turning and heading away.

Once she's gone, I take a deep breath and try to pull myself together. I let my guard down just now, and I should never have allowed Claire to overhear my conversation with a potential customer. I guess I've made a few little mistakes lately, and I need to get a lot more discipline back into my operation. As I head over to the window, I spot Claire heading out into the garden, counting the money as she goes. I might have dodged a bullet for today, but I'm worried that she's starting to get suspicious. It was dumb of me to start bragging about money, but I just get so angry when they treat me like some pathetic little nobody. Hopefully, her suspicions aren't deep-rooted.

I've got plenty of children dotted around the country. If necessary, I can afford to lose one more. However, I'd rather not.

Joanna Mason

"Mason," I say, flashing my badge at the fire chief without giving him time to notice that it's expired. "What have we got here?"

"I just finished explaining to your colleague -"

"So explain to me," I tell him, glancing over at the burned-out husk of what used to be an ordinary suburban family house in an ordinary middle-class neighborhood. "What happened here?"

"We've recovered four bodies," he replies, leading me past the cordon. "They've been sent for examination, but based on the sizes, I'd say two of them were children. I'm no expert, but judging from their condition, I'd say it's gonna take dental records to identify them. Accelerants were used on the house *and* its occupants, which means most of the usual identifies are gonna be long gone."

"Someone really wanted to get rid of them, huh?" I reply, forcing a smile.

"We got the first reports at around midnight," he continues. "We were here eight minutes later, but as you can imagine, there was nothing we could do. That smell in the air is from all the gasoline that was used. Usually, arsonists use a small amount liberally spread throughout the property to ensure that the fire gets started, but in this case it looks like the whole place was soaked."

"So you're sure it was deliberate?" I ask, stopping next to a burning pile of twisted black wood.

"Unless you can think of an innocent reason why someone might douse their entire house in gasoline and then play with matches," he replies. "Someone wanted this place to burn good, and that's exactly what happened."

Spotting movement nearby, I see Dawson coming around from the rear of the site. He glances over toward me, and there's an instant, and kind of satisfying, look of shock on his face when he sees me, followed by a hint of resignation. I guess he knew I'd show up eventually, even if he probably hoped he could avoid me for a while.

"If you want my opinion -" the fire chief starts to say.

"That's okay," I reply with a smile, "I already have enough opinions of my own. Thanks for the offer, though." Heading over to Dawson, I watch as he stares at the ruins of the house. The entire place has been completely destroyed, and it's hard to believe that we can learn much from the remains. I mean, sure, the forensics guys are gonna be crawling all over the site for days, and there's a chance they'll find something useful, but the whole property has basically been turned to ash. Someone wanted to remove all traces of the house's prior state, and it looks like they succeeded.

"Is this a social call?" Dawson asks eventually, not looking over at me, "or did you just happen to be in the neighborhood?"

"I just happened to be looking through the files on your computer," I tell him, "and I saw you'd been assigned to this case."

"Nice try," he replies, "but I know you're bluffing. I changed my password."

"Damn," I mutter, feigning irritation. "I guess you got me." I wait for him to say something, but he simply turns back to look at the remains of the house. "So you had a big juicy case," I continue after a moment, "with a bunch of random broken-backed girls dragging themselves away from some kind of captive environment, plus a burned-out building in the middle of nowhere, and you *chose* to drop that case and come investigate some kind of petty arson in the suburbs?" I pause again. "What the hell's *that* all about?"

"I let Jordan Carver take the other case," he replies, as if that simple fact settles the debate.

"Why would you do that?"

"I could tell he wanted it. He's a big-shot, thinks he's headed to the top. I figured he'd have a better chance of getting somewhere with that case."

"But he won't have me helping him," I point out, hoping to at least get a smile in return.

He looks down at his notebook.

"And we all know how useful I am," I add. "Right?"

"I don't need your help, Jo."

"You kinda do," I reply. "I mean, you pretty much just admitted it. You know damn well that I'd have come and given you some pushes on that case, and we'd have solved it long before some guy named Jordan Carver has even finished writing his preliminary report. Instead, you shoved it onto this new guy and came to poke around in the ashes of..." I look down at the ruins of the house. "What is this, anyway? An insurance job? Family discord?"

"Four people died here last night," he replies. "I really don't see this as a minor case."

"You think it was a murder-suicide?"

"There were four bodies," he continues. "Two were children, and the other two... It's too early to say for certain, but I think they were both female. I've got a hunch that the man of the house wasn't home when all of this happened."

"Or if he *was* home," I add, "he bolted as soon as he'd lit the match."

"The occupants were supposed to be a married couple and their two children," he replies. "So far, it's looking as though I'm missing the guy and I've got an extra woman."

"You think he came home and found his wife in bed with a girlfriend?" I ask. "Maybe this was a crime of passion. Please, Dawson, don't tell me you jumped at this case just because there might be lesbians involved."

"A crime of passion doesn't explain the children," he continues. "I can't believe that a man would burn his children just because he's mad at his wife."

"Why not?" I reply. "I can believe it."

He turns to me.

"There are people who'd do something like that," I add. "It'd be naive to think otherwise."

"You're calling me naive?"

"I'm saying it'd be naive to think that there aren't circumstances in which a man would kill and burn his children." I wait for a reply, and it's clear that he's pretty touchy today. "So I can tell you're pissed off at me," I add after a moment. "It's tempting to think that you switched cases and changed your password as part of some kind of attempt to give me a hint that you wanna be left alone. Did Elaine put you up to this?"

"Not everything's about you, Jo."

"Still, you're being kinda passive aggressive."

"So are you." He pauses. "Maybe not so passive."

"I can still help you," I continue, determined to get things back on track. "Come on, I appreciate this little act of rebellion, but we work better together."

"You need someone dull and reliable?" he asks, clearly not amused. "Someone for the great Joanna Mason to bounce ideas against?"

Hearing a knocking sound nearby, I glance over at the next house and see that someone's banging on the door.

"I don't need you," Dawson says firmly after a moment. "You think I can't solve a case without your help, but you're wrong. I'm going to get to the bottom of this fire, and I'm going to do it alone."

"I know you are," I reply, still watching as the visitor knocks on the window of the neighboring house. "And if you don't," I add, "you can keep switching cases until you find a nice easy one you can solve in a few hours. I'm sure that'd give you a nice ego boost, huh?"

"Jo -"

"Meanwhile," I add, not letting him get a word in, "maybe you should be paying more attention to things like that."

"What?" He turns and looks over at the woman standing in the next yard.

"Hey," the woman says, speaking into her phone, "it's me, I'm here like you wanted. Where the hell are you, Patricia? I came all the way out here and now you're standing me up?"

"You've got an extra female body in the morgue," I say, turning to Dawson, "and now it looks like the female neighbor's done a vanishing act. If I were you, I'd think about joining those dots." Without waiting for him to thank me for the help, I turn and head back toward my car. Dawson's in a weird mood today, and I feel as if I'm banging my head against a brick wall. If I'm going to get his attention again - hell, the attention of the whole department - I'm gonna have to make a breakthrough in at least one of these cases, even though technically I'm assigned to neither.

By the time I reach my car, I've already come up with a plan.

John

Checking my watch, I see that it's exactly one minute past twelve, which means that I'm being kept waiting. I specifically told the customer that he had to be here at twelve o'clock precisely, and now there's no sign of him. I'm starting to think that he's going to be a no-show; it happens sometimes, when people get scared or manage to convince themselves that they're being set up. Still, I had a feeling that this particular customer was going to come through, so I'll be disappointed if he simply vanishes. He sounded pleasingly desperate on the phone.

"Any sign?" Leonard asks as he comes out from the office, with a cup of treacly coffee in one hand and a rolled-up newspaper in the other.

"I think we might be getting stood up again," I reply calmly. "Either that, or he's got lost along the way."

"You sure you don't wanna come inside for a bit?" Leonard asks. "There's no point standing out here in the sun." He pauses. "Aren't you hot in that suit? I mean, Jesus, man, would it kill you to wear a t-shirt for once?"

"I'm fine," I reply, as I spot a tell-tale cloud of dust in the distance.

"You need a haircut?" he adds. "I've been practicing on some of the assets, but I'd like to have a go on a more willing customer. I'm seriously thinking about setting up a little salon once we've cashed out of this joint."

I turn to him. "Seriously?" I ask.

"Everyone's gotta have a dream," he replies. "What's yours?"

I open my mouth to reply, but to be honest, I don't really know what to say.

"Someone's coming," he continues, looking over at the gate.

"I think the meeting might be back on," I reply, following his gaze and spotting a car heading along the dirt road.

"Same procedure as last time?" Leonard asks.

"Same procedure as *every* time," I tell him as the car bumps along the road and finally comes to a halt just a few meters from me. I watch as an unkempt and nervous-looking man climbs out of the driver's-side door, and as he turns and looks back the way he came, it's clear that he's worried he might have been followed, or perhaps that he's being set up. He looks up at the sky, almost as if he thinks a helicopter's gonna swoop down.

"Looks jittery," Leonard whispers.

"Welcome," I say, stepping toward the man and reaching out to shake his hand. "You're a little late, but we can let that slide for once. I understand that it can be hard to find this place, since we've been very careful not to appear on any maps. It's not easy to be invisible in the modern world."

"I've got your deposit," the man says, ignoring the offer of a handshake; instead, he pulls a brown envelope from his jacket pocket and throws it at my feet. "The rest of the money's somewhere else, though. It's a long way from here, so don't try anything. I've taken precautions."

"If you don't have the full amount," I reply calmly, "we can't conclude our business."

"I want to see what I'm getting first."

"That's acceptable," I tell him, smiling at the realization that despite everything he's just said, he clearly has the rest of the money stashed in his car. He's trying to act tough and smart, but I can see through the mask. "I just want you to remember that we're not running a charity here. Our service has a price, and that price is non-negotiable."

"I'm armed," the guy replies. "Don't think I'm defenseless!"

"Would you like to follow me?" I reply. "There's no need for us to stand on ceremony. I'd like to show you the assets at our disposal. I've already picked out one that I think will suit you perfectly, but of course the final decision is yours and yours alone."

"You know what I want," he mutters, still very much on edge. "If you've got it, I'll go fetch the rest of the money from the car."

"I thought the remainder of the payment was a long way from here?" I reply, smiling at his slip-up.

"Just show me," he says firmly.

"Leonard," I say, turning to my erstwhile colleague. "Perhaps you'd be so good as to lead the way." As Leonard heads over to the main shed, I gesture for the customer to follow. "I should warn you," I continue, "that what you're about to see might seem rather disturbing. You indicated on the phone that you wanted to understand how our operation works, and I fully appreciate your need to have confidence in the product we offer, but it's very important that you -"

"Just get on with it," he says, clearly not in the mood to take advice.

"As you wish," I reply quietly.

Up ahead, Leonard starts unlocking the barn.

"Stop here," I tell the customer, before turning to him. Moans and wails are starting to drift toward us from inside the barn, and I can see that the customer is becoming concerned. "I'm afraid you can't be allowed to look directly into the containment facility, but my colleague will shortly bring the selected specimen out for you to inspect. I'm sure you'll understand that it's better if you don't get too close." I pause for a moment, trying to hide the fact that I'm amused by his look of fear. "There's really no need to worry," I add eventually. "Our system is completely -"

"Holy fuck," the customer says, his eyes widening as he takes a step back.

Turning, I see that Leonard has returned with the asset whose identity is going to be sold. Naked and covered in his own filth, the male figure stumbles a little as he's led by the chain attached to his neck; Leonard gives him a solid kick that sends him sprawling across the ground, and the asset lets out a pained groan. Althougg his back is crooked and misshapen, this particular asset was lucky to only sustain a fracture rather than a full break: he can't move fast, but unlike many of the others, he can still walk. I should have broken his back properly, but I guess I can be a little sentimental sometimes.

"What the hell kind of operation have you got going on here?" the customer asks, his voice filled with panic.

"Meet Tommy Symonds," I reply with a smile. "Twenty-two years old, son of a drug addict mother and a male whose identity, I'm afraid, was known not even to the bitch who incubated his seed. Evidently she was fond of little assignations behind bars, and I believe she simply lost track of the various men with whom she enjoyed carnal relations. Tommy has spent his entire life here with us at this facility, although he has attended a small number of appointments with doctors and educational specialists. Just enough to establish his identity, you understand, and to get him listed in various state and federal databases."

"What's this guy got to do with me?" the customer asks.

"Your hundred thousand dollars is going to buy Mr. Symonds' entire life and identity," I tell him, reaching into my pocket and pulling out a small brown envelope, from which I remove a passport and various identity cards, along with a birth certificate and various other records. "As you can see, you and Mr. Symonds share a reasonable likeness. You'll have to part your hair on the left side, at least until you get new copies of some of these documents. I generally advise customers to make themselves look as much like the original individual as possible, and then to gradually revert to their preferred appearance over a number of years. I appreciate that this is inconvenient, but it's the safest way to proceed."

"But..." He pauses, clearly shocked by the situation. "Won't someone notice that this Tommy Symonds guy is missing?"

"As I explained," I continue, "he has spent his entire life at this facility. He has no friends, and his mother hasn't seen him since the night she gave him to me. We have scores of men here, and we endeavor to match each new customer to an asset whose appearance offers some promise of approximation. After all, you're going to need to get your documents renewed at some point. His name and basic details are in various government databases, although they have no record of his DNA or fingerprints. To all intents and purposes, *you* are Tommy Symonds now. Never forget that."

"So I take his identity?" he asks. "And, what, does he take mine?"

I shake my head. "No," I tell him. "He won't be needing it."

"This is fucked up," the customer replies, with a sense of awe in his voice.

"Nevertheless," I reply, "I think it's time for us to conclude today's business. Will you be happy to take this new identity?"

He pauses to examine the documents for a moment. "I need a new name," he mutters. "Fuck, man, I've messed up my life. The cops want me and... It's either this or..."

We stand in silence for a moment.

"Then this is your only sure-fire way to acquire a whole new identity," I point out. "There's nothing fake about Tommy Symonds. He's a real person with real credentials that have been carefully built up over the years. Those credentials are now yours, and since they're real, there's no way you can be caught out. If you choose to take this opportunity, that is."

"Fine," he replies, "I'm in. Let's do this thing."

"Of course," I say. "There's just the small matter of the payment."

While he heads over to his car, I look across at Tommy Symonds and see the look of hopeless confusion in his eyes. He has no idea what's happening to him, and since I never bothered to teach most of the assets how to speak properly, he can't even try to communicate; he just stares at me with a look of hatred, perhaps mixed with fear, as I smile back at him. I still remember the night I acquired Tommy. In fact, I remember the night I acquired every one of the assets, and there's a small part of me that'll be sorry to see him go. Then again, there's no room for sentimentality in this business.

"One hundred grand," the customer says as he comes back over to me, dumping a hold-all at my feet. "You can count it if you want. It's all there, minus the deposit I already gave you."

"I have no doubt," I reply, before turning to Leonard. "I think the deal is concluded," I say calmly.

Reaching down to his waist, Leonard pulls a large hunting knife from his belt. After putting one arm firmly around Tommy's chest, he slices the knife straight through the unfortunate young man's neck, and although Tommy struggles, he's powerless to fight back as blood pours from the wound. It's a rather disgusting sight, and I still remember how I flinched when I first saw it happen many years ago, back when I was a young man and such things disturbed me.

"What the fuck's he doing?" the customer shouts.

"There can only be one Tommy Symonds," I reply calmly, watching as the original Tommy struggles in Leonard's grip like a fish floundering on dry land, eventually vomiting a little blood. "I'm sure you wouldn't want to risk any confusion." As the words leave my mouth, Tommy's lifeless body slumps down to the ground. With a smile, I turn to the customer. "You are now Tommy Symonds. Whatever reason you have for abandoning your old identity, you can rest assured that you now have a whole new life. As long as you take a few minor precautions and ensure that you gradually change the appearance of Tommy in official photos, there's no reason why you shouldn't live out a long and happy existence with your new identity."

"And you... grow these guys here?" he replies. "What do you do, buy them as babies and then raise them until you can sell their identities?"

"I think our business is concluded," I say calmly. "There's no need for any further discussion, so perhaps, Mr. Symonds, you should turn around and get out of here, and focus on assuming your new identity. Forget about this place. As far as you're concerned, you were never here. Remember, if anything happens to us, your new name might be at risk."

Clearly needing no further encouragement, the customer turns and hurries back toward his car. Like everyone who comes here to cut a deal, he seems genuinely stunned by the process that we use, and I guess he'd rather get as far away as possible from the gritty reality of our operation. As he drives away, I reach down and pick up the bag of money; unzipping the top, I can't help but smile as I see the wads of cash stuffed inside. Even after all this time, the sight gives me a thrill.

Glancing over at the body of Tommy Symonds, I'm momentarily struck by the memory of that night, twenty-two years ago, when I paid his mother a thousand dollars in order to acquire him. He was one of my first purchases, and in a way I feel that his sale marks some kind of important moment. Still, it's important not to be sentimental or nostalgic. I just need to focus on the money. After all, money is the whole reason I started doing this in the first place.

Without money, a family can't survive.

"Clean that mess up," I tell Leonard, before turning and heading to the office so I can count the cash.

Joanna Mason

"I know this must be difficult for you," I say slowly, keeping my voice low and trying to sound calm and reassuring, "but we need to work quickly if we're going to catch the people who did this to you. Your answers could save other people from the pain you've gone through."

It's a little after midday and I'm sitting in a room at the hospital where some of the freed women are being looked after. Since they showed up at the Wash house a couple of nights ago, disoriented and injured after crawling from wherever they were being held, they've been checked and examined over and over. It's clear that they're all in a delicate and vulnerable state, which is why investigators are taking their time and being very cautious as they try to get them to open up about their ordeal. Unfortunately, I don't have time to be quite so patient, which is why I bluffed my way through the door and snagged a quick sit-down with one of the less traumatized women.

"Let's start with a simple question," I continue, glancing briefly at the door and seeing to my relief that no-one seems to be coming to interrupt us just yet. "Can you confirm your name for me?" I look down at the paperwork I 'borrowed' from one of the nurses.

The woman stares at me, with pure fear in her eyes. She's flat on her back in a hospital bed, and thanks to a series of old fractures in her spine, she's completely paralyzed from the waist down. It's a miracle that she managed to crawl away from wherever she was being held.

"Angela," I say after a moment. "You told the doctor last night that your name is Angela. Do you know your surname?"

No reply.

"Do you know how old you are?"

Again, no reply.

"You look like you're about twenty," I continue, trying to sound reassuring, "maybe a year either way. Do you know how long you were held prisoner?"

She doesn't reply; she just stares at me, as if she's convinced I'm suddenly going to hurt her at any moment.

"What's your earliest memory?" I ask. "I mean, your absolute earliest memory in your entire life... Can you think back to when you were younger?"

Nothing.

"You *can* understand me, right?" I wait for an answer. "Just nod if you understand the words I'm saying to you."

She pauses, and then finally, hesitantly, she nods.

"That's good," I reply with a smile. The truth is, I know I'm bad at this kind of thing. I usually leave Dawson to interview subjects who are in a vulnerable state, and I'm pretty sure my attempts at a reassuring tone are a miserable failure. Still, I have to keep trying. "So why don't we go for a different approach?" I continue. "Why don't you -"

"Where's Manuel?" she asks suddenly.

I stare at her.

"Where's Manuel?" she asks again.

"Who's Manuel?"

She looks over at the door, and it's clear that she's starting to panic.

"If you tell me who Manuel is," I continue, "maybe I can go get him for you." That's a lie, of course, but I need to keep her talking.

"Manuel hasn't come this morning," she says. "Is he okay?" She turns to me. "He said we'd be okay."

"Manuel's the man who was holding you prisoner?"

"He told us to leave."

"Manuel set you free?"

She nods.

"So you didn't escape?" I continue. "You were released on purpose and then, what, just sent to go crawling out into the night?"

"He told us to leave," she says again. "He told us to hurry, and that someone would help us. Did Manuel send you?"

"No," I reply calmly, "Manuel didn't send me. In fact, I don't really know who Manuel is. Not yet, anyway, but it sounds like I should find out as quickly as possible, 'cause he sounds like someone who might be able to answer a few questions for me."

"Manuel's a good man," she replies. "He's much nicer than the other one."

"The other one?"

She nods.

"So there were two?" I wait for an answer. "Two men were holding you in that place, and one of them was Manuel?"

She nods again.

"What was the name of the other man?"

"Albert." She pauses. "I heard them talking sometimes," she continues in a panicky, staccato kind of tone, "even though I don't think I was supposed to. Albert was in charge. He was mean to Manuel. I hated Albert. Sometimes he phoned someone named John. I don't think John was very nice either. Only Manuel was nice."

"Suddenly we're getting quite a cast of characters," I reply, quickly making some notes. "So Manuel was looking after you," I continue, "and Albert was in charge of Manuel, and..." I pause for a moment as I try to put the pieces together. "John was working with Albert, or maybe in charge of Albert..."

Looking down at my notes, I realize that whatever was going on with these people, it must have been pretty complex and well-organized. "But it was Manuel who set you free," I add, trying to make sense of the sequence of events.

"Manuel had kind eyes," she replies.

"But you don't know where he is now?"

She shakes her head, and after a moment I realize that she's on the verge of tears

"If I can find Manuel," I continue, "I'll bring him to you. Would you like that?"

"Please..." she whimpers.

"But in order to find him, I need some more information. I need a surname, or a license plate, or anything I can use to track him down."

"I don't know," she replies, her voice cracked with tears. "I want Manuel. Why can't you get Manuel?"

"Manuel doesn't seem to be available right now," I tell her. "But *I'm* here. I mean, I'm on your side, Angela, but I really need you to try to think of something that might help me work out where Manuel is. Can you tell me what he said the very last time you saw him?"

"He came in and started unlocking us all," she replies. "He seemed worried, and he kept looking back over at the door as if he thought someone might come and stop us."

"I know the feeling," I mutter, glancing at the door and seeing that we're still not being interrupted. To be fair, I assumed the hospital's security team would be all over me by now, but they seem to be having a particularly slow day. It's good to know that these women are in such safe hands.

"He was scared," she continues. "Eventually he left the key and told us to get ourselves out, and then to crawl away. He told us he couldn't help us anymore, but that we'd be okay if we could just..." She pauses, and suddenly she seems shocked by something. "It was like he was saying goodbye," she adds eventually. "It was like... He was telling us to go away, because he wasn't going to be able to come to us anymore. Is that what happened? Is Manuel gone for good?"

"If I can find him," I reply, hoping to keep her calm, "I can bring him to you."

With tears flowing down her cheeks, she looks over at the window, and it's clear that the thought of never seeing this Manuel guy again is causing her a huge amount of distress. After all that time in captivity, she must have formed a pretty strong bond with him.

"Listen," I start to say, "if we -"

Before I can finish, there's a knock at the door and three doctors enter the room, eying me with great suspicion.

"Ms. Mason," the first doctor says, "do you mind if I see your badge again?"

"I'm done here anyway," I reply, getting to my feet. "I'll show myself out."

"I really need to see your badge again," he says, while his colleagues conspicuously block the door.

"I showed it already," I point out, starting to worry that my sneaky attempt to gain access has been rumbled. "The nurse saw it."

"*I'd* like to see it."

Sighing, I reach into my pocket and pull my badge out; I hold it up quickly, but before I can put it away, the doctor grabs it from my hand and takes a closer look.

"The thing is -" I start to say.

"This badge is expired," he says firmly. "I just had a phone call from Jordan Carver. I believe he's a colleague of yours?"

"I haven't had the pleasure yet," I reply through gritted teeth.

"He told me I should expect a visit from you. He said that if and when you attempted to gain access to one of the women we're currently treating, I should politely turn you away and tell you to go and speak to him personally."

"Where's Manuel?" Angela asks plaintively from the other corner of the room. "Do you know if Manuel's coming back? I thought maybe he might come to visit me today."

"Do you have any idea how much damage you could have caused?" the doctor hisses at me, as one of his colleagues goes over to console Angela. "These women need to be treated with caution. By blundering in here, you might have set Angela's recovery back by months!"

"Save the lecture," I reply, pushing past him before turning and trying to grab my badge. "I need that," I tell him.

"So you can bluff your way through more doors?" he asks. "Sorry, but Jordan Carver told me not to let you have it."

"Jordan Carver can kiss my -" I pause as I realize that this whole situation is getting way out of hand. "You're too slow," I say eventually. "By the time Jordan Carver has finished teasing information out of Angela and the rest of the victims, it'll be too late to stop other people from suffering. These women are already fucked up, so is it really wrong to fuck them up a little more if it means we get some answers?"

"Yes," the doctor replies. "I believe that's a gross violation of our duty of care, and I also happen to believe that it's an indefensible moral position." He pauses. "Do you really think your investigation is more important than the well-being of these victims?"

"If my investigation helps more people," I reply, "then... sure. I do."

"That sentiment horrifies me," he says firmly.

"Good for you," I tell him. "Enjoy the safety of your little moral kiosk. I'm sure Manuel would be very pleased to know that these women are in such good hands and that no-one's asking them any difficult questions."

"Who's Manuel?" he asks.

"Exactly," I reply, before turning and heading toward the exit.

"Who's Manuel?" he asks again.

"Find out for yourself," I mutter darkly.

"You're not welcome back here, Ms. Mason," the doctor calls after me. "Don't think for one second that you can pull this stunt again! I will have you arrested if you try to pull a stunt like this again!"

Ignoring him, I head out into the reception area and then over to the elevators. I was making progress with Angela, and I'm convinced that I could have got some more information out of her if only I'd been given the time. Unfortunately, it seems that someone's decided to start meddling in my working methods, and while I'd usually prefer to spend a little more time gathering information, this time I'm mad as hell. Whoever the hell this Jordan Carver guy is, I think it's time I made him realize that he's picking the wrong fight.

John

"Your share," I say to Leonard as I slide a bundle of notes over to him. "I gave you a little extra this time since you had to perform that rather public execution. Sorry, I just wanted to give the customer a bit of a shock."

"All the same to me," he replies, stuffing the cash into his jacket pocket. "What I really want though is a day or two off so I can actually spend some of it. I'm saving and saving, but at the same time I'm getting older and older. I want to fuck some nice Vegas whore while my hips are still up to it. I don't suppose there's any chance -"

"You knew the deal when you signed up," I reply firmly. "You'll get all the time off that you need once we've finished with this set-up."

"And when's that gonna be?"

"We just need a few more sales," I tell him. "I don't know about you, but I'd like to be a millionaire many times over after all the hard work we've put in."

"And then we liquidate the remaining assets?"

I nod.

"How're we gonna do that?"

"Gasoline?" I suggest. "I'm sure you'll think of something. Don't worry about it yet, though. We've still got a couple of years left at this rate." Pausing for a moment, I can't help but think back to the moment when I shot Sharon; I've had to do similar things in the past, of course, but this time I feel as if it's getting harder and harder to ignore those hints of emotion in the back of my mind. I always thought I was more or less emotionless, but now I'm not so sure. Some kind of humanity is starting to break through at the worst possible moment.

"Jesus," Leonard says with a sigh. "I'm getting too old for this shit. Don't forget, I'm the best part of a decade older than you. If we finish in two years, I'll be in my goddamn sixties by the time I get my salon opened. It doesn't matter how much cash I've got once I'm a doddering old fool. How the hell am I gonna be able to spend it?"

"I'm sure you'll think of something," I reply calmly.

"I think I'll head down to Florida when we're done," he continues. "I know that's kind of a cliche, but I don't care. Cliches are cliches for a reason, and all I want is some sunshine and some women. Not old women, either. I figure I can afford to get a nice little girlfriend, maybe in her early twenties. I don't care if I have to pay her for the privilege of getting between her sweet cheeks. I mean, fuck, at my age it's just a matter of getting it when you can, while you can. Certain mechanical aspects of the body won't keep working forever, if you know what I mean. I just want that soft, smooth flesh and a great pair of tits hanging in my mouth every night while she -"

"I get it," I say firmly, closing the bag and getting to my feet. "I appreciate that it must be hard for you spending all your time out here at the facility, Leonard, but I refuse to make any changes to the routine. After the mess that happened with Albert and Manuel at the other site, I think a little caution would be in order. Let's just carry on as before. The situation with the other site was caused by deviation from the routine, not by any kind of flaw in the routine itself."

"You're the boss," Leonard mutters.

"That's right. So let's do things my way." Heading to the door, I pause for a moment and turn back to him. "I'll be in touch early next week, unless a new customer comes along. I figure we should lay low for a few days, just to be sure that there's no interference."

"Gonna spend some quality family time, huh?" he asks.

"Something like that," I reply, before making my way out into the sun-bleached yard and heading over to my car. I feel as if I need to get home as fast as possible. After all, given everything that happened with Sharon and my first family, I rather like the idea of consolidating my current set-up. Sooner or later, I'm going to have to pick one family and commit to them, and I want to have all the information at my disposal first. There's also the matter of my daughter, Claire. She seemed a little suspicious this morning, and I need to smooth things over with her.

After all, to lose one family is bad luck, but to lose two in as many days would be downright careless.

Joanna Mason

"Where is he?" I ask, pushing the door open and making my way into the office.

"Dawson?" Mezki replies, looking over from his computer. "He's out somewhere. I think he's -"

"Not Dawson," I say firmly, feeling as if I'm about to explode in a fit of rage. "This Carver guy. I want to speak to Jordan Carver and I want to fucking tear him a new asshole. That's if he's got an asshole to begin with, though; so far he sounds so perfect, I'm starting to wonder if the guy even shits."

"Interesting choice of words."

"You know what I mean!"

"He's -"

"I just had to talk my way into the building," I continue, interrupting Mezki as I pace over to the window, stare out for a moment, and then pace back toward my old desk. "Do you realize how ridiculous that is? This Jordan Carver idiot, whoever the hell he is, had my badge confiscated back at the hospital, and then the guy on the security desk downstairs just now was some new jerk who didn't recognize me, so I had to act all nice and plead with him to let me through. He only agreed after he'd spoken to someone else and made sure I was really who I claimed to be. I mean, what the hell is that all about?"

"Well..." Mezki pauses for a moment. "I mean, Jo, technically, you're on sick leave -"

"Not anymore," I tell him. "Soon, anyway. I'm going to see Schumacher and tell him to bring me back, and then I'm gonna get a new badge, and then I'm gonna shove it up Jordan Carver's ass." Taking a deep breath, I try to calm down, but it's no use. Whoever this Carver guy is, he clearly doesn't understand who *I* am or why I'm so goddamn good at my job. I'm sure he's heard a few other things about me, though, and he's probably on some pathetic little crusade to bring me down just so he can show the others that he's in charge. If that's the case, he's picked the wrong target.

"Are you okay?" Mezki asks. "You look a little red in the face."

"What the hell was Schumacher thinking?" I continue. "Why did he bring some new asshole in to mess things up? This office worked perfectly well before, and now it's just..." I pause, trying to find the right word. "It's all changed," I add eventually, my frustration starting to boil over. "Even Dawson's changed! Dawson never changes!"

"Actually, Jordan Carver's made some improvements around the place," Mezki replies. "He's streamlined the forensic requests routine, and he's brought in someone to improve the IT system, and the old coffee machine's been replaced by a new model that actually makes coffee instead of that sludge that used to come out."

I turn and glare at him.

"I'm just saying," he continues, "that sometimes change can be good."

"You don't know what you're talking about," I reply after a moment.

"Jo, he's not the enemy. Jordan Carver -"

"Stop saying that name!" I continue. "I feel like everywhere I go at the moment, it's Jordan Carver this and Jordan Carver that! Hell, I've only been off sick for a few months, it's not like I went and spent a year traveling around the world. And now I come back and everything's completely different! Even Dawson's acting all weird! It's like Jordan Carver got into his head and made him..." I pause again as I realize that maybe I'm starting to sound paranoid. "Everything just seems different," I add after a moment, suddenly overcome by a wave of sadness. "Things were okay as they were."

"Not everything's different," Mezki replies. "Just a few little things." He pauses. "I think you might have to change too, Jo."

"Me?"

"The way Carver's got things set up now... I think we're all going to have to be a little more..."

I wait for him to answer.

"More what?" I ask eventually.

"Professional?"

"You think I'm not professional?"

"You cut corners," he replies. "I know it works for you sometimes, but the overall department seems to be heading in a direction that requires greater oversight and a stricter application of good practice in pursuit of a more efficient service delivery model." He pauses. "That's actually a direct quote from a seminar Jordan Carver led the other day covering -"

"I don't need to hear this," I say, interrupting him again. "I think I get it now. This Jordan Carver guy is some kind of middle-management, by-the-books asshole who thinks he can come in with some fucking theory about police work, and he wants to squeeze all the fun out of what we do here."

"It's not supposed to be fun," Mezki replies. "At least, I don't think that's -"

"We all work better when we're having fun," I snap back at him, before realizing that I've been argued into a corner and now I'm starting to say ludicrous things. "You know what I mean," I add, finally managing to calm down. "If we follow all the stupid rules, people die. If we sit in an office and go in a boring line from point A to point B and then point C, bad things happen out there in the real world and, hey, guess what? People die! At least -"

"Shit," Mezki mutters, glancing over at the door.

I turn just in time to an unfamiliar figure heading this way, with his eyes fixed directly on me. I'm momentarily taken aback by the calm, calculated expression on his face, as if he's practiced this approach hundreds of times and thinks he knows exactly what he's going to say to me and how I'm going to respond. If this is the famous Jordan Carver, then it's kind of not hard to see how he could have had such a strong effect on the department in such a short period of time: he looks to be young, maybe in his late twenties, and with dark skin and a perfectly-fitted suit he certainly stands out in a building that has tended to be a little behind the times when it comes to diversity and good tailoring. For perhaps the first time in my entire life, I feel genuinely lost for words.

"I've got the files you wanted," Mezki says, springing up from his seat and hurrying over to the door as Carver enters. It's amusing, but also pitiful, to see how keen Mezki is to please this guy.

"That's great," Carver says slightly dismissively, dropping them straight back onto Mezki's desk, "but can you get them to me digitally? I want to check them over while I'm on the move. That way, I can give you my feedback this afternoon and we can get on with implementing those changes we discussed yesterday in our one-on-one session."

"Sure," Mezki replies, hurrying back to his desk. "Anything to help."

"So," Carver says, stopping directly in front of me and fixed me with a determined stare, "you must be the famous Joanna Mason."

"And you must be the guy who got me thrown out of a hospital room when I was making progress with one of the victims," I reply.

"I believe your credentials have expired," he says firmly.

Biting my tongue, I smile politely. I know this guy and I are going to end up arguing, but I want him to be the one who throws the first verbal punch.

"I think we need to discuss some things," Carver continues. "Would you happen to have time to join me in my office, Detective Mason? I always think it's better to identify conversations that need to take place in private, and zone them off from the public space."

"I'm kinda busy," I reply, "but... Sure, I can spare you a few minutes to... zone stuff off from the public space."

"Please," he replies, "come and join me when you're ready."

As he heads through into his office, I find myself feeling uncharacteristically unsure of myself. Something about this Carver guy is sending shivers through my body, almost as if I've come up against someone whose way of working is the complete opposite to my own. In fact, I'm starting to think that maybe Jordan Carver is the antithesis to my working methods in every possible way. What's more, he seems to be a very confident individual, which means it's going to be harder to knock him off his perch.

"See?" Mezki whispers. "The guy's on a mission."

"Sure," I mutter, unable to think of anything more incisive or cutting.

"He's totally dedicated," Mezki continues, "and he always goes by the book."

"Great," I say with a sigh. "Just what I need right now. A nemesis."

John

"Where've you been?" Claire asks as soon as I enter the kitchen.

"I just had to take care of a few things at work," I reply with calculated, practiced nonchalance. "Nothing for you to worry about."

"Like what?"

"Like a few minor things," I continue, trying to hide the fact that these constant questions are becoming extremely irritating. "Do you really want me to give you an in-depth rundown of an insurance salesman's day-to-day activities? I can, you know. It'd bore you to death, but I'm willing to give it a try. I can list all the phone-calls I made, all the forms I filled in, all the websites and quote databases I had to check. It's a really long list, but if you're interested, I'd be happy to share."

She stares at me.

"Nah," she says finally. "You can keep all that stuff to yourself."

"What do you *think* I do all day?" I ask with a faint smile. "Run a criminal gang and have people shot?"

Figuring that I seem to have dodged a bullet, I head over to the other side of the kitchen and start filling the coffee machine. After the drama of the past few days, it feels good to be back at one of my homes, doing normal things. Still, I can't shake the feeling that Claire is tense about something, and although I want to turn and check whether or not she's watching me, I can't afford to let her know that I'm feeling jumpy.

"Jesus," she says after a moment. "That's so sad."

"What is?" I ask casually, glancing over and seeing that she's watching a video on her tablet.

"You seen this?" she replies, holding the screen up for me to take a look

I open my mouth to reply, but suddenly I feel as if someone has punched me in the gut; a news feed is showing video images of the house that I burned down last night. Seconds later, an image of Sharon flashes up, and I realize that the police investigation must be in full swing. There's no way they can ever link that scene to me, of course, but after a moment the image changes and a grainy but recognizable shot of my face appears, evidently culled from an old family photo.

"Fucking tragic," Claire says, tilting the tablet back toward her.

"Wait -" I say, hoping to stop her.

"Fuck," she adds, staring at the screen. "This guy looks a bit like you, Dad. His hair's parted differently and he's wearing different glasses, but there's quite a resemblance." She holds the tablet up again, and for a moment there's a look in her eyes that hints she might know more than she's letting on. It's as if connections are being made in her brain.

"I suppose it does look *slightly* like me," I reply, focusing on the need to stay calm. "The nose looks a bit bigger on that poor guy, though."

"You think?" She takes another look at the screen. "I think it looks about the same as yours." She pauses as the image changes, showing more pictures of the burned house. "Apparently they're looking for that guy," she continues after a moment. "They think he killed his family and one of the neighbors, and then torched the place. Why the hell would someone do that? He had two kids in there, but he just covered everything in gasoline and burned them. What kind of monster would do that, huh?"

"Indeed," I reply uncomfortably.

"I guess he wasn't much of a family man," she replies. "People who do things like that should be fucking burned alive in public. I'd show up to watch that kind of fucker get roasted."

"Do you mind toning the language down a little?" I ask with a faint smile. "You weren't raised in a barn, you know."

"You know what I mean," she continues. "I hate capital punishment, but for someone like that, I'd totally make an exception. I'd take popcorn and everything. Hell, I'd toast marshmallows over the fucker's sizzling corpse."

"That seems a little extreme," I point out.

"Bullshit. It's the least those bastards deserve. Seriously, that level of cruelty is inhumane. When someone does something so fucking monstrous, the best thing is just to take 'em out into the street and end their miserable life as painfully as possible. At least that way, they'll die knowing what it was like for their victims. I mean, hell, one of the kids he killed was just, like, a baby."

"Huh," I reply, somewhat startled by her outburst. "I always thought the younger generation was rather liberal and averse to violence."

"Not when it comes to people who kill children." She pauses. "Not me, anyway. So what would *you* do with the bastard if you caught him? Send him away for therapy?"

"Me?"

She stares at me, and once again I find it hard not to wonder whether or not she knows a little more than she's admitting. I'm probably being paranoid, but Claire's an intelligent girl and I wouldn't entirely put it past her to come up with a few theories of her own. Then again, I've always been careful to keep my families separate from one another, so I figure I just need to stay calm, talk to her normally and not do or say anything that might arouse her suspicions.

"Jesus, Dad," she continues with a smile, "you look fucking terrified."

"I'm just a little surprised," I reply. "This vindictive streak is kind of a new side to you."

"I just think you should protect society from bad apples," she replies. "If -"

Before she can finish, my cellphone starts ringing. Reaching into my pocket and pulling it out, I see that Leonard is trying to get hold of me. There's no reason why he should call, so I'm immediately worried that there's a problem.

"Aren't you gonna answer that?" Claire asks after a moment.

"I think I'll take it through to the office," I reply, heading to the door.

"Why do you always hide away when you get a call?" she asks.

I turn to her, with the ringing cellphone still in my hand.

"If I didn't know better," she adds, "I'd think you were up to something."

"Up to something?"

She smiles. "Relax, Dad. I'm just winding you up. Why are you so touchy all the time?"

"Long day," I mutter, before turning and hurrying to my office. Once I've shut the door, I head over to the desk and finally answer the call. "What do you want?" I whisper, "I told you I'd be in touch soon! You can't keep calling me at home like this!"

"I was thinking," he replies, not sounding too stressed about anything, "wouldn't it be better to meet customers away from the compound in future? It seems kinda risky to bring them here."

"Fine," I hiss. "Whatever. Is there anything else?"

"It was just a thought," he replies. "Speak to you after the weekend, I guess."

"Just focus on the task at hand," I tell him. "Your job isn't to think, Leonard. Your job is to keep an eye on things. If there's any thinking to be done, *I'll* do it."

Sighing, I end the call and take a deep breath. That old fool picked a perfect moment to bother me about some random, totally unimportant matter. I swear to God, I could wring his neck sometimes. Glancing over at the door, I spot something moving near the floor, and suddenly I realize that there's a faint shadow, as if someone has been loitering out in the corridor and listening to my conversation. I watch as the shadow moves away, but there's no doubt that Claire is starting to get suspicious, and I wouldn't put it past her to make a few extra connections if she keeps digging.

Closing my eyes, I realize that I need to take action in order to make sure things don't get out of hand. I've already killed one family this week. If I have to kill another, I'll only have one left. I hope I don't have to arrange for Claire to have a little accident, but if that's what it takes to get things back under control, I guess she won't be leaving me any other option.

Part Four

Ashes

Joanna Mason

"You think you're smart, don't you?"

I open my mouth to reply, but there's something about Jordan Carver's steely gaze that makes me feel extremely uncomfortable. He's staring at me with unblinking eyes, and I can tell that he thinks he's got my measure. I want to prove him wrong, but he's got me at a hell of a disadvantage; he seems to know a lot about me, probably from my files, whereas I know next to nothing about him. Damn it, why didn't I prepare myself better first?

"My record speaks for itself," I say eventually.

"Your record," he replies flatly. "You mean the number of cases you've solved?"

"Sure."

"It's average."

I can't help but smile at this ludicrous claim. "Average?"

"There seems to be some kind of myth about you, Detective Mason," he continues, taking a seat behind his desk. "I'm fairly certain this myth is one that you yourself have devised and propagated. The gist of it seems to be that you're somehow smarter than your colleagues. People talk about you having a gift for making great instinctive leaps of logic. You're quite revered in some quarters, and..." He pauses. "Less so in others."

"Like I said," I reply, "my record speaks for itself."

"You antagonize people," he continues.

"People allow themselves to be antagonized by my working methods," I counter, feeling as if this guy's trying to rip me apart. He won't succeed, of course, but it's kind of brave of him to try. If he keeps this up, I might actually start to respect him a little.

"You enjoy putting people on the spot and making them sweat," he continues.

"It has a certain amusement value," I reply with a faint smile.

"Would you like to try doing it to me?" he asks.

"Not right now."

"Why not?" He stares at me for a moment. "I've met people like you before, Joanna. You have some kind of personal mythology thing going on. You've got this image of yourself in your head, and you're determined to make sure that other people see you in the same way. You want to be regarded as smart, so you work hard to maintain an image of cool, calm and detached indifference. You want to be regarded as a genius, so you focus on a few core cases, snatching them from your colleagues and making wild assumptions as part of your investigation. You trumpet your successes and, I'm quite sure, bury your failures"

"To be fair," I reply, trying not to let my irritation become too obvious, "I get results."

"From time to time."

"From time to time?" I pause. "What's that supposed to mean?"

"It means that your working methods are no longer going to be tolerated."

"What are you gonna do?" I reply. "Fire me?"

"Not at all," he says calmly. "In fact, quite the opposite. You seem pretty healthy to me, Detective Mason. Can I take it that you'll be resuming your normal duties soon?"

"As soon as possible," I reply.

"How soon?"

"How does Monday sound?"

"How does right now sound? I'm curious to see the infamous Joanna Mason in action. I guess there's a chance you might actually be as good as you claim, but I have to admit, I have my doubts. You're not a mind-reader, Detective Mason, and you certainly don't have some kind of supernatural level of instinctive insight. You're a cop, like everyone else here. Let's face it: if you were really anything special, you'd have risen up the ranks long ago."

"Maybe I can hitch myself to *your* wagon," I reply.

"Don't try to be smart with me," he says, opening a desk drawer and taking out a badge, which he slides toward me. "Welcome back,

Detective Mason. Now you can log in to the system with your own credentials, rather than breaking into Detective Dawson's account or blackmailing Dr. Mezki with threats of weaponized pornography."

"Snitch," I mutter darkly.

"I should warn you, though," he continues, "I'm going to be expecting results. I'm assigning you to the case of those girls who turned up out at the Wash farm. You and your partner are going to have to work pretty damn hard to get some answers, and if you turn up anything substantial, I'm really going to be impressed."

"I'm sure Dawson and I can put a smile on your face," I reply.

"You won't be working with Detective Dawson," he says firmly. "He's requested to be transferred off that case, and just between the two of us, I don't think he's too keen to be around you." He pauses. "I know that you and he have a certain amount of history -"

"So who's my partner going to be?" I ask, keen to cut him off. "Someone boring and slow?"

"Me."

I stare at him.

He smiles.

"I told you I want to see you work up close," he continues, getting to his feet and walking around the desk to join me. "We're going to work together, Detective Mason, and *that's* how I'm going to determine if you're really as good as you claim, or if you're just another middling cop with a big ego."

"You're just full of compliments, aren't you?" I reply.

"I'm going to let you lead the way," he says firmly, clearly trying to intimidate me with this constant eye contact game he's got going on. "I hope, Detective Mason, that you can surprise me by showcasing these supposed abilities of yours. Otherwise, I guess we'll just have to accept that you're an ordinary detective who enjoys puffing up her reputation from time to time."

"Is that a challenge?" I ask.

"Sure," he replies with a grin. "Why not? Come on, let's get to work. If you think I'm being unfair, then now's your chance to prove me wrong. Let's go solve this case."

John

"Can you go a bit slower?"

"Sure," I mutter, taking a moment to catch my breath before starting again, this time trying to make love to Barbara in a more laid-back manner. I thought she wanted it to be fast and rough, but obviously she's changed her mind and somehow I'm supposed to be able to read her mind and work out every little altered nuance.

"What's wrong?" she asks after a moment.

"Nothing," I reply quickly.

There's an awkward silence as we continue to make love for a few minutes.

"Honey..."

I wait for her to finish the sentence, but the silence resumes.

"Is this how you want it?" I ask eventually, even though I know that only pure stubbornness is keeping me going. I'd rather withdraw and do something else. Hell, anything would be better than this. It's not as if she's even wet anymore. It's like making love to a dry sponge.

"Are you sure you're okay?" she asks.

"I just want to know what you want," I continue, "and to make love without us each asking the other what's wrong all the time."

"Well..." She pauses. "Maybe we should quit it for tonight, John. There's no point forcing it if it's not working."

"If you'd just tell me what you *want*," I reply, unable to hide the irritation in my voice, "then I could give it to you. Jesus Christ, Sharon, this is supposed to be a two-person operation. You need to do a little more than just open your legs and..." I pause as I realize that I'm being way too harsh. Still slowly thrusting into her, I try to regather my composure. "Let's just take a re-set," I add eventually. "I'm being slow, like you asked. Now what would you like me to do next? Just think about it, focus, and work out what you want, and then tell me."

I wait for her to respond, but another awkward silence descends upon us. Leaning down, I try to kiss her, but she moves her face away from me.

Sighing, I decide to continue in silence.

"Who's Sharon?" she asks eventually.

"Huh?" I reply, still gently thrusting.

"You just called me Sharon," she continues, staring up at me in the darkened room.

"No," I reply, trying not to panic. "I didn't."

"You did."

"Do you want this fast or -"

"Can you get off me, please?"

"Barbara -"

"John, get off."

I pause, half in and half out.

"Get off me right now," she says firmly. "I'm not kidding!"

Sighing, I roll off. In all the years I've been married to Barbara - hell, in all the years I've been married to all my wives - I've never had a problem like this before. I've always been so good at keeping the different families separate, but since the disaster a few days ago when all those girls escaped, my mind has been elsewhere. It's amazing how quickly one fuck-up can snowball and cause countless others. Sitting up in the bed, trying to think of an explanation that might appease Barbara, I realize that I need to find a way to clear my head as quickly as possible if I'm to have any chance of holding this all together.

"Who's Sharon?" Barbara asks eventually.

"Sharon?" I pause. "I'm not sure, sweetheart. I don't think I know anyone called -"

"Don't lie to me, John," she continues. "Are you..."

I wait for her to continue.

"Are you having an affair?" she asks eventually.

"Of course not," I reply quickly, disgusted by the idea.

"Then why did you call me Sharon while we were having sex?" She pauses. "Trying to have sex, anyway." Another pause. "Do you *want* to have an affair? Is that it? Is Sharon someone you've met, and you think about her while you're with me?"

I shake my head.

"You seem so distant," she continues. "I knew there was something wrong when you came home this time, but I couldn't put my finger on it."

"There's nothing wrong," I say firmly, trying to fight the urge to wrap my hands around her goddamn neck. Getting out of bed, I grab my dressing gown.

"Where are you going?" she asks.

"Downstairs," I mutter. "There's nothing for me to do up here, is there?"

"You could tell me who Sharon is."

"I don't know anyone named Sharon!" I shout, turning to her. For a fraction of a second, in the darkness, Barbara's face seems to twist and distort itself until, suddenly, it's Sharon who's staring back at me, complete with a bullet wound in the side of her head. I stare at her, trying to force myself to remember that this is just some kind of illusion or hallucination brought on by stress, but Sharon's face won't go away. It's almost as if she's haunting me.

"John?" she says after a moment. "What's wrong? Are you starting to wish you hadn't blown my brains out? Are you starting to regret killing our children and burning the house down with us all inside?"

"I had to," I whisper.

"You had to what?" Barbara asks.

I blink a couple of times and realize that Sharon's face has dissipated; it's Barbara sitting in the bed again, staring blankly at me. I swear to God, I feel as if I'm losing my mind right now.

"What did you have to do, John?" she continues. "Who the hell is Sharon?"

"I don't know anyone named Sharon," I reply firmly. "As it happens, I've never even met anyone named Sharon in my entire life. Not to my knowledge, anyway. I mean, I suppose in all my years on the road I might have, at some point, and completely innocently, bumped into *someone* who happens to have that name. I'd be a liar if I said I was certain I've *never* met a Sharon, and you know I don't want to lie to you, honey, but the truth is..." I pause as I try to work out what, exactly, I'm trying to say. "There's no Sharon," I add eventually, "and even if there is, she's someone I've met by accident and not even paid attention to, and therefore not someone who, uh, I'd be thinking of when I'm trying to make soft, sweet love to my one and only, beautiful, gorgeous, wonderful wife."

I wait for her to reply.

She stares at me.

I swallow hard, even though my throat is dry.

"You're a bad liar," she says eventually, before rolling over and turning the bedside lamp off. "We'll talk about this in the morning."

I stand in darkness, wondering whether I should try to say something else. Finally, realizing that I need some time to think of a better explanation, I turn and head wearily over to the door, before stepping out into the brightly-lit hallway. As I pull the bedroom door shut, I can't help but sigh. I've always prided myself on my ability to separate out the different elements of my life. How is it possible, then, that such a well-organized and disciplined mind could suddenly start to make so many goddamn fuck-ups?

Slowly, achingly, I trudge downstairs.

Joanna Mason

"My first memory?" Angela says, staring into space for a moment. "I don't know. All my memories are kind of the same, so it's hard to separate them out or say which one comes first."

It's just after 8am and Angela is being interviewed by a police psychiatrist. Jordan Carver and I are sitting in on the interview, although Carver has made it abundantly clear to me that we're not allowed to interfere or say anything during this entire session; apparently he's worried about some bullshit issue concerning fragile witnesses or something like that. To be honest, as he droned on and on while we were driving over to the hospital, I kind of zoned out. He's blatantly testing me, to see if I can keep my mouth shut, and I'm determined to make him realize that he doesn't understand me at all.

"Tell me about a strong memory, then," the psychiatrist continues. "When I ask you to think back to an important moment in your life, what's the very first thing that comes to mind?"

Angela pauses, before glancing over at me.

"Don't look at them," the psychiatrist says, her voice hushed and calm. "Look at me, Angela."

Angela turns to her.

"Tell me about a strong memory."

"There was..." Angela pauses again, as if she's reliving a moment from her past. "We used to live in a kind of barn," she continues eventually. "We each had our space, but not much, and we were chained to the wall. There were these bars and..." Another pause. "We never really moved. Some of us could only move our heads, most of us could use our arms, and one or two could make their legs move, but... Occasionally, one of the others would get taken out and we'd never see her again. I don't know what happened to the ones who left."

"Who took the girls out?" the psychiatrist asks.

"The man," Angela replies. "Sometimes, later, it was Manuel, but Manuel was different. He cared about us. He wanted us to be okay. That's why he let us go."

"Did you ever talk to him?"

She shakes her head.

"Then how do you know his name was Manuel?"

"I heard the other man call him that once," she continues. "There were two other men. I never heard their names. One of them only came in to see us a few times, but I think he was in charge. He told the other men what to do, and he was always around when one of the other girls got taken away." She looks down at the floor for a moment. "I remember leaving the barn once. I had to go in a car. I'd been taught some things to say, and we went to a place, it was a bit like this."

"A hospital?" the psychiatrist asks.

Angela nods. "But smaller."

"A doctor's surgery, maybe?"

"I don't know."

"And what happened there?"

"I had an injection."

Feeling a nudging sensation on my arm, I realize that Jordan Carver is trying to get my attention. When I look at him, he indicates that he wants to speak to me outside; figuring that I should be an obedient and pliable little thing for a while, just to piss him off, I follow him out into the corridor.

"Let's hear it," he says, keeping his voice down as Angela continues to be questioned in the next room.

"What?" I ask.

"You're supposed to be some kind of genius," he continues, "so surprise me. Help me make sense of this mess."

"I think it's tragic," I reply, determined to surprise him. "The poor girl -"

"Just tell me what you really think," he continues, interrupting me. "This barn where they were held. The trip to see a doctor. The injection. What the hell was going on?"

"I think they were being farmed," I reply, figuring I should try to impress him with a decent theory. "I think someone was holding these girls, possibly from birth, and raising them until they were adults so that..." I pause for a moment as I realize that I'm not entirely certain what to say next. The theory is still coming together in my head, and it's going to take a while before all the pieces fit together perfectly. Still, I'm convinced I'm on the right track.

"Some kind of sex ring?" he asks.

I shake my head.

"Then what?"

"Identity," I reply. "What if these girls were being kept so that their identities could be cultivated and then sold to people who, for whatever reason, needed to disappear?"

"That's insane."

"Is it? If someone acquired a bunch of babies somehow and raised them dirt-cheap in a barn, he or she could sell their whole identities once they were old enough."

"You're talking about something that would take decades to come to fruition," he replies. "No-one would go to so much trouble for a pay-off they might never even get to see."

"I still think it's possible," I tell him. "All the pieces fit. You just have to make a bit of a leap and accept that somewhere out there, there might be someone who's patient enough to set something like this up. Most criminals are in it for the short-haul; they want a quick pay-out and they want to get away with the money. But what if this guy, whoever he is, understands that he can take it slow and eventually sell the identities of these girls for six or even seven-figure sums once they've reached adulthood?"

"Is this an example of your instinctive leaps, Detective Mason?" he asks.

"It's the only thing that makes sense to me right now," I reply. "If you've got a better idea, I'd like to hear it."

He stares at me for a moment, and it's clear that he's trying to decide whether or not he trusts me. "Fine," he says eventually. "I'm going to keep things open for now, but I have to admit, your idea is just so crazy, it might actually have some truth to it."

"I'll take that as a compliment," I mutter.

"You've managed to surprise me, Mason," he continues. "Not a lot of people are able to do that."

Although I force myself to smile, I can't help but feel a little dirty; the last thing I wanted to do was to help this asshole have a good day, but at the same time I also wanted to shatter his expectations. I guess he's one of those people who can find the positive in any situation, which is an outlook that I find to be extremely annoying. In many ways, it seems that Jordan Carver is my complete opposite.

"If you're right about this," he continues, "we need to get a handle on it fast. All the victims who escaped were women, which means there are probably more people caught up in this. If someone's selling identities, males are likely to be more profitable than females, so I'd be surprised if there wasn't a whole warehouse full of men going through exactly the same ordeal."

"We need to find this Manuel guy," I reply. "If he chose to let the girls loose, he might be the weak link in the operation, although..." I pause for a moment as I try to work out what's really happening here. This Manuel figure doesn't quite make sense to me.

"We need more than a name to go on," Carver replies.

"Forget it," I continue as I'm hit by a sudden moment of realization. "Manuel's dead."

"What makes you say that?"

"Because he hasn't got in touch with anyone," I continue. "He didn't even stick around to help the women get away properly. Most likely, he turned and ran, and before he could reach safety, his bosses picked him up. Given the fact that he must have cost them millions of dollars, I imagine he's suffered a very slow and very painful death by now."

"Or he just decided to hide," Carver suggests.

"He's dead," I reply. "I'm certain. It's the only thing that makes sense. Otherwise, he'd have come to us for protection."

"You're making a bit of a leap here," he replies.

"I guarantee I'm right, though," I tell him.

"I'll get Angela to work with someone to produce a composite of the men who were holding her," Carver replies. "I'll also see if we can get the other women talking. Angela seems to be the most cooperative so far, but I'm sure we can at least get something from the others, even if it's only confirmation of everything Angela's telling us."

"While you're doing that," I reply, "I'll go get pizza."

He stares at me.

"I'm tired," I continue, hoping that I've surprised him a little. "I think I've done pretty well this morning, don't you? First few hours back on the job and I've already got further than any of the rest of you. I deserve pizza."

"Fine," he replies with a faint, taunting smile. "But I'm coming with you."

John

"I'm going to the office today," I say, sitting at the kitchen table and watching as Barbara pours herself a glass of juice. "I don't know how long I'll be, but I should be back for dinner. I think I'll just grab lunch while I'm out, though. Is that okay?"

Studiously ignoring me, Barbara puts the carton back in the fridge before heading to the door.

"I'm sorry about last night," I add.

She stops for a moment, and then finally she turns to me. "What exactly are you sorry for?" she asks. It's the first thing she's said to me all morning, so at least the silent treatment seems to be at an end.

"All of it," I reply. "Everything."

"Be specific. *What* are you sorry for, John? What do you think you did that made me get upset?"

"I'm sorry I called you Sharon," I continue. "I don't know where that name came from, but it just seemed to pop into my head from nowhere. I actually was thinking just now about the fact that the other day, in the newspaper, I was reading an article about Ariel Sharon, the former Israeli leader, and I suppose it's possible that maybe -"

"Stop lying," she says firmly, with a hint of tears in her eyes.

"I'm just trying to -"

"So in the middle of our awkward, failed attempt to make love," she replies, "you inadvertently called out the name of a former Israeli prime minister?"

I open my mouth to reply, but suddenly I realize that maybe this isn't the finest explanation I could have come up with.

"You're a Catholic, John," she mutters, before turning and heading through to the hallway. "And a liar too."

"Barbara -" I call out, before Claire comes hurrying through to the kitchen in a typical rush.

"Hey, Dad," she says, "got anything fun lined up today?"

"Not particularly," I reply with a sigh.

"Going out?"

"I'm wearing a suit, aren't I?"

"What time are you gonna be back?"

"I have no idea."

"But if you had to guess."

Glancing over at her, I realize that there's a hint of suspicion in her eyes. She seems strangely keen to know my plans, and I can't help but worry that she's trying oh-so-casually to get a better idea of my movements.

"I honestly don't know," I tell her, forcing myself not to get too paranoid.

"Do you know what's got Mom so mad?" she continues. "She's acting like there's a wasp up her ass. More than usual."

"It's nothing."

She turns to me. "So you *do* know?"

"It's just parent stuff," I continue. "A little disagreement over nothing. It'll blow over pretty soon. It's just your mother reacting a little vividly to something I may or may not have said. She's a little stressed at the moment and unfortunately the smallest things can set her off. If I were you, I'd try to avoid too many conversations with her today."

"Is it my fault you and Mom are fighting?" she asks, staring at me with a pained expression for a moment before finally a smile crosses her face. "Relax, Dad. I know it's not my fault. It's probably yours. I mean, no offense, but you *can* be a bit of a jerk sometimes."

"Thanks for the vote of confidence," I reply, getting to my feet and grabbing my briefcase. "If you must know, I'm going to go and spend all day sitting in an airless little office, going over the figures from my last trip. It's a dull job, but someone has to do it, and I might lose my bonus if I allow even the slightest error into my reports."

"Sounds boring," she replies, taking a bite from an apple.

"Absolutely," I continue, "but after all these years, I've kind of come to appreciate the boring parts of life. They allow me to rest my head a little." I head to the door, before turning back to Claire. "Let me give you some advice," I add. "If you can find a way to keep from getting bored while you're performing menial tasks, you'll never struggle to hold down a job. Things like filing, checking forms, performing extremely repetitive actions over and over and over again all day long... Most people struggle with that kind of thing, but if you can handle it, you'll always be able to slot yourself into the workforce somewhere."

"Thank you," she replies flatly, "for that very inspiring little pep-talk."

"You're welcome," I tell her, before heading through to the hallway and then, finally, making my way out through the front door. It's a glorious morning, made even better by the feeling that I finally managed to impart some fatherly advice to my daughter. Claire's a difficult girl at times, and her teenage years have really brought out a kind of insolence that I'd hoped she might avoid. Still, if she started listening to her father a little more than usual, that wouldn't necessarily be a bad thing. The girl has to learn how to comport herself in society.

Stopping next to the car, I pause for a moment. I feel as if I've forgotten something important, but in my current agitated state, I neglected to bring my diary. Still, whatever it was, it can't be too important.

A few minutes later, as I pull out of the driveway and head toward the intersection, I can't help thinking about Tommy Symonds. It's such a silly thing, but I keep replaying the moment when I first acquired him from his mother. Of all the children I've purchased and raised over the years, Tommy was the one who really stood out; I suppose it's because, in a slightly strange way, he looked a little like my grandfather. Now that Tommy is dead, and another man is out there using his identity, I feel strangely saddened by the thought that perhaps this whole operation is getting to the point where it needs to be wound down. I've been selling these kids' identities for many years now, but I honestly believe that in another five or maybe six years, I'll be able to retire and -

"What the hell is that noise?" I mutter as I suddenly realize that something's rattling on the underside of the car. Pulling over at the side of the road, I hurry out of the driver's seat and make my way around to the curb before getting down on my hands and knees; leaning further and further under the car, I finally spot some kind of metal box attached to the bottom of the fender, and there's a small green light flashing in the shadows. My first thought is that it might be some kind of explosive device, but as I force myself to look more closely, I realize that there's another, equally sinister, explanation.

Someone's trying to track me.

"Jesus Christ," I mutter as I sit back and look along the sidewalk.

Filled with panic, I take a deep breath and try to stay calm.

Someone has attached a tracking device to my goddamn car, presumably so they can record my every movement. My mind races with possibilities as I try to work out who the hell would have done something like this: the most obvious suspects are the police, who might finally have begun to suspect my involvement in this whole mess; then again, since the police are too dumb to have made that kind of connection, I suppose there's a danger that Leonard is trying to double-cross me; alternatively, a rival gang might be trying to move onto my patch. Finally, there's -

I take a deep breath.

Suddenly my mind clears and I realize *exactly* who's responsible for this.

"Claire," I whisper.

It's true. She's a smart kid, and it certainly wouldn't be beyond her abilities to order some kind of cheap tracking device from a website. Right now, she's probably sitting at home, watching a flashing light on an online map that shows exactly where I've parked. Hell, I'll be lucky if she hasn't got a camera hidden inside the car as well. The question, therefore, is how long she's had this device in place, and whether she's managed to gather any particularly incriminating information.

Does she know everything?

Does she even suspect?

More importantly, does she have evidence?

Forcing myself to stay calm, I realize that I have to leave the device in place. If I move it, she'll realize that I'm onto her, and I don't want to have any kind of confrontation, at least not yet. Still, it's obvious now that Claire is becoming a major problem, and as much as it pains me to realize such a thing, I've got a very strong feeling that I'm going to have to deal with this issue as quickly as possible.

"Damn it," I mutter as I get to my feet and brush grass off my trousers. It looks like I'm going to have to get rid of Claire as soon as possible. This is the absolute *last* thing I need to be dealing with right now.

Joanna Mason

"So what's wrong with you?" Carver asks as we sit in a small pizza place near the hospital. "You were off sick for months, and if you don't mind me saying so, you still seem tired."

"Haven't you been through my files?" I reply, taking a sip of cola.

"The information in your files is very vague," he continues with a faint smile. "So vague, in fact, that I'm starting to think that you went through and removed anything that might point to the truth."

"You're paranoid," I tell him.

"And you're seriously ill," he replies. "Aren't you?"

"I don't..." Pausing, I realize that somehow this asshole has managed to outmaneuver me. I guess I under-estimated him, and although I still think he's a total pain, it's clear that he's a pretty good judge of character. "I had a medical problem," I say slowly, choosing my words carefully, "and now it's... at a point where I can return to work."

"You're cured?"

"Like a ham," I say with a smile.

"So you're completely healthy?"

"Sure," I reply, even though I'm aware that he still seems suspicious.

"You don't *look* healthy."

Sighing, I sit back as the pizza is placed on the table between us.

"My mother died when I was young," Carver continues once the waitress has headed back to the counter. "She had breast cancer, and it spread pretty much throughout her entire body. It was almost like an infestation. She fought it for a year, but then later, when she started to slide, she got this look in her eyes, or *around* her eyes... It was very distinctive, and I've rarely seen it since. People with cancer, they just seem to have this air about them. Sometimes I think that I've got this kind of radar where the disease is concerned." He stares at me as if he's on the verge of telling me that I have that same look in my eyes. "I don't mean to pry into your personal affairs," he says eventually, "but if there's something that might affect your performance, I think it would be good if I knew. Anything you tell me will only be between the two of us."

Picking up a slice of pizza, I take a bite while I try to work out what to say. I never expected this guy to be so direct, but it's as if he thinks he's really got my number and now he just wants to confirm his suspicions. No-one has ever managed to get past my defenses so easily, and I can't deny that I'm feeling a little wrong-footed.

"Are you dying?" he asks suddenly.

"Jesus Christ," I mutter, putting the slice of pizza down.

"I believe in being honest and direct," he continues. "I thought that you, of all people, would appreciate such an approach." He pauses. "I'll ask you again, Detective Mason. Are you dying?"

I open my mouth to tell him to fuck right off, but something holds me back. I try to come up with another response, but finally I realize that I've left it too long. The answer must be written all across my goddamn face.

He sighs.

"So what?" I reply. "Everyone's dying. Some people are just doing it faster than others."

"How long have you got?"

I take a deep breath.

"Years?"

Looking down at the pizza, I try to work out how I managed to get cornered like this. As much as I hate to admit it, Jordan Carver seems to be very good at finding the right buttons to push; somehow, without setting off any of my alarms, he's managed to get me to pretty much admit something that I've barely even admitted to myself. I want him to die in a very painful way, preferably as soon as possible.

"How long?" he asks again.

"Two years," I say eventually. "Maybe. That's kind of the best case scenario if I take all my medicine like a good little girl."

"And are you?"

"I'm looking after myself."

"What pills are you on?"

I stare at him, and although I know I could easily just lie and tell him I'm swallowing half a dozen different types of medication each day, there's some part of me that actually *wants* to tell him the truth, just so I can mess with his head. Besides, it's not as if he's going to be around for long; I'm pretty sure I can drive him out of the office within a few weeks, and since he's a stickler for routine, I'm certain he'd never spread any gossip about me. Either that, or he'll end up being promoted and soon he'll have forgotten that I even exist.

"The pills make me fuzzy," I tell him. "They mess with my head, like I'm not even myself anymore."

"So you've stopped taking them?"

I nod.

"What does your doctor say?"

"He doesn't know."

"So let me get this straight," Carver continues. "If you take the pills, you could last another two years, but your head would be... fuzzy? So, instead, you're *not* taking the pills, in order to keep your head clear, and now your life expectancy is down to..."

"I don't know," I reply. "Probably less than it could be."

"And that's a sacrifice you're willing to make?"

"I'd rather be myself for whatever time I've got left," I reply, "than try to live as long as possible while floating along in a daze like some kind of dumb-ass."

"That's a very interesting approach to the situation."

"Jesus," I mutter, looking over at the door and considering a sudden dash for the exit. I'm so riled right now, I'm having to focus on keeping still: my right foot is shaking slightly, and I'm starting to feel a little out of breath.

"I'm surprised you opened up to me so easily," he continues. "I guess I've just got that kind of face."

"Careful," I reply darkly turning back to him, "or I might tell you *exactly* what kind of face you've got."

He smiles.

"As fun as it's been to open up to you and share my deepest, darkest secrets," I reply, preferring to cut the chat off before it gets even more personal, "we have a case to be working on, and I'd like to get it solved before I'm in my bath-chair. Right now, the way I see it, we don't really have a lot of leads, and the few we have are kinda sketchy. Even if I'm right about the whole identity market thing, we still don't know who's behind it or where they might be storing their other prisoners."

"If they're selling identities," he replies, "then they need customers. They must be advertising their service somehow."

"There are websites that deal with stuff like that," I tell him. "It might be worth checking out some of the dark-net sites, just to see if anything seems to match."

"Do you know how to access those kinds of sites?" he asks.

"Of course."

"Now why doesn't that surprise me?" he replies.

"We still need something else," I continue, "and given the way things are looking, our best bet is to -"

Before I can finish, Carver's cellphone starts ringing, and I sit back and take another slice of pizza while he answers.

"We'll be there in a few minutes," he says quickly, before hanging up. "Angela's had a reaction," he tells me as he grabs a slice of pizza and gets to his feet. "She might have recognized the face of one of the men who kept her chained up. It looks like we might have had a stroke of luck."

John

As I pull up in the driveway, I can't help but think about the tracking device still blinking on the underside of my car. Claire has probably spent all day watching my progress via her laptop, and I guess she thinks she's got me right where she wants me; I've spent the day doing very ordinary, very mundane chores, but I'm worried that perhaps the device was on my car yesterday, in which case she might have noticed my drive out to the facility where the assets are kept.

"Dumb little bitch," I mutter as I switch the engine off.

The worst thing is, I'm *paying* for all of this. Claire's never managed to hold down even a basic part-time job, especially since her scoliosis got bad and she needed surgery, so the laptop and all of her spending money comes out of my pocket. It's absolutely insane to think about how easily she's been able to start tracking me, but I'm determined to make sure that her little plan comes up short. It's a terrible shame, and I wish things could be different, but there's absolutely no doubt: I'm going to have to deal with Claire permanently. I just need to find the right moment.

Taking a deep breath, I realize that I need to be patient.

As I head toward the front door, I keep telling myself over and over again to just stay calm and make sure that I don't act in a way that might attract attention. The last thing I want to do is give Claire any kind of hint that I'm onto her little scheme, so I need to make her think I haven't got a care in the world. I'm usually pretty good at covering things up, so I just need to make sure that I don't panic.

Opening the door, I remind myself to stay calm.

The house seems to be completely calm and quiet. I wouldn't be surprised if Barbara has gone into town, so it's entirely possible that Claire is here alone, in which case I should perhaps take the opportunity to strike while I have the chance. Carefully pushing the door shut, I'm careful not to make too much noise as I set my briefcase down. Reaching into my coat pocket, I quickly find the pen-knife that I keep for emergencies. I walk over to the bottom of the stairs and look up at the door to Claire's room; all I have to do is go up there, sneak up on her, and cut her throat open.

I take a deep breath.

I hate the fact that I have to do this.

I wish I had another choice.

Taking another deep breath, I start walking upstairs.

"Surprise!" shouts a voice, and suddenly I'm surrounded by a gaggle of laughing, cheering people who immediately drag me back down into the hallway. Within seconds, they break out into song, and I stand in the middle of the crowd, completely shocked as they wish me a happy birthday. I want to ask them what the hell they're doing, but for a moment my mind goes completely blank. Given everything that's been happening lately, I can't even remember whether or not today really *is* my birthday. Is it possible that this is all some kind of horrific trick?

"Happy birthday, Dad!" Claire shouts, reaching out and giving me what appears to be a very genuine and happy hug. "You thought we'd forgotten, didn't you?"

"It did seem possible," I reply, before turning and realizing that some of the neighbors are here, along with a few of my wife's friends. It's a surreal experience, and I'm rather stunned as they lead me through to the front room and I find that a small buffet table has been set up, along with a tray of champagne. I try to work out whether it really *is* my birthday, or at least the birthday of this particular identity, but it's hard to concentrate.

"Happy fiftieth," says a familiar voice nearby.

Turning, I find that Barbara has come over to me. There's a look of sadness in her eyes, and it's clear that she hasn't forgiven me for the mistake I made last night, but at least she's making an effort. She's wearing the dress I bought her a few years ago on our trip to Austin, and she's pinned her hair up; her eyes, however, betray her skepticism, and I can't help but feel profoundly sorry for her.

"I had no idea you were planning this," I tell her, as guests push past in order to get to the food.

"We've been working on it for a while," she replies. "A few weeks."

"I'm not sure I deserve such a wild celebration," I continue, trying to strike up a normal, relaxed conversation. "This is rather over the top, although obviously I appreciate it very much. You really didn't have to go to all this trouble, though. I'd have been happy with just a quiet evening and some good food. And your company, of course."

"It's nothing," she mutters. "We just thought you'd like a bit of a party. That's all."

"Barbara..." I pause, briefly stunned into silence by the tears in her eyes. "I really *am* sorry about last night," I continue. "I honestly have no idea why I said what I said. It must have just been one of those random brain spasm things, you know? I don't know anyone named Sharon, and I was absolutely focusing on you while we were making love. The whole thing was just a horrible mistake on my part."

"Sure," she replies, clearly not convinced. "Don't worry about it, John."

"You don't believe me," I continue. "Barbara -"

"It doesn't matter," she replies, clearly trying to control her irritation. "You've given me your explanation, and that's going to have to be enough for me, isn't it? I mean, hell, you've given me a couple of explanations, so one of them has to be true, doesn't it?" She stares at me for a moment, and it's abundantly clear that she still thinks I'm keeping something from her. "I should go and talk to the guests," she adds, turning and hurrying away.

Standing alone in the middle of my own party, surrounded by a bunch of people who are my wife's friends rather than my own, I try to work out what the hell I should do next. This must be the most tense party in the history of the world, and I feel like just going upstairs and sitting alone until everyone has gone. Still, I figure I need to act like a good host and at least try to engage with the people who've bothered to show up, so I grab a glass of champagne and start making my way through the crowd. Unfortunately, I barely know anyone here, so when I reach the end of the crowd, I end up turning around and contemplating a return journey.

"Having a good time?" Claire asks, having quietly sidled over to me.

"Of course," I reply, taking a sip of champagne. "This is a wonderful surprise."

"I'm onto you, you know," she continues.

I turn to her.

"I *know*," she adds.

"Know what?" I ask, determined to wait and see what she actually means before assuming the worst.

"Everything," she says with a faint, devious smile. "Almost everything, anyway. Enough to put the rest of the pieces together." She stares at me for a moment, and I swear it's as if she's enjoying every second of this horror. "You think everyone else is so dumb, don't you?" she continues. "Especially me and Mom. You think we're just dumb little idiots who don't understand what you're really doing. That's fine, Dad... You just keep on seeing things like that if it helps you feel better about all the pain you've been causing people. Live in your own little bubble until it's too late, but what do you think all these people would think if they knew the truth about you?"

"I don't know what you're talking about," I reply, trying my best to sound innocent.

"Yeah," she replies with a grin, "you do, Dad. You really, really do. So do I. And the best part is, soon - not today, but soon - everyone's gonna know. I'm not gonna embarrass Mum in public, but you won't get away with this crap forever."

As she walks away, I'm left seething in the corner of the room, gripped by a kind of blind panic. I still don't know exactly what Claire has found out, but there can no longer be any doubt about the matter: she knows that I'm up to something, and whether it's linked to my business activities or my other families, I can't allow her to start causing trouble. I watch her smiling and laughing as she talks to one of the guests, and with a heavy heart I realize that there's only one solution.

For the second time in a week, I have to kill my family.

Joanna Mason

"We managed to sedate her eventually," the psychiatrist says, as we stand at the glass door and stare at Angela's prone form on the bed. "It wasn't easy, though. She fought until she was blue in the face. I think she thought we were somehow linked to those people. I don't think I've ever seen anyone look so scared."

"Exactly what happened?" Carver asks.

"I'll show you," the psychiatrist replies, leading us through to the next room. "Someone came from your department, Detective Carver, and asked if Angela could participate in a short interview to generate a composite image of the men who did all of this to her. I was a little dubious at first, but given the urgency of the case, I agreed to allow Angela to give it a shot, on the basis that I would sit with her at all times and end the session if I felt that she was suffering unduly."

"And this is what she came up with?" Carver asks, picking up a print-out of a man's face.

The psychiatrist nods.

"So what made her get upset?" I ask.

"I'm afraid that's my fault," she continues. "Once the composite image was complete, one of the nurses happened to note that it reminded her of a face she'd seen on the news a few hours earlier. I should have intervened, but instead I let Angela see the photo from the news broadcast, and that's when she experienced an extremely strong and very terrified reaction. It was difficult to get any words out of her, but based purely on the look in her eyes and the way she responded, I think there's a very strong possibility that the face from the news might be the face that she was trying to describe. It certainly acted as some kind of trigger."

"Show me," Carver says firmly.

Picking up a tablet computer, the psychiatrist opens a browser and quickly finds the page she's looking for, before turning the screen for us to see a slightly grainy image of a man's face.

"His name, apparently, is John Benson," she continues. "He's wanted in connection with a fire a couple of nights ago in which his wife, their two children, and a neighbor were burned to death. If the news reports are to be believed, the guy's a cold-blooded murderer, but I figure you guys probably know what's really going on here."

"Dawson's case," I mutter.

"Excuse me?" Carver replies, turning to me.

"Nothing," I say quickly.

"I know it seems rather incredible," the psychiatrist continues, "but I've honestly never seen a reaction like this before. As unlikely as it might be,

I think there's a very good chance that this John Benson individual might be linked to the site where the women were being held."

"That's quite a long-shot," Carver says, interrupting her.

"No," I say, grabbing the tablet and taking a closer look at this John Benson guy's face. "I think there might be a connection."

"Based on what?"

"Based on the face," I continue, "and based on the fact that both cases seems to involve someone who likes burning places to the ground. Remember that ruined barn that was found near the Wash family home? I'm pretty sure that someone doused that place in gasoline before setting it on fire. Now it looks as if, just a short time later, someone did more or less the exact same thing to this house. It's not impossible to think of a situation in which John Benson might need to extricate himself from his family life in a hurry, especially if all his pretty ladies managed to crawl away into the night." The guy probably panicked."

"Still," Carver replies, "we can't assume that they're linked." He pauses. "Is this another example of your fabled intuition, Detective Mason?"

"Sure," I reply, passing the tablet to him. "If that's what you want to call it, then go ahead, but to me it just seems like common sense. Unless you've got any better leads for us to be following, I want to consider the possibility that this John Benson guy might be linked to whatever happened to these women. There's no need to narrow our investigation down just yet. There's two of us, so why don't we go in two different directions?"

Carver pauses, and I can tell that he's not entirely convinced.

"Fine," he says eventually. "It's seems a little coincidental, but I'm willing to run with it until something better comes up. I'll leave you to liaise with whoever's covering the Benson case, Detective Mason."

"Absolutely," I reply with a faint smile. Dawson's going to be so pleased...

"I'll focus on the other victims," he continues. "Angela can't be the only one who's able to answer our questions. Once we get them all talking, we should be able to correlate their stories and start building up a much better picture of what was really happening. It's still possible that these girls are unreliable witnesses, and I want solid evidence before I start banging on doors." He looks down at the photo of John Benson. "Maybe some of the other women might recognize this guy."

"I'll be in touch," I reply, heading to the door.

"Detective Mason," he calls out.

I turn to him.

"Good job today," he adds. "I've got to be honest, I thought you'd be more of a handful, but you proved me wrong. It seems some of the more lurid stories about your behavior might not be true after all. I look forward to working with you some more."

"The feeling's mutual," I reply, before stepping out into the corridor and making my way toward the elevators. The truth is, I *hate* the thought that Carver approves of the way I work, and I was only so goddamn cooperative today because I wanted to set him off-balance; now that he thinks he understands me, I can start ignoring him completely and get back to the way I prefer to work: alone, with occasional attempts to bug Dawson and bounce some ideas off him. As far as this case is concerned, Jordan Carver is completely irrelevant.

John Benson's the guy we're after. I can feel it in my gut.

Epilogue

22 years ago

"At least this one isn't crying," Leonard mutters as he leans into the back seat of the car and carefully lifts little Tommy Symonds out of the pile of blankets. "Most of 'em are bawling their heads off when they get here, almost like they know what's happening."

"Don't get sentimental," I remind him.

"I'm just saying," he continues. "Compared to the others, this one's like a little angel."

"He seems to be remarkably calm," I reply, catching sight of Tommy's face in the moonlight. Leonard's right: this child, more than any of the others we've gathered here, seems strangely placid, and I can't help but wonder if perhaps there might be something wrong with him. Grabbing the documents that his mother left behind, I quickly look through the papers before realizing that there's no mention of any kind of abnormality. "Huh," I mutter. "I think he's just a quiet one. I suppose they can't all be exactly the same."

"I'll get him settled in," Leonard says, turning and carrying the baby across the cold, dark yard.

After taking a moment to double-check Tommy's paperwork, I make my way to the office and grab a bottle of whiskey from on top of the filing cabinet. Pouring myself a glass, I head back out to the yard and wander over to the barn, where I find Leonard carefully placing the new arrival into a crib alongside all the others. It's a strange sight, at once both touching and tragic.

"I've been thinking," I say after a moment. "As we gather additional assets, it might be wise for us to branch out and acquire a second site."

"Seriously?" Leonard replies, turning to me. "I thought you always said it was too much of a risk to start spreading the operation?"

"I've changed my mind."

"And where the hell are you gonna get the money?"

"I've got some cash stored up," I tell him. "It's worth investing early on in order to make sure that we can grow the operation over the next couple of decades. This is a long-term project, and any little errors or short-cuts at the beginning could grow exponentially over time until we have a real problem." I pause for a moment as the child gurgles in his crib, but he falls short of actually crying. "Just think," I continue. "One day, when Tommy's all grown up, we can sell his identity to anyone who fits the bill and who can manage to draw the cash together."

"Are you sure we have to keep 'em alive until then?" Leonard asks.

"Of course," I reply. "In a couple of years' time, we'll have to take Tommy to get some shots at the hospital. It's important to ensure that he has a paper-trail so that, when it comes time to sell his name, he's fully included in all the systems and databases."

"I still think it's too much of a risk," he replies. "What if one of them gets away?"

"Then find some other way to immobilize them," I tell him. "I don't know, hobble them, or break their backs, but not until we're sure we don't need to take them to any appointments. Wait until they're older."

"And then what?" Leonard continues. "When someone comes and buys up this kid's name, what are you gonna do with the original?"

"That's the point at which we can dispose of him," I reply calmly, before looking across the darkened room and spotting several other babies sleeping in their cribs. "There's no need to be squeamish," I continue. "As long as we stick to the plan, nothing can go wrong."

"Have you ever killed a man before?" he asks.

"No."

"So how do you know you can do it?"

I pause for a moment. "I'm quietly confident," I say eventually. "It's simply a matter of freeing the mind from distractions, avoiding too many unpleasant ruminations on one's actions, and getting on with the job. A gun or a knife... Whatever, it doesn't matter. For the money we're going to make from these assets, I can certainly do whatever's necessary. I suppose fire might be one of the best methods."

"I hope you're right," Leonard replies as we both head to the door. "I also hope none of 'em start crying tonight. I'm trying to train 'em so they don't think crying gets 'em what they want. They're basically like dogs, you see. If they cry and you come running, it's like you're training 'em to cry so they can make you appear. By only going to 'em when they're not crying, I reckon I can get 'em to see things my way."

"Whatever you feel works best," I reply, heading back out to the yard and waiting while Leonard locks the door to the barn. "I'm fully aware that you've got the toughest job here," I continue, turning to him. "In some respects, anyway. At least I get to meet people and have a little excitement when I'm acquiring these children. All you get to do is hang around and watch out for trouble."

"And how long do you think it's gonna be until we can make a return on our investment?" he asks.

"For most of them," I reply, "we'll have to wait until they're in early adulthood. I suppose it might be possible to sell one or two before then, but I'm not counting on it. Adult identities are where the real money can be made, and that's why we're in this for the very, *very* long haul." Heading over to my car, I stop and glance back at him. "You're not having any doubts, are you?" I ask. "Sitting out here night after night, it wouldn't be difficult for stray thoughts to enter your head."

"No doubts," he mutters. "I just find it hard work on such a large timescale. Most of my previous jobs have been in and out, boom, that kind of thing."

"Try to get used to this way of working," I reply, glancing back at the barn and imagining Tommy sleeping in his new crib. "We've got a long wait ahead of us," I add, "but I promise, one day people are going to start coming to buy the identities of Tommy Symonds and all the other babies. We just need to hold tight and make sure we don't get lazy. Can you do that, Leonard?"

He grunts and heads to the office.

"I'll take that as a yes," I reply, climbing into the driver's seat before pulling the door shut and looking over at the barn. "Goodnight, Tommy," I whisper, unable to stifle a faint smile. "Here's to a very profitable relationship."

Part Five

The Paper Man

Prologue

Five years ago

"Daddy?" she asks, standing in the doorway. "What's wrong?"

At first, her father doesn't seem to notice her. He's sitting at the kitchen table with his head in his hands, and he hasn't even bothered to switch the lights on. He has a cellphone nearby, though, with the screen all lit up, and until a moment ago he seemed to be talking to someone. Now, however, he turns and stares at Claire for a moment, with a startled look on his face.

"Nothing's wrong," he says as he composes himself. "Is your back hurting?"

She shakes her head.

"Then go back to bed," he tells her. "You need all your strength for the exam tomorrow."

A tinny voice can be heard shouting from the cellphone.

"Who are you talking to?" Claire asks.

"No-one," he replies, before quickly shutting the cellphone off. "It was just a wrong number."

"You were talking to them, though."

"I was being polite," he replies. "It's always important to be polite, sweetheart, even if it's late at night and someone's called you by mistake. After all, you never know if later on some day that person might recognize your voice and be in a position to give you a hand with something. We all need to think about karma, right?"

Wrinkling her nose as she thinks, Claire eventually turns and reaches up to the light switch.

"Don't," her father says firmly.

Claire pauses and turns to look over at him, while keeping her hand next to the switch.

"Just..." He pauses. "Go to bed. It's almost midnight. Do you want to be all tired and grouchy when the doctor looks at your back?"

"I don't mind," she replies. "Why don't you want the light on?"

"I'd rather just sit and think," he replies with a sigh. "Where's Mom?"

"In bed."

"So how come *you're* awake?"

She shrugs.

"There's nothing to worry about," he continues, forcing himself to smile. "I just had a bad week at work, that's all, but I'll bounce back."

"Did you get fired?" she asks.

"Fired?" He smiles. "No, sweetheart, of course not. No-one would ever fire me." He pauses. "You don't seriously think I could ever get *fired*, do you? I mean, Claire... I'm the best insurance salesman in the country. Better than that, I'm..." He pauses again. "You have no idea how brilliant I am. Maybe one day you'll understand."

"Were you traveling all this time?"

"Of course," he replies. "You know I have to be on the road a lot, Claire. It's just how my job works. The people who need insurance, they're out there but they don't come to me, so I have to go and find them. I go to their homes and talk to them about what they need, and then I give them the right forms so they're covered properly." He pauses, waiting for her to go back to bed and leave him alone. "You'd like it if I was home more, wouldn't you?" he asks eventually.

She stares at him.

"I'd like it too," he continues, "but someone has to bring the money home, right? I mean, if you wanna go out there and start selling insurance, I'll be glad to sit around in my pajamas and be a kid." He pauses again, still smiling even though he's painfully aware that Claire doesn't seem to be responding. "So until young girls start entering the workplace," he adds, "I think we'd better keep things as they are, and I'll go out to work while you stay home and help Mom. Is that a deal?"

Wrinkling her nose again, Claire keeps her eyes firmly fixed on her father, but she doesn't say anything.

"Go on," he adds. "Go back to bed. I've got to go up too. Your Mom's gonna be wondering where I've got to."

Nodding, Claire turns and heads back to the bottom of the stairs. She starts going up to her bedroom, but after a moment she stops and listens as she realizes her father has started talking to someone again on the cellphone. Holding her breath, she sits on the stairs and tries to eavesdrop on the conversation. In order to hear better, she has to lean around the corner a little, and finally she's just about able to make out her father's figure in the dark kitchen.

"I told you," he says, sounding stressed, "I've got three buyers lined up. All we need is for one of them to come through and then we'll have hit our quota for the year. Hell, all three might turn out to be up for it, in which case we're swimming in money."

He stops speaking, and Claire can hear the faint buzz of a voice coming from the cellphone, although she can't make out what it's saying. The voice sounds agitated, though, and a little angry.

"Exactly," her father continues. "You've really gotta learn to control your nerves, Leonard. It pisses me off when you call me up late at night, moaning about things that haven't fucking happened yet. It's not your job to worry about stuff like that, so just back off, okay? You deal with your side of things, and I'll deal with mine, and the world can keep turning happily. Deal?"

The buzzing voice replies for a moment.

"Just stick to the normal routine," her father adds wearily, "and try to -" Before he can finish, he happens to glance toward the door, and for a fraction of a second he makes direct eye contact with Claire.

Leaning back out of view as quickly as possible, Claire stays frozen in place for a moment. She knows her father looked directly at her, but she hopes that since she's in the darkened hallway, he might not have seen her.

She waits.

She can hear her heart beating.

"I'll talk to you tomorrow," her father says after a moment, his voice suddenly sounding strangely cautious. "Goodnight, Leonard."

As quietly as she can, Claire makes her way upstairs and hurries to her room, before stopping once she's through the door and turning to listen for any sign that her father might be coming to tell her off. Moments later, she hears him walking to the bottom of the stairs, and as she peers back out from her room she can just about make out his shadow on the wall. He's clearly looking up to see if she's still awake, so she hurries across her dark bedroom and gets back under the covers. Although she knows she should go to sleep, however, she can't help wondering about that weird conversation she just overheard.

What she wants to know, more than anything else, is the truth about whatever her father's hiding. She knows there's something, even if no-one else has realized. After a moment, she hears her bedroom door being gently pushed open. She stays completely still, until finally she hears her father going back downstairs, leaving her alone in the dark room with a racing heart.

Joanna Mason

"Morning, perky," I say, putting my hands on Dawson's shoulders from behind and forcing his chair around until he's facing me. I can see that he's not in the mood for any of this, but I figure I can *make* him get in the mood. "How are you doing on this fine morning?" I continue. "You drunk enough coffee to be vaguely human yet?"

"What do you want?" he asks dourly.

"Why do I have to *want* anything?" I ask, taking a step back. "I just happened to wake up this morning and realize that, gosh, the world is a wonderful place, and we should all try to embrace the positives whenever possible. And then I thought about the fact that I really haven't seen you much over the past couple of days, so I was hoping you'd be here when I arrived." I take a deep breath, determined to project the happiest possible countenance. "It's good to see you, Mike," I add. "I just wanted to be open about how I feel. That's what the world needs: more people who say what's really on their minds."

He stares at me.

"That was a joke," I add.

"Ha ha," he mutters.

"Come on," I continue, "you know I was just messing with you, right?"

"Whatever you want," he replies, turning back to his computer, "I came into the office to do some paperwork, not to get involved in one of your dumb games."

"I'm not playing a game," I reply, even though I'm painfully aware that I've already started to become far too annoying. "It's about the Benson fire," I continue, figuring that I should get straight to the point before he turns around and tells me to fuck off again. "Carver and I have been looking into that other case, the one you ditched 'cause you thought it was too difficult, and now we're starting to think that it might be linked to the fire you're covering." I pause for a moment, waiting for him to reply. "That's Jordan Carver, by the way," I add. "You know, my current partner. In a professional sense, anyway. We're just a pair of new pals investigating a case together. Someone should make a detective show about us, maybe starring -"

"I already gave Carver everything I've got," he replies, interrupting me. "You need to go see him if you want to look through the stuff. It's all cataloged and annotated, so it shouldn't be a problem."

"Can't I look through it with you?"

No reply.

"Why not?" I ask.

"Because we're not working the case together," he replies. "Remember? Carver's your partner now, so he's the one you need to be talking to and making jokes with and all that other crap."

"You're no fun these days," I reply, hoping to get him to at least crack a smile. "What happened, Mike? Bad night at home with the vagina from hell? I've always wondered about Elaine's vagina. Is it like a Sarlac? Does it have teeth? I always imagine it as some kind of big round pit with barbed teeth, and maybe there's a small skiff floating nearby, preparing to execute people by -"

"I'm fine," he says firmly, interrupting me. "Just... Let it go, okay? It's great that you're in a good mood, but some of us are trying to use coffee alone to get through the morning, so can you please just go and work on your own case? Or have you already solved it with one of your legendary moments of intuition?"

"Not quite," I reply, "but I'm close. Why, does that bug you?"

"The fact that you're standing here bugs me," he replies. "The fact that you're preventing me from filing this report... *that* bugs me. This is a work environment, Jo, not a playground. Dumb-ass banter was fine when we were partners and we had to fill up time while we were going places, but now we're just colleagues, and you're disrupting two cases instead of one. I really, *really* don't have time for any of this, okay?"

"What crawled up your ass and died?" I ask.

"It's called professionalism," he mutters, turning to face his computer again. "You should try it some time. It's what most people try to use instead of rambling on about inspiration."

"Sounds boring," I reply. "I think I'll stick to my approach. I tend to, you know, solve more cases this way." I wait for him to reply, but it's pretty clear that Dawson is in a foul mood this morning, and to be honest, this back-and-forth isn't really much fun. "So I'm gonna go and get on with some work," I add, "and when I've solved my case, I'll swing by and solve yours too. Do we have a deal?"

No reply.

Leaning closer, I take a sniff. "You smell of booze and cigarettes," I say. "Are you hungover?"

Again, no reply.

"Seeya around, then," I continue, heading to the door just as Mezki comes through from the lab. "What's up with Dawson?" I whisper, grabbing him by the arm and yanking him out into the corridor. "He's in a bad mood. Like, a *really* bad mood. What gives? Did he accidentally catch sight of Elaine naked again? I imagine that could really put a man off his breakfast. Just the thought of it makes my non-cancerous parts tingle."

"No idea," Mezki replies, keeping his voice down, "but he was already like it when he came in this morning."

"I blame the wife," I reply. "Anyone who has to spend his free time with that bitch is probably gonna struggle to smile."

"You don't think it's a bit deeper than a bad mood?" Mezki asks. "Like... Maybe he's actually upset about something?"

I turn and look over at the back of Dawson's head. He's busy typing away on the computer, and if I'm honest, I'm a little worried; he's always somewhat resistant to my attempts to strike up early morning banter, but there seems to be something darker about him today.

"Nah," I say after a moment, turning back to Mezki. "He probably just had to have sex with Elaine last night. That'd put a crimp in any man's style for a day or two. I guess he's still having to apply anti-itching cream to his dick." Without waiting for Mezki to reply, I turn and head toward the elevators, but despite my attempts to laugh the whole situation off with jokes about Elaine, I can't shake the feeling that something has fundamentally changed in my relationship with Dawson. Unfortunately, I know from bitter experience that in this kind of situation, I tend to become even more annoying than usual. If Dawson would just go back to how he used to be, I'm sure I'd be far easier to be around.

Now that he and Elaine are having a kid, I think he might be turning to the dark side. If this carries on for much longer, I'm going to become insufferable.

John

"I'm off now!" Barbara calls out from downstairs. "See you later!"

"Have fun!" I shout from the bedroom, and seconds later I hear the front door slam shut.

Silence.

And then the sound of a chair leg scraping across the kitchen floor.

Claire.

I stand completely still, listening to her moving about in the room directly beneath my feet. She doesn't have school today, and it's been so long since I was at home for a weekend, I don't have a clue what she usually does in her free time. Is she the type of teenage girl who goes out all the time with friends, or does she prefer to skulk in her room? I simply have no idea, but I'm quite certain of one thing: she's going to want to cause me problems, and she's going to -

"Hey, Dad!" she calls out suddenly from the bottom of the stairs. "Can you drive me into town later?"

I open my mouth to reply, but no words come out. Is this some kind of trick? Is she testing me? A million possibilities race through my mind.

"Dad?"

"Sure!" I shout. "In about half an hour. Is that okay?"

"Perfect! Thanks!"

She heads back into the kitchen, and I'm left standing in the middle of the bedroom, almost shaking with fear. That brief little conversation seemed so natural and so unforced, it's tempting to think that maybe I'm imagining the threat in my head. Those things she said to me at my birthday party might just have been some kind of joke, designed to put me off my guard. After all, I don't have a clue what teenagers are like these days; maybe it's some kind of rite of passage for them to threaten their parents during a family occasion, in which case it's just bad luck that she happened to pick a very bad moment.

Or maybe she really knows something.

Figuring that I'll never solve the mystery by standing here like this, I finish getting dressed before making my way downstairs. I can still hear Claire preparing breakfast in the kitchen, and so far the whole situation seems so normal and everyday... Still, I can't afford to let my guard down, not even for a second. I love Claire, but if she threatens to bring my business crashing down, I'll have absolutely no choice but to -

"You want coffee?" she asks brightly.

"Since when do *you* make coffee?" I ask as I reach the kitchen door.

"Since I started drinking it," she replies, pouring herself a cup. "Surprised?"

"A little," I reply, and it's true: every time I go away for an extended period of time, I come home to find that Claire has grown up some more. This time, she seems to be on the cusp of becoming a woman, and as she adds some kind of powder to her coffee, I can't help but feel that the maelstrom of puberty might almost have finished tearing through her body. In other words, she's growing up fast, and she might well be becoming more devious at the same time. It's clear that I can't trust her, not even for a second.

"It helps with weight loss," she says after a moment.

"I'm sorry?"

"Cinnamon," she replies with a faint, knowing smile. "It's healthier than sugar." She takes her cup over to the table and places it next to her bowl of cereal. "There's plenty of coffee in the pot if you want some, and you should totally try the cinnamon instead of sugar. I swear, your life will be transformed."

I pause, momentarily gripped by indecision. Is all this talk of coffee part of some ploy to get me to relax? Or is the cinnamon perhaps tainted by something? Claire's a smart girl, and I wouldn't put it past her to have bought some sodium pentothal online and slipped it into the things she expects me to eat and drink. Damn it, this whole house could be laced with the stuff, and she's probably just waiting for me to make a mistake so that she can sit me down and get me to tell her everything about my other lives. The idea is clearly absurd, but then again, I can imagine that Claire might take some delight in the prospect of tricking me with such a simple plan.

Then again, I need to be careful and make sure I don't start over-thinking things.

"Dad?" she says after a moment. "What's wrong? You've gone, like, totally white."

"I'm fine," I reply, realizing that I need to pull myself together. "I think I might get some coffee in town, though. Just to be on the safe side."

"The safe side?"

"You know what I mean."

She stares at me.

"What is this, anyway?" I reply. "Some kind of interrogation?" As soon as the words have left my mouth, I know I've made a mistake; I should never have used that word; even if she wasn't already planning something, I probably gave her an idea. For a genius, I sure as hell make some dumb mistakes from time to time.

"You want a cracker?" she asks, holding a small box out to me.

"No," I reply.

"Go on," she continues. "You'll love them. Just try one, I swear you'll be hooked."

I shake my head.

"For me? Please? I got them from this health-food store at the mall. They're, like, the best thing I've ever eaten. They've got fig jam in them, so they're really good for your stomach." She smiles. "Come on, don't be a spoilsport. Just *try* one. What's the worst that could happen?"

"You could have filled them with a truth serum," I *almost* say, before deciding to hold my counsel for now.

"Suit yourself," she mutters, putting the box on the table. It's clear that she's a little annoyed, which further piques my curiosity.

"You know me," I reply. "I take a while to get used to new things."

Shrugging, she starts eating her cereal, before glancing over at me again. "So... Are you just gonna stand there watching me eat?"

"No!" I blurt out. "I'll go and get the car running. You know, to warm it up."

"It's almost, like, eighty or something out there," she replies. "Isn't that warm enough for you?"

"Come out and let me know when you're ready to go into town," I tell her, before turning and heading back to the bottom of the stairs. I keep reminding myself to stay calm and not act as if I'm stressed, but something about this whole situation is driving me crazy. It's clear that Claire has got me in her sights, and she's undoubtedly enjoying watching me squirm; with that tracking device on my car, she probably thinks she can just sit back and wait for me to make a fatal mistake, and her little outburst at the party was most likely an attempt to make me panic so that I'll slip up. I feel as if I've managed to sleepwalk into a trap. I don't have long to work out what to do, but one thing's certain: I can't let Claire control me like this.

A genius should never be pushed around by a dumb teenage girl.

Heading out to the car, I double-check that no-one's watching before getting down on my hands and knees and taking another look at the tracking device. It's still blinking away on the car's underside, no doubt collecting data and silently beaming it back to Claire's laptop so that she can track my every movement. She thinks she's so goddamn smart, and it's just a matter of dumb luck that I happened to become aware of this thing. Still, I have a small advantage over her because, for now at least, she has no idea that I've discovered her little trap. All I need to do is stay calm, act cool, and work out what to do.

"Dad?" she calls out suddenly.

I stand up quickly and see her coming out the front door.

"What are you doing down there?" she asks, putting her jacket on as she comes over to the car.

"Just... looking for my keys," I reply. "I dropped them and they kind of slid under the side."

"Huh," she says, opening the passenger-side door and getting inside. "Can you take me to the mall? I need to pick up some stuff."

I take a deep breath. This situation is becoming intolerable, and I can't afford to be weak.

I've worked too hard, for too long, to let a suspicious teenage girl bring my empire crumbling down, and even though Claire's my daughter and I'm fond of her, I'm certain that the best course of action is to kill her. I'll drop her off at the mall and then start making plans so that I can resolve this whole messy situation within twenty-four hours. And then, I think I should start the process of cashing out on the whole operation. I can't live like this anymore. With two families dead, I'll only have one left, and I think that might just be enough for me. It's time to settle down.

"Dad?" Claire calls out from inside the car. "Are you getting in? I don't have all day!"

After pausing for a moment, I take another deep breath, plaster a fake smile across my face, and open the door. Fortunately, I'm very good at pretending to be calm. Hell, I've had a lifetime to practice faking my emotions. I'm a natural these days, and I fit in anywhere.

Joanna Mason

"He was weird," says Priscilla, standing in her doorway. "Real weird. Like, always kinda sweaty and beady-eyed, like he expected that someone was gonna ask him a difficult question or..." She pauses for a moment. "Well, I'm just saying, I never liked John Benson. The guy had bad vibes."

"The world is full of weird people," I reply, feeling a little defensive as I jot down a few comments in my notebook. "Not all of them turn out to be murderers."

"You can tell the weird ones," she continues, as if she didn't hear what I said. "I've always had a special ability that way, you know. I can spot freaks a mile off, and I can tell you what *kind* of freak they are too. Whether they're into doing bad stuff with kids, or they're killing people, or they're into kinky stuff in the bedroom... I can sniff 'em out from a hundred paces. Everyone around here knows that about me. Whenever someone new moves into the street, people come knocking on my door after a few days, asking me what I make of 'em. I'm always right, too. Always. I'm quite famous in this neighborhood."

"That's a hell of an achievement," I reply, realizing that this woman probably isn't going to be very useful. So far, she seems to be completely deluded. Handing her a card, I decide to make my excuses and get moving. "Thanks for your cooperation," I continue. "If you think of anything else, don't hesitate to call me."

"It's intuition," she replies.

I pause for a moment.

"That's what I've got," she continues. "Magical intuition."

I take a deep breath, bristling at the idea.

"What's wrong with you?" she asks. "You look like you've seen a ghost."

"I'm fine," I reply. "Just... get in touch if you think of anything, okay?"

"Huh," she mutters, staring at the card as if it's the most disgusting thing she's ever seen. "Whatever. It's too late to save that poor woman and her cute little kids, though. She was lovely. I never got any bad vibes off her. Only him. And now it's too late to do anything to help them." Sniffing back tears, she seems genuinely upset. "If only people had listened to me sooner, those two little angels might still be alive."

"Aren't angels dead by definition?" I ask.

She stares at me.

"That was a joke," I add.

"I don't think it was funny," she replies with a frown. "You shouldn't joke about stuff like that."

"Well, maybe -"

"I'm done talking to you," she says firmly.

"Sure, but -"

"Done!" she shouts.

As she closes the door, I turn and make my way back to the sidewalk. I hate talking to members of the public and I hate pretending to be interested in what they have to say; the only reason I bother to plaster a fake smile on my face is the knowledge that for some unknown reason, people tend to respond better to that kind of bullshit. When I was working with Dawson, I used to let him handle this kind of door-to-door crap, but with Jordan Carver on my back, I figure I need to show a little initiative. I'm definitely not a people person.

"Anything?" Carver asks as he comes over to meet me.

"Apparently Benson was weird," I reply, slipping my notebook into my pocket. "Other adjectives I heard included 'odd', 'creepy' and 'funny'. He wasn't a popular guy, and of course everyone now claims that they were onto him from the start, and that his wife was a saint. It's amazing how hindsight works, huh?"

"It was the same down the other end of the street," he replies. "It seems most people around here were vaguely aware of him, but no-one really talked to him very much. The guy was generally seen as being pretty standoffish, although I heard lots of good things about his wife and children. She was popular in the local community, got involved with events and fund-raising programs, and no-one seems to have ever heard her arguing with her husband, although a lot of people I spoke to seemed to have a hard time understanding what she was doing with him."

"Money?" I reply. "From what I heard, Benson was always on the road. He sold insurance or something like that. I didn't think people even *did* that door-to-door crap anymore. I mean, what's next? Vacuum salesmen? Elmer Gantry knocking on the door and trying to sell people a Bible?"

"Something about this guy doesn't add up," Carver replies, turning to look over at the ruined shell of the burned-out house. "I've run some preliminary inquiries, and I can't find anyone named John Benson who was involved in the insurance business, not in the whole goddamn country. He had no professional accreditation, no license to practice, no office, no coverage, no commercials... Whatever he was doing when he was on the road, I don't think he was selling insurance. Most likely, that was just a cover story that he used to keep his wife in the dark."

"Then it's definite," I reply. "This case is linked to ours. John Benson is almost certainly the guy who was holding those women -"

"Hold on," he says, interrupting me. "It's still only a possibility."

"I'm telling you," I reply firmly. "I *know* they're linked."

"Part of your instinct, huh?"

"I'm always right about things like this."

"Always?"

"Always."

He sighs. "We don't really have much else to go on right now, so I'm gonna let you run with this, but don't think for a moment that I'm buying into your bullshit."

"But my bullshit often works remarkably well," I point out. "Haven't you heard the rumors? Most times, the whole department is singing the praises of my bullshit. Seriously, as bullshit goes, my bullshit is better than anyone else's bullshit by a factor of -"

"You're trying to be funny," he replies dourly.

"And you're a tough crowd," I mutter.

"We've wasted enough time here," he continues. "The John Benson case is for Mike Dawson to investigate, and I'm sure he can keep up to date with any new developments just fine without our help. In the meantime, I think we need to check in with the forensics team that's been working out at the main site. If we're going to get to the bottom of what was happening to those girls, we're going to need hard facts, not gut feelings and instincts. It's time for some good old-fashioned legwork."

"Surely there's still *some* room for my gut feelings?" I reply as we head toward the car. "I mean, I get it: you're new here and you can't quite bring yourself to believe that I could make these leaps of logic, and I totally understand why you're being so skeptical. Still, you need to give me at least one chance to show you that I can do this. If I'm wrong, I'll happily hold my hands up."

"I'm not Mike Dawson," he says firmly as he unlocks the door and gets into the car.

"I noticed that," I reply, getting into the other side. "You're taller, less tolerant of my foibles, and if I might say so, you're clearly over-compensating for something."

He turns and glowers are me.

"Was that insensitive?" I continue. "Sorry, I'm always so bad at working out exactly where to draw the line. Consider me suitably chastised by your menacing expression."

"Can I ask you a favor?" he replies.

"Shoot."

"It's a forty minute drive out to the Wash family home. Do you think you could be completely silent for all the time, and not bother me at all?"

"If you -"

"Great," he adds, starting the engine before conspicuously leaning across to turn the radio up.

Sighing, I turn and look out the window. Pissing this guy off is kind of fun, but it's getting a little repetitive. The thing about Dawson is that I never run out of ways to get a rise out of him, and he always gets annoyed in just the right way. I guess my best bet now is to rile Carver so much that he asks to be reassigned. I give him forty-eight hours, maximum. No-one can handle me at full blast for too long.

The worst part is, I can tell I'm getting cocky, and when I get cocky, I make mistakes. I need to get Dawson back on my side. He knows how to get the best out of me, and he also knows how to make sure I don't become a total bitch in the process. I don't like myself when I'm in this kind of mood.

John

"I thought you weren't coming home until later," I say, shocked to find that Barbara is in the hallway when I get back from dropping Claire at the mall. This was definitely not part of my plan.

"Yeah, I just..." She pauses, and as she hangs her coat on the hook, I can see a look of concern in her eyes. "It was supposed to be some kind of big meal lasting all afternoon, but I wasn't really feeling up for it so I just showed my face and gave Harriet a gift and decided to come home." She glances at me, and I can tell that she's still annoyed about my accidental use of Sharon's name the other night. "Don't worry, though," she adds. "I'll keep out of your way."

I watch as she heads through to the kitchen. I'd been hoping to have the whole afternoon to work out how to deal with this situation, but Barbara's sudden return means that I've been presented with an extra opportunity. Following her into the kitchen, I watch as she tries one of Claire's crackers from earlier. I half expect her to exhibit some sign of having been drugged, but she simply goes about her usual business, making a pot of tea while grabbing some things from the cupboard. I guess the crackers were clean after all.

"Are you going to stand and watch me the whole time?" she asks eventually, still not looking over at me. "It's very creepy, John."

"I'm sorry," I reply, heading over to the counter and immediately finding myself staring down at a set of carving knives. They were a gift from Barbara's cousin at our wedding. Or maybe that was a different set of knives that Sharon and I were given by *her* cousin, and they just look similar. I used to be so good at remembering these things, but lately it's getting much harder.

"You're very antsy today," she continues, sounding distinctly unimpressed. "It's annoying."

"Sorry."

"Don't you have anything to do?"

I stare at the largest knife.

"John?"

Turning, I realize that she's staring straight at me.

"You've been away for weeks," she says, with a harsh tone, almost as if she's admonishing me. "You're probably going to head off again in a few days' time. Do you really not have anything to be doing?"

"I..." Pausing, I realize that I'm making a terrible job of this whole thing. "I thought I'd grab some lunch," I tell her falteringly, "and then head into town and catch up with some work at the office."

"That sounds great," she mutters, turning away from me as she makes herself a sandwich. "Will you be home for dinner?"

I pick up the largest knife and try to work out what I'd do with Barbara's body if I killed her here and now. After a moment, I realize that there are tears in my eyes; Barbara and I have been together for a couple of decades now, and I think I always secretly thought that of my three wives, she'd be the one I'd end up settling down with when this whole mess was over. Taking a deep breath, I figure that the best option would just be to burn her. I always try to come up with ingenious plans, but I usually just end up burning things. Fire cleanses the soul.

"John?" she asks, sounding distinctly unamused. "I asked you if you'll be home for dinner."

"Um, sure," I reply, holding the knife behind my back. "I think so. Sure. Sounds good."

"It'll just be something from the freezer," she replies with a sigh, still focusing on her sandwich. "Don't get your hopes up."

"Absolutely," I say, grabbing a packet of cookies and walking over to her. The truth is, killing Barbara is going to be a thousand times more difficult than killing Sharon. I always found Sharon to be a little annoying and shrill, whereas Barbara understands me. I wish there was some other way to extract myself from the mess I've created, but over the past couple of weeks I feel as if my grip has been slipping. I need to get things back under control, and even though I know I'll be haunted by Barbara's death, I also know I can get over it. No matter what happens to me, I always manage to reset my emotions eventually.

"Jesus Christ, John!" she says suddenly, turning to me, "are you really just going to -"

And that's when I do it, almost without thinking. Dropping the cookie packet, I drive the knife straight into her chest with such force that I feel the six-inch blade grating against her ribs as it goes deep into her body. There's a shocked, horrified look on her face, as if she's frozen in terror and can't believe what's happening. She opens her mouth, and for a moment I'm terrified that she might scream.

I wait.

She stares at me, her ice-blue eyes fixed on my face. Slowly, her bottom lip starts to tremble.

"Barbara?" I say after a moment.

"W... Wh..."

I try to twist the knife, hoping to catch her heart and kill her quickly, but the blade is wedged between two of her ribs and I have to wiggle it free. Blood pours from the wound, flowing down her red blouse and staining it a darker shade, and after a moment she grips the counter, as if she's having trouble standing. Her breathing is becoming harsher and more labored, but she's still just staring at me.

"I'm sorry," I say, before stabbing her again, this time taking more care to go straight for the heart. The blade slips effortlessly between two more ribs, and I might be imagining things, but I swear I feel the tip puncturing her heart and going all the way through.

She tries to say something, but blood starts to flow from her mouth, dribbling down her chin as she gasps; after a few seconds, she tries again, but all that comes out is a faint gurgle. She reaches up and puts her hands on mine, holding the knife. For a moment, she seems to be trying to pull the blade loose, but she doesn't have the strength.

"I'm so sorry," I continue, with tears flowing down my cheeks. "I wanted this to be quick. I didn't want you to know, but the truth is, I had no choice. Things have just spiraled out of control, and if I hadn't done this, trust me, everything would have been much worse. At least this way, you won't have to suffer. Forgive me. Please..."

I wait for her to say something, but she just continues to stare at me.

"Please," I say, trying not to let my voice crack. "Please. Please. Please."

Her eyes start to close for a moment, as if she's about to die, but then she opens them again, catching herself at the last second.

"I promise..." I take a deep breath, feeling as if I'm losing control of my emotions. "I promise I'll make it much quicker with Claire."

Suddenly she shifts her weight forward, as if she's trying to knock me over, but I simply step out of the way and watch as she crumples down onto the kitchen floor with the knife still sticking out of her chest. I wait for her to move, but she's completely still, and after a few seconds have passed I realize that she might already be dead. Crouching down, I gently roll her onto her back and see that her glassy eyes are staring up at the ceiling; when I check her pulse, I find that there's no sign of life.

It's over.

Damn it, that took way too long.

I've killed many people in the past, of course, but I've always been careful to do it quickly and from behind. I never wanted to see their faces, or to let them realize what I was about to do to them. With tears flowing down my cheeks, I sit back and stare at Barbara's dead body. My hands are trembling, and I can't stop thinking about the look in her eyes as she stared at me. At least Sharon died quickly, without knowing that I was the one who killed her; Barbara, in her final moments, saw my true face and must have thought that I was some kind of monster.

I take a deep breath.

This isn't how it was supposed to end. Not with Barbara. Not with any of them. I was supposed to bring my business to a nice, neat conclusion and then pick one family to stay with for the rest of my life. That's what I am, at heart: a family man. The problem is, I just can't decide what kind of family I want, so I had to do things like this. I'm sure Barbara would disagree with me, but I swear to God, all I'm really looking for is a quiet life with a wife and child who love me. Sure, I'm going about things in a very unusual way, but that doesn't make me a bad person.

I pause. All around me, time seems to be standing still.

I know I should start cleaning up and getting rid of Barbara's body, but it's as if I'm paralyzed by the thought of what I just did. I keep replaying the whole thing over and over in my head, thinking back to the feel of the knife as it slipped between her ribs and the look in her eyes as she stared at me. These images keep spinning through my mind, preventing me from doing anything else, even as a pool of Barbara's blood continues to grow until, finally, it reaches my shoe.

"I loved you," I say tearfully, staring at the back of her head. "Always know that I loved you. It was just better this way. I saved you from so much more pain."

Joanna Mason

"Middle of fucking nowhere," I mutter, shielding my eyes from the relentless afternoon sun as I turn and look back toward the Wash house.

It's true: this *does* feel like the middle of nowhere. The Wash house is basically a rundown old farmhouse, surrounded by acres of land that seems to have gone to ruin. It's hard to believe that anyone ever managed to make this place work as a proper farm, and the only thing that seems to be growing in the area now is a bunch of straggly old weeds. In other words, this is exactly the kind of place where someone might want to hide out from the rest of the world; it's like a patch of land that the rest of the country forgot.

Looking down at the map in my hands, I stare at the vast nothingness and realize that the chances of something being discovered out here is low. Hell, you could build a small city in this kind of wilderness and I doubt anyone would notice. There are no cameras out here, no roads, no passing traffic; in a world where every human being has their every movement recorded and stored, I can kind of understand the impulse to retreat to an un-surveilled location. Throughout human history, people have always been able to cut loose from civilization and head west to a place where they can start their own rules. These days, there's no more west, so people have to look for these pockets of solitude and freedom in other, darker locations.

The world is fucked up.

"Mason!" a voice shouts from the distance. "What the hell are you doing out there?"

Turning, I see that Carver is standing by the house, waving at me.

I wave back.

"Are you coming?" he shouts, obviously wanting me to join him in the house so we can talk to the couple some more. There's no point, of course, but I guess he wants to feel like he's getting something done.

I wave again.

He turns and heads inside.

Thank God. Peace at last.

The truth is, spending time with Jordan Carver is bad for my soul. When I'm around him, I become a total asshole; I play dumb games and I spout all this gibberish, and I only think about ways to piss him off. It's fun for a while, but eventually it becomes tiring and I just want to retreat for a while and try to calm down. Dawson was always so good at understanding what I needed, and it's at times like this that I miss hanging out with him. One thing's for sure: I can't keep working with Carver. I don't want to spend my final months as a complete bitch.

"So," I say out loud, staring out at the wilderness and trying to imagine all those women crawling to safety. "Come on. Give me something."

I take a deep breath.

Silence.

Nothing.

There's a faint pain in my left shoulder. It's been there for a couple of days now, and I'm fairly sure it's something to do with my cancer. I can't go and get it checked out, though, because then I'd have to face Dr. Gibbs, and he'd undoubtedly be able to tell that I haven't been taking my pills. Then again, since I'm dying anyway, I guess it's no big deal if I don't know the details. For now, I feel strangely calm, although I know that eventually, as my body starts to weaken, I'll become increasingly scared. Either that, or one night I'll go sleep and I simply won't wake up the next morning. Someone'll find my body, and that'll be that.

I guess that would be the easiest way out.

Hearing a noise nearby, I look down and spot some kind of mouse running through the bushes. He scurries past my shoe and continues on his way, evidently off to some kind of pressing engagement.

"Have fun," I mutter.

And that's when it finally hits me.

I've got nothing.

There's no inspiration here, no moment of sudden clarity, and I don't even feel anything stirring in my soul. I'd at least hoped that once I stopped taking the pills, my mind would go back to how it used to work, like Superman when he steps away from the Krypton, but I guess maybe the cancer is starting to affect the way I think. If that's the case, then there's no point in me even working anymore; hell, there's no point in me being alive. I'm just another ordinary person, and if there's one thing that I've always felt, one thing that's always sustained me, it's the belief that I'm a little better than most of the people around me. If I've lost that edge, suddenly life doesn't seem very appealing.

Reaching into my pocket, I pull out some folded maps that I printed out this morning.

"Nope," I mutter, checking them one by one. "Nope, nope and... nope."

Sighing, I put the maps back in my pocket.

I turn and look back toward the farmhouse, and suddenly I realize that something else is different here. There's no Dawson. It's crazy, but maybe I actually *need* Dawson in order to work properly, in order to think properly. With that realization, I finally start to feel really, truly lost.

John

"Hey," I say, as I peer out the window for the hundredth time and see that there's still no sign of Claire yet. "I'm just calling to say that I'll be home sooner than planned. Tomorrow, in fact."

"You will?" Susan replies, sounding genuinely pleased on the other end of the line. "That's great, honey! You want to get the grill out and we can have a little party in the garden on Sunday? I can invite Rob and Sheila!"

"Sounds like a blast," I reply, still staring out the window. Maybe I'm old-fashioned and a little behind the times, but I fail to understand how a teenage girl can spend so goddamn long at the mall. When I go shopping, I know what I want and I get in and get out as quickly as possible; I swear, sometimes I think Claire and her friends see the mall as some kind of social hub.

"So what gives?" Susan continues. "You finishing work early or something? Nothing's wrong, is it?"

"Everything's fine," I tell her. "The truth is, I was just sitting at my desk, doing a spot of paperwork, and I realized that I missed you." I pause for a moment. "In fact, I think I'm going to change my schedule around and start having more time at home from now on. All these weeks away are really grinding me down. I want to spend more time at home with you and the kids. I mean, if you want me to be home -"

"Are you kidding?" she replies, with obvious excitement. "Honey, that's the best news I've heard in a long time! You know we love it when you're here, and I can tell that life on the road really stresses you out. Maybe we can even think about taking a vacation together some time. You know, as a family?"

"That sounds wonderful," I tell her. "It's just the kind of thing we need to do in order to..." I pause, trying to work out how to end that sentence without letting her realize that I'm feeling a little emotional. "We'll talk about it when I get back tomorrow," I add eventually. "Can you get some food in for the grill, and I'll light her up for a spot of Sunday afternoon fun?"

"Can't wait. But honey, I have to go now! I think someone's at the door."

"Oh?" I pause, suddenly worried that maybe a link has been established between my different lives, and that perhaps the police have turned up to talk to Susan about me. "Who?" I ask, trying to sound very casual and indifferent.

"No idea," she replies. Moments later, I hear the sound of the door opening and voices talking. "It's just Sheila," Barbara says after a few seconds.

"Honey, we'll talk tomorrow, okay? Can't wait for you to get home!"

"Me too," I reply.

"Oh, and honey?" she adds. "Can you pick up a new set of carving knives on the way home? You remember those ones we got from my cousin Shirley as a wedding gift? They're looking kinda shabby."

I pause for a moment. "Sure," I mutter. "Fine. No problem."

Once the call is over, I stand for a moment, contemplating the possibility that my life is soon going to be just one long run of backyard grills and dull conversations with Susan. How did it happen this way? How did I end up facing life with my least interesting family? Sighing, I set the phone down on the table and resume my silent vigil at the window, still waiting for Claire to come home so that I can finish the job. After a moment, however, I find myself thinking about those goddamn carving knives. For some reason, it's getting harder and harder to remember the differences between my three families.

Joanna Mason

"Where's Dawson?" I ask as Mezki wanders into the office.

"Is that all you're ever gonna ask me from now on?" he replies, dropping a pile of papers on his desk. "Are you under the mistaken impression that I'm Michael Dawson's secretary?"

"Yes," I reply, "I *am* under that impression. So where the hell is he?"

Sighing, he takes a seat and logs onto his computer. "I have no idea," he says after a moment, "but you're not the only one who's been asking. Schumacher wants to talk to him too, but apparently his phone's off and no-one's quite sure what he's up to today."

"He's gone AWOL, huh?" I reply, feeling a faint glimmer of concern in the pit of my stomach. Glancing over at Dawson's desk, I can't help but think that this is very much out of character for him. In all the years I've known him, Dawson has never had his cellphone off, and he's always been busy working away on whatever case he's been assigned. The idea that he'd suddenly skip out of sight, even for half a day, seems strange. I need to find him.

"He'll be back," Mezki adds. "He *always* comes back."

"Tell him I need to talk to him," I reply, unable to shake a sense of concern.

"Tell him yourself."

"Just tell him," I say firmly, turning to Mezki. "Cut the bullshit and *tell* him if you see him. I need to talk to him about something important."

"Fine," Mezki replies with a faint smile. "What's up with you, anyway?"

"Mason!" a voice calls out from across the office. "Get in here! Now!"

"You're in trouble, huh?" Mezki continues, his smile becoming a full grin. "What've you done this time?"

"No idea," I reply with a sigh as I realize that whatever's wrong, Schumacher's probably going to tear a strip out of me. "Just tell Dawson to stick around if he appears, okay? I need to talk to him. It's important." With that, I turn and head across the office before reaching the door to Schmacher's room and leaning inside. I'm ready to deliver some kind of highly amusing quip, but to my surprise I see that Jordan Carver is sitting with Schumacher, and the pair of them look pretty pissed off about something.

"Come in," Schumacher says sternly. "Sit down."

Pushing the door shut, I approach the desk. "I'd rather stand," I say cautiously. "Medical advice."

"Do you know why I've called you in here?" Schumacher asks.

"Because you've missed my smiling face and witty remarks?"

He stares at me.

Jordan Carver stares at me too.

"What is it?" I ask wearily, realizing that whatever bullshit problem they've cooked up, it's going to take some of my time and attention to fix. It's not as if I have a whole lot of time *left* anyway, so I'd rather not have to waste it dealing with made-up issues.

"I've been speaking to Detective Carver," Schumacher continues, "and I have to say that I'm highly disturbed by some of the things he's told me about his experiences working with you over the past few days. I know you can be a little caustic, Jo, but this really seems to have gone a step too far and I truly believe that this is the last opportunity to fix the situation before it gets out of control."

"Snitch," I mutter, turning to Carver. Suddenly I can't help but think back to our conversation the other day about my illness, and I start to feel nauseous as it occurs to me that he might have come in here and told Schumacher the whole damn thing. If that's the case, then there's no way I can hide it anymore; pretty soon, the whole department is gonna know that I'm dying, and then I might as well just go ahead and quit now. I can't believe I told him the truth about my cancer.

"It has come to my attention," Schumacher continues, "that your attitude to your new partner could potentially cause this department some serious problems. Detective Carver has been keeping track of some of the things you've said to him over the past few days, and when he informed me of those things, I realized that we have a problem here, Jo." He pauses, as if he's hoping that I'll have some grand moment of realization. "I'm only going to ask you this once," he adds. "Is there anything you've said to Detective Carver that you think might have been... over the line?"

"In what way?" I ask, starting to think that maybe this isn't about my health after all.

"Just anything you can think of. I'm sure you must be able to come up with a few things that perhaps were a little ill-judged?"

I pause for a moment, trying to give the impression that I'm thinking real hard. "Nope," I add eventually. "I think I've been pretty much perfect."

Sighing, Schumacher picks up a piece of paper from his desk. "According to Detective Carver," he continues wearily, "after three days, you've insulted his intelligence numerous times; you've refused to accompany him to important meetings because you wish to indulge your own, more mercurial working methods; you've constantly argued with him and tried to denigrate his ideas; you've made numerous attempts to link your case to the case being worked on by Michael Dawson, for reasons that Detective Carver and I both believe are completely spurious; and on three separate occasions, you have referred to Detective Carver as Detective Hitler."

"But that -"

"Detective Hitler," Schumacher says again, more firmly this time. "Do you have any idea how offensive that is, Detective Mason? In just three days, you've insulted, harangued and ignored your new partner at every available opportunity, and your verbal abuse of him has taken reached the point where it could be a problem for the entire department."

"It was a joke," I reply, realizing that I need to calm things down a little. "Surely you can see that I was just joking, right?" I wait for him to say something, but I feel as if this whole situation is starting to unravel pretty damn fast. "The idea that I meant anything else is crazy," I continue. Again, I wait for him to say something, and slowly a sense of panic starts to grip me as I realize that he doesn't seem to understand. "It was a joke," I say again, "just... a joke. Right? Everyone jokes."

"And who laughed?" he asks.

"Well, I did," I reply, before turning to Carver. "You kind of smirked a little."

Carver stares blankly at me.

"It wasn't *that* kind of joke," I continue. "Come on, you guys both understand, right?"

"I'm just grateful that Detective Carver came to me about these concerns directly," Schumacher continues. "Frankly, he would have been justified in going straight to a lawyer. This department could have been sued for millions of dollars, Jo, simply because we allowed your behavior to continue in this manner."

"It was never my intention to cause trouble," Carver says calmly, turning to Schumacher. "My only aim in bringing this to your attention is to help protect the department from further trouble. There are some very litigious people in the world today, and any form of workplace bullying -"

"Bullying?" I reply, interrupting him.

"I think this amounts to bullying," Schumacher says, holding up Carver's list of complaints. "You wanted to get your own way, Jo, so you tried to bully your new partner into giving you what you wanted. You thought you could manipulate the situation to your own advantage. You've got a hell of an ego, Jo, and it helps you most of the time, but when it gets out of control, you have a tendency to go too far."

"Bullshit," I continue, my heart racing as I try to work out what's really happening here. There's no way Carver was *actually* bothered by my behavior, so he must be trying to twist the knife in an attempt to get rid of me. "I was just joking," I add. "Come on, you know what I'm like. Carver was winding me up and I wound him up a little in return. It's just healthy banter, and I thought he was man enough to take it. That's how things work between partners. Ask Dawson!"

"This isn't about Dawson," Schumacher replies. "This is about you and Detective Carver."

"At least Dawson can take a joke," I mutter.

"This is not a joke!" Schumacher shouts, louder than I've ever heard him shout before.

I stare at him, and suddenly I realize that I need to be careful in order to keep from bursting into tears. Damn it, I guess this must be another side effect from all those pills I was taking. I never used to get so emotional, but now I find myself having to bite my bottom lip in an effort to stay in control.

"Jo," Schumacher continues, a little more calmly this time, "these are serious allegations. You might have *thought* you were joking, but you need to consider other people and their feelings, and the fact that your actions, even if they're intended as a kind of mocking banter, might be interpreted by others in a very different way."

"So we should just be robots when we talk to each other?" I ask.

"Jokes are supposed to be funny," he replies. "No-one's laughing here."

"If I might interrupt," Carver says, turning to me, "I want to stress that my intention here is not to cause you any distress, Detective Mason, or to embarrass you in any way. I feel that the matter can be settled if you simply commit to being a little more tolerant and thoughtful in future. Not just around me, but also around other colleagues and, indeed, the general public. A small adjustment to your attitude could make a big difference."

Staring at him, I realize that I've walked straight into this trap. He's been planning to drag me down all along, and that little heart-to-heart conversation the other day was just the icing on his cake. I let my guard down and gave him all the ammunition he needed, and now he's managed to take complete control. I feel angry, not only at him but also at myself. What the hell is wrong with me these days?

"Plus an apology," Schumacher adds.

I turn to him.

"I want you to apologize to Detective Carver," he continues.

"I don't really *do* apologies," I start to say. "I -"

"You're gonna do one this time," Schumacher replies. "If you want to avoid being suspended without pay and subjected to a lengthy disciplinary hearing, you'll damn well apologize."

"I'm sure Detective Mason doesn't want to spend the next six months or even year wrapped up with a disciplinary panel," Carver says, with a faint smile that makes clear his satisfaction. "I'm sure she has more pressing matters to attend to, and hopefully she'll understand that sometimes one has to set aside one's ego in order to create a more effective workplace environment."

"Jo?" Schumacher continues. "That apology?"

"I need to think about it," I reply, almost trembling with rage at the ease with which I've allowed Carver to skewer me.

"Don't think too long," Schumacher adds. "You need to apologize to him in person, with no sarcasm or bullshit, within twenty-four hours, or I'm gonna have to feed you to the wolves."

I take a deep breath. "Fine," I say eventually. "I'll definitely take that into consideration. Now is it okay if I get going? I have things to do."

"Don't make this harder than it has to be," Schumacher replies.

"Of course not," I tell him, before turning and heading out of the office as fast as I can without making it seem as if I'm panicking.

"Hey," Mezki says as I make my way past him. "You got -"

"Fuck off," I mutter, hurrying into the corridor and making my quickly to the bathroom, where I quickly lock myself in one of the cubicles.

Standing completely still, I stare at the wall as a kind of white-hot rage starts to wash through my body, filling my every atom with pure hatred. In all the years I've been alive, I've never once allowed someone to pull something like this on me, but I have to give Jordan Carver credit: he's really managed to corner me. The worst part is, I gave him all the ammunition he needed. I mean, sure, I might have been a little tough on him, and I guess I might have gone a little over the top from time to time. I was just joking, though, and any ordinary person would have been able to see that.

Dawson always understood when I was joking.

With tears starting to stream down my face, I lean back against the door and try to work out what I can do next. Although it's tempting to just walk away from the whole thing, I know deep down that I need to put Carver in his place and solve the case, just to prove a point. If that asshole thinks he's managed to get one over on me, he's wrong, and he's about to learn that I've still got a few tricks up my sleeve. There's no damn way I'm letting my career end like this.

John

By 8pm, I'm starting to think that something must be seriously wrong. There's no way that anyone, even a teenage girl, can spend seven hours at the mall, so it's looking increasingly likely that Claire must be up to something. She's probably looking for more ways to trip me up or, worse, she might even have gone to the police with what she knows. I can only pray that it's not too late, and that she comes home soon.

Just as I'm starting to give up hope, however, I hear a key in the lock, and moments later there's the telltale sound of a teenage girl crashing into the house.

"I'm back!" she calls out. "I ate while I was out!"

"That's fine," I mutter, staring down at the uneaten microwave waffles I made for dinner. To be honest, I don't really have much of an appetite.

"Where's Mom?" Claire asks as she comes through to the kitchen.

"Out," I reply, realizing that somehow I neglected to come up with a convincing cover story. Still, it should only take me a minute or two to dispatch Claire. I just need to keep my resolve. "She went out with Sheila."

"Who's Sheila?"

"Her best friend," I reply, before remembering that Sheila is actually *Susan's* best friend, not Barbara's. "I don't really know," I add. "You know how these things are. Believe it or not, I don't keep tabs on all your mother's acquaintances. I mean, there are so many people she meets when she's out and about, and it'd be a little weird if I knew all their names."

She stares at me.

"Don't you think?" I continue. "It'd be weird, wouldn't it?"

"Huh," she replies, grabbing a glass and heading to the sink.

Figuring that there's no time to waste, I stand up and walk over to her. Reaching into my pocket, I pull out the gun I loaded earlier and I hold it up, aiming straight at the back of her head while she pours herself a glass of water.

"The mall was crazy today," she says, still facing away from me.

"Uh-huh," I reply, preparing to pull the trigger. I just need to summon the strength; I've killed so many people lately, so why not one more?

"I thought I was never gonna -" she starts to say, before pausing suddenly.

I wait for a moment. Does she know? Seconds later, I spot movement on the faucet, and I realize that Claire's staring straight at my reflection.

"Jesus," I mutter, pulling the trigger.

At the last second, Claire ducks out of the way and the bullet smashes through the window. Stunned by the fact that I missed, I turn just in time to see Claire hurrying toward the door. I take a moment to aim and then I fire again; this time, I hit her leg just below the knee and she lets out a cry of pain as she tumbles down onto the kitchen floor.

I open my mouth to say something, but no words come out. Instead, I take a couple of steps closer and aim at the side of her head as she struggles to get up. Blood is pouring from the wound in her leg, and she's leaving a smeared trail as she desperately tries to get away. Holding the gun closer -

Before I have time to react, Claire suddenly kicks out at me and knocks my legs clean out from under me, sending me crashing down against the table with such force that I bite a slice off the side of my tongue when I land. Crying out as the pain and blood hit my mouth, I momentarily drop the gun, and as I reach up to my lips, I can already feel hot blood flowing from the injury. I spit a small slice of flesh out onto the floor, accompanied by a torrent of blood. The pain is excruciating, and as I turn and reach for my gun, I realize that Claire has managed to drag herself out into the hallway.

"Fuck!" I grunt, grabbing the gun and getting to my feet. I can see Claire hobbling toward the front door, and the pain in my mouth spurs me on to aim at her and fire several times. She ducks into the dining room as the glass in the hallway window shatters, but I can hear her still moving. Spitting more blood against the wall, I walk slowly and steadily through to find Claire, only to reach the bottom of the stairs and realize that there's no sign of her.

    I stand in silence for a moment.

    I know she's still here.

    She's hiding.

    "Claire!" I call out, my voice barely recognizable as my mouth overflows with blood. "It's me! I just want to talk to you!" Sighing, I realize that this approach is useless. Heading through to the next room, I check behind the chairs before hurrying to the front room and -

    Suddenly a heavy wooden object smashes into my face, knocking me cold down to the ground. I let out a grunt as I land, and more blood flows from my mouth. With the gun still in my hand, I start getting to my feet, only to have the wooden object slam into my chest with such force that I swear I feel a cracking sensation in my ribs.

    "Where's Mom?" Claire screams, standing over me with a chair in her hands, ready to strike me again.

    "You don't understand -"

    "If you've hurt her," she continues, her voice trembling with fear, "I swear to God, I'll make sure you suffer." She pauses for a moment. "Where is she?"

"I'm sorry," I reply, trying to buy some time. "Claire, really -"

"You didn't kill her," she replies, staring at me with a look of horror on her face. "Please, tell me you didn't kill her."

Before she can hit me again, however, I hold the gun up and fire, blowing the chair out of her hands. Determined not to give her time to get away, I grab hold of her legs and rugby tackle her to the ground, before using one arm to force her body beneath my own; I aim the gun straight at her face and get ready to pull the trigger.

"Please, Dad," she whimpers, her eyes full of tears. "Don't hurt me -"

"Stop whimpering," I reply angrily, before realizing that despite everything that has happened, this is still my daughter. "I'm sorry," I add. "If I had time to explain, I would and you'd understand, but I don't. It's just better this way. Please, you just have to trust me. I love you, honey." With that, I pull the trigger...

All that happens is a hollow click.

I try again.

Another click.

"You're out," she whispers.

"No," I reply, pulling the trigger several more times. "This isn't -" As the words leave my mouth, Claire manages to shift her weight a little, and seconds later she slams her knee up into my crotch, creating a crunching sensation that knocks me down to the floor. I try to get up, but the pain is too strong and I almost black out as I struggle to haul myself up onto a nearby armchair. By the time I'm able to turn around, I see that Claire is already limping toward the front door.

"Claire!" I call out, with more blood pouring from my mouth. "Sweetheart! Come back!" Getting to my feet, I hurry after her, and somehow I manage to catch her before she can get the front door open. Pulling her back toward me, I spin her around and then slam her head against the wall once, then twice, and finally a third time until I feel her body fall limp in my arms. Letting go, I watch as she slumps down to the floor, and I take a step back as I realize that despite the slight complication, I've managed to keep her from getting away.

I stand in silence for a moment, staring down at her motionless body.

"Why did you have to fight?" I ask breathlessly, with blood still pouring from my mouth. "Why the fuck couldn't you just make this easier for all of us?"

Part Six

Hunted

Joanna Mason

"Hold up!" Jason shouts, sounding a little panicked. "Jo! You're actually kinda hurting me!"

"Deal with it," I reply breathlessly, riding him as fast as I can. All I want right now is an orgasm, and I'm damn well not gonna stop until I get one. "I don't care if your fucking dick falls off," I continue, leaning over him as sweat drips from my forehead and I continue to grind against him. "This is what I pay you for, right?"

"Yeah, sure," he replies hesitantly, "but -"

"Aren't you supposed to at least fake something?" I continue, feeling the first tingling sensation in my clitoris. "I mean, can't you pretend to be enjoying yourself?"

"I guess -"

"Never mind," I add, shifting position a little as the orgasm begins to build. "It doesn't matter. Just stay hard and I'll do the rest."

"Would you -"

"Shut up!" I shout, closing my eyes and focusing on the orgasm that finally, after almost half an hour, seems to be reluctantly offering itself to me. As I continue to ride Jason, I feel a kind of harsh, blunt pleasure starting to grow, and I hold my breath as I desperately try to bring myself to a climax. For a moment, I feel as if it might be fading away again, so I push harder and harder, still holding my breath, until I damn well force the orgasm kicking and screaming into the light, and I finally let out a gasp as it hits me.

For several minutes after it's over, I stay where I am, with Jason still inside me. I'm still breathless, and to be honest, that wasn't exactly the greatest fuck I've ever had, but it was necessary. I was about to go mad.

"So how was that for you, honey?" he asks eventually.

"Honey?" I reply with a raised eyebrow.

"Calm down," he says with a smile. "It was a joke." He pauses, and after a moment his gaze moves to my scarred chest.

"It wasn't funny," I say, climbing off and sitting on the side of the bed. I'm still a little out of breath, but at least some of the tension has left my body. Jason might not be much good for conversation, but at least I always know I can get an orgasm when I call him up.

"You mind if I finish myself?" he asks after a moment.

I turn and see that he's begun to peel the rubber off his penis.

"No," I say, trying to hide the sense of disgust in my voice. "If you want to do that, you can wait until I've left."

"You don't wanna give me a hand?" he replies with a smile. "Or a mouth?"

"Jesus," I mutter, getting to my feet and heading over to the chair in the corner of the motel room, where I tossed my clothes earlier. "What you do on your own time is your own business," I continue, starting to get dressed, "but I'm the one who's paying you for this session, remember? You can jerk off all you want once I'm gone."

"Would it bother you?" he asks.

"What?" I reply, barely even paying attention.

"If I did that," he continues. "After you're gone, I mean."

"Makes no difference to me," I reply as I slip my shirt back on, before suddenly a horrifying thought strikes me and I turn to him. "You don't mean... You wouldn't be thinking *about* me while you're doing it, would you?"

He stares at me.

"Whatever," I tell him, feeling a shiver pass through my body. "Do what you want, but just... not when I'm around." As I continue to get dressed, however, I become increasingly aware that Jason is staring at me; he usually starts cleaning himself up while I'm getting ready to leave, but this time something seems to be fascinating him. "What?" I snap eventually, turning to him. "Are you storing up images for later?"

"No," he replies, "it's just..." He pauses. "I've never seen you quite so angry. I mean, I've seen you when you're angry, but this is the first time you've looked like you're set to really lose your temper."

"I had a bad day at work," I tell him, feeling a little uncomfortable with even this small amount of intimacy. Still, Jason's the only person I can actually talk to right now, and so I find myself contemplating the unthinkable. "What would you say," I continue after a moment, "if I called you... a few mean names and again? I mean, you wouldn't completely overreact, would you?"

He stares at me.

"Would you?"

He doesn't reply.

"I mean," I add with a sigh, "it's not my fault if other people don't have a sense of humor, is it?"

"Did someone get pissed off at you?"

I take a deep breath.

"You might have overstepped a line," he continues. "Just apologize."

"Never."

"Why not?"

"Because then he's won," I point out. "I'm not a bully. I mean, you know me. Fairly well, anyway. I say things, jokes and stuff like that, but it's only to provoke a reaction. He knows it was all just banter, but he's twisting it around so he can make me look bad."

"But you *did* say mean things to him, right?"

"I gave him the ammunition," I continue, before sighing again. "He set the trap, but it's my fault I blundered into it."

"You can be a little sharp sometimes," he replies. "Maybe people don't always know it's a joke. Just apologize to this guy and hope that he accepts it, and then be a little more careful next time. I know you're not an asshole, Jo, but some people are a little more sensitive and not everyone has your kind of view of the world. It's not easy to offend you -"

"It's impossible to offend me," I tell him.

"Right. Sure. But other people aren't like that. They have these things called beliefs, and values, and if you cross those, sometimes it turns out to be a bad thing." He pauses. "Seriously, Jo. There are people who actually care about that kind of thing. They're like fucking aliens, I know, but... Everyone cares about something. Even you."

I shake my head.

"Well then you're a one off," he continues, "but if you're gonna walk among us mere mortals, you need to occasionally tone things down a bit. For your own sake. Otherwise, you'll make it easier for other people to cause trouble for you."

"Fine," I mutter, pulling some cash from my pocket and placing it on the nightstand, before heading to the door. "Sometimes I forget that the world's full of assholes who can't wait to be offended so they can get on their moral high-horse. I guess I'll just have to watch what I say sometimes." Opening the door, I step out into the corridor before turning back to him and once again feeling as if I've been a little too open with. "You were mildly useful today," I add, "but this really was the last time I'm gonna call you. From now on, I'll be playing the field a little and trying out some new guys. It's nothing personal. Thanks for the memories."

"Uh-huh," he says with a smile.

"I mean it this time," I tell him.

"I'm sure you do," he replies, still sitting on the bed, with his erection still looking hard and proud. "See you when I see you."

I pause for a moment. "Do you think I have an ego problem?" I ask finally.

"Um..." He pauses. "Yeah? Kinda. I mean, I don't know if it's a problem, but it's definitely... pretty big."

I open my mouth to argue with him, but finally I pull the door shut and head along the corridor. That little respite with Jason was just what I needed, and now I've finally got my head straight. Jordan Carver thinks he's backed me into a corner, and he's right about one thing: I guess I shouldn't have been quite so blunt with some of the jokes I made. That doesn't mean, however, that I'm going to just roll over and let him walk all over me. As I hit the button for the elevator, I check my watch and see that it's getting late. I have to get to the hospital, and then I figure I'll spend the rest of the day doing some work of my own. I've got all the maps I need for my little side-project, so now the hard slog needs to begin.

I'll apologize to Jordan Carver tomorrow, and I'll make it seem convincing and heartfelt, but it's only a means to an end. By the time this case is over, he's going to realize that he crossed the wrong person.

John

Why does this keep happening to me?

As I pour more gasoline onto the kitchen floor, I can't help but reflect upon the fact that my life seems to be falling apart. Or rather, my *lives*. Until this week, I was able to keep everything running smoothly: I had my three wives, my three families, and my business operation, and I had relatively little difficulty when it came to juggling all these different elements. Since the disaster at the Staten facility and the escape of all those women, however, everything has begun to collapse. First, I had to kill Sharon and the two children I fathered with her, and now I'm pouring petrol over the bodies of Barbara and Claire. Once I've burned this house down, I'll have only Susan left.

Poor, dull, sexless Susan. The least favorite of my wives.

I guess there's a certain irony to the situation.

Realizing that the gasoline can is getting lighter, I decide to use the last few liters to make doubly sure that the bodies burn. I head over to the middle of the room, where I've piled Barbara and Claire together, and I slowly pour the remaining gasoline over their corpses. The whole house stinks now, and although I've become familiar with the stench in recent days, it's still hard to keep from vomiting. Somehow, though, I've learned over the years to put my emotions to the back of my mind and focus on the task at hand.

After a moment, the last of the gasoline dribbles from the can, splattering noisily onto Claire's shoulder, and finally it's done.

I stand in silence for a few minutes, until I realize that there's nothing left to do.

Placing the canister on the kitchen table, I reach into my pocket and take out a box of matches. For a fraction of a second, it occurs to me that I could just light a match right now, drop it to the floor, and end everything. I'm sure there'd be pain, but it wouldn't last too long and at least the longer agony would be over. I certainly deserve to die, and there's definitely a certain attraction to the idea that I could just stop running and relax. The fall of the burning match would only last a second or two, but it would be a moment of absolute peace and calm; I'd be able to forget all my worries and just breathe.

But no. Suicide would be a failure. After everything I've done, I'm not going to -

Suddenly something strikes my leg, not hard enough to knock me over but certainly enough to make me step back. Looking down, I see that Claire has somehow managed to cling to life, and she's dazedly reaching out toward me. I stand in stunned silence for a moment as I realize that this nightmare isn't over. Glancing at the table, I spot one of the carving knives and try to decide whether I should finish her off or just head outside and light the fire. The thought of burning her to death fills me with dread, but at the same time I know that I'd get over the sorrow fairly quickly.

"Stop..." she whispers as she starts pulling herself from under her mother's corpse.

Turning and walking quickly out of the kitchen, I grab my briefcase from the hallway and set out into the driveway. My heart is racing: I'd been planning to wait a few hours until darkness settled and *then* light the fire, but now I realize that I don't have that luxury. Still, I should be able to get away from the scene of the crime without too many problems, so I head around to the rear of the house and stop once I reach the spot where the line of gasoline ends. Glancing over my shoulder, I double-check that no-one can see me, and then I set the briefcase down before taking out the matchbox, selecting a match, and striking it against the side. The flame flickers into life and I pause for a heartbeat before leaning down and letting the match fall down onto the line of gasoline.

Within seconds, the match has ignited a line of fire running straight up to the house and through the back door. It takes only a few more seconds for the whole lower level of the building to light up, as flames quickly take hold and rip through the kitchen. I step back, and a moment later the kitchen window shatters. By now, the bodies are undoubtedly burning, and this time there can be no doubt that Claire is gone. Her pain hopefully didn't last too long, and as I wait a couple more seconds I realize that it must finally be over, and that means it's time for me to get the hell out of here.

I turn to run.

And that's when, out of the corner of my eye, I spot a dark shape climbing over the fence and dropping down into the next-door garden. It's only a brief glimpse, but I know for certain that I saw someone, and although I'm poised to get moving, I can't help but wonder if somehow, through some colossal stroke of bad luck, I might have been spotted as I burned the house. For a few seconds, I'm frozen to the spot, completely unable to even contemplate the possibility that I need to kill again, but finally I hurry across the garden, grab hold of the top of the fence and pull myself up so that I can look over.

Claire.

I can barely believe it, but she's hobbling across the garden, soaked in gasoline but somehow still alive. My first thought is to call out to her, but finally I realize that a better bet would be to sneak up on her and finish her once and for all. The house is burning fast and I can already hear shouts in the distance, but Claire seems to be heading away from the commotion, which I guess means only one thing: she's terrified that I might still be around, and she'd rather hide for a while until she's certain that I'm gone.

Letting go of the fence, I hurry to the back of the garden and use the old potting table as a means to climb up and clamber over into the next garden; missing my footing, I tumble down hard against the lawn with such force that I'm momentarily dazed. Getting to my feet, with my briefcase still in my hand, I run across the lawn, determined to cut Claire off in the next garden. I just have to hope that no-one spots me in the meantime, and as I climb over another fence, I can't help but think that this entire situation has crossed into the realm of the absurd.

Landing hard on the next lawn, I scramble to my feet and race over to the low fence at the far end. I climb over with ease and make my around the side of one of the houses, before making climbing over another fence. I'm starting to wonder which way Claire went, and as I hurry from garden to garden, it occurs to me that perhaps I should have just chased after her and killed her when I had the opportunity. Then again, she probably would have screamed. Better still, I should have made sure she was dead the first time, instead of allowing my sentimental side to dictate the course of action. I should be well on my way from the scene of the crime by now, but instead I'm being forced to hurry from garden to garden, desperately looking for my injured daughter while our family home burns in the background.

"Fuck!" I mutter as I climb over another fence and find, yet again, that there's no sign of Claire. For a moment, it occurs to me that perhaps I should call out to her, but then I realize that I should be careful not to give her any kind of warning. Still, I have no idea where she's got to, and right now my biggest fear is that she might come out of hiding and run for help. As long as she's terrified of me, there's a chance that she'll stay hidden, in which case I can still find her.

I stand completely still for a moment, listening out for any sign of her, but the only sound comes from the burning building in the distance.

Sighing, I realize that I need to act fast. Simply turning and running isn't an option; that girl knows too much about me, and I can't let her get away. Reaching into my pocket, I pull out my cellphone and realize, with a faint smile, that I might as well give it a try. I bring up Claire's number and hit the button to call her, and to my surprise I realize, just a few moments later, that I can hear a ring-tone coming from the other side of the garden. The ring-tone falls silent, but I'm pretty sure it was coming from one of the bushes nearby. I guess the dumb little bitch thought she could hide from me.

Seconds later, Claire's gasoline-soaked form rushes out from behind a tree, making a dash for freedom; before she can get more than a couple of steps, I'm able to grab her by the neck and pull her down to the ground, and I clamp a hand over her mouth just in time to stop her screams for help.

Joanna Mason

"Is this really necessary?" I ask, as the scanner slowly hums and whirrs its way past my body for the third time today. "I mean, it's not like the cancer has gone anywhere."

The radiologist smiles politely.

"I know it's your job and all," I continue, trying and failing to hide my irritation, "but seriously, is there any need to keep on looking inside me? We all know what's happening, so why not just let it take its course?"

Checking one of the dials, the radiologist merely continues to smile. It's almost as if she finds me amusing; either that, or pathetic.

"I guess you need to keep yourself busy," I add, "so you can bill the insurance companies. I mean, that's what this is about, right? You run a scan, send a bill for a few thousand dollars, and everyone's happy. Meanwhile, I carry on dying, and the bills keep racking up."

"Dr. Gibbs wants to check how your pill regimen is going," the radiologist says after a moment, still smiling even though she's focusing on the screen. "If we can determine the effect of your pills, it might be possible to tailor the regimen a little more closely to your needs."

"Yeah, but I'm -" I start to say, before realizing that I should probably stop talking so much. I haven't taken any of my pills for months, but I'm damn well not gonna get into an argument with anyone; it's not as if they'd understand why I made this decision, so I figure it's better to just roll along, acting as if I've been a good little girl, until they eventually lose interest.

"Trust me," the radiologist continues, "there's a good reason to be taking these scans. What would you prefer? Should we just cut you loose and send you out there into the world without any help? There might be a time when you need stronger pain relief, in which case these scans can show us how the cancer has been spreading. I'm sure that Dr. Gibbs is running a series of models to determine the nature of your particular condition." She pauses, before pressing a button that causes the machine to stop moving. "There," she adds. "All done."

"So I can get up now?" I ask.

She nods.

Climbing off the table, I walk stiffly over to the desk where the radiologist is studying various screens.

"So what do you see?" I ask cautiously, figuring that I might as well know the bad news as soon as possible. "Let me guess. The cancer's spreading faster than ever, right?"

"All your numbers are really good," she replies. "Much better than I'd have expected, actually. The pills are really working for you."

"Huh," I reply, resisting the temptation to tell her point-blank that I'm not even taking any of the goddamn pills. Still, it's surprisingly difficult to process this sliver of good news, and I can't help but allow my mind to wander. What if, by some miracle, my cancer clears itself up? What if my body, unlike anyone else's body, manages to work out how to stop this thing? For a few seconds, I allow myself to entertain the possibility that somehow I could be better than everyone else, and that I might actually beat this thing. Finally, however, I force myself to remember the truth: I'm dying, and a good scan today just means that the next one will be doubly grim.

"I'm sure Dr. Gibbs will be very happy," the radiologist continues. "Between you and me, I think he was starting to suspect that you'd stopped taking your pills."

"Perish the thought," I reply, doing a decent impression of someone who's genuinely shocked by the idea. "Does he really think I'd be so dumb?"

"I'm going to get these results to him," she replies, as the nearby printer starts up, "and he'll call you in the next few days to discuss your next step. With results like these, though..." She pauses, and it's clear that she's not sure whether to continue.

"What?" I ask cautiously.

"There are some test programs in the hospital," she replies. "Please don't allow yourself to get your hopes up too much, Ms. Mason, but your numbers are now looking pretty respectable. There's a chance that, if you want, you could maybe be referred onto one of these test programs. They're experimental, of course, and you mustn't start thinking that they could lead to a cure, but there's always a chance that you could get some real benefits."

"Like not dying?"

"Like not dying so soon," she continues. "Less pain. Less fear. I don't want to fill your head with flights of fancy, but some of these experimental programs can have a very positive effect on your quality of life." She pauses. "I happen to know one of the doctors in charge of a particularly promising line of research. If you're interested, and if Dr. Gibbs agrees, I'd be happy to put your name forward to him. I think there's a good chance he'd take you on."

"I don't know," I reply, reluctant to let myself get too carried away. "I mean, I don't like the idea of being some kind of guinea pig."

"At least talk to him," she replies. "What harm could it do, right?"

I open my mouth to turn her down, but finally I realize that it might be worth giving it a shot. "Sure," I tell her, even though I'm convinced I'll regret the decision. "Go for it."

As I'm getting dressed a little later, I can't help thinking about this test program, and wondering whether it might help. I know I should keep a lid on my expectations, but as hard as I try, I can't stop myself wondering if by some miracle I might wind up getting some real help. When I came to the hospital today, I knew I was going to die; now, totally unexpectedly, I find myself contemplating the impossible. I've spent so long trying to come to terms with the inevitability of my death, but suddenly there's this hint of optimism that seems to have been rekindled in my heart. Finally, feeling a little breathless, I take a seat and stare at my reflection in the mirror on the opposite wall. I look tired, but not necessarily ill. I know that hope is dangerous, and that it's just a dead end, but no matter how hard I try to remind myself that there's no such thing as miracles, I can't help it.

What if I survive?

John

"If I let go," I hiss, still holding my hand firmly across Claire's gasoline-soaked face, "do you promise not to scream? I mean, do you *really* promise?"

My heart pounding, I wait for some kind of response, but she merely stares up at me with a look of absolute terror in her eyes. I've got a knife pressed against her chest, with the tip of the blade pushing between the buttons of her shirt and digging gently into her flesh. She knows that I could easily finish her off right here and right now, and that's exactly what I *should* do. However, now that I'm certain she understands a little about my true nature, I can't help but think that maybe, just maybe, it'd feel good to tell her the truth about my actions before she dies.

She should know that I'm not just some crumby insurance salesman.

"I can't trust you," I say eventually. "I'm sorry, but I can't take my hand away. You'd scream. Hell, you'd be a fool not to. I'm sure this has all come as a huge shock to you, and I swear, I wanted it all to be over quickly. Now, though, I guess I owe you an explanation." In the distance, I can hear the sound of sirens, as police cars and fire trucks arrive at the scene. I wanted to be well away from the area by now, but I figure I shouldn't have too many problems. They won't even have started looking for me yet, so I can spare a few minutes here.

I take a deep breath.

"I'm not the man you thought I was," I continue, struggling to put things into words as Claire's horrified eyes stare up at me. "All those times I told you I was going off to sell insurance... I know you suspected that something was wrong. We've been playing this little game, haven't we, you and I? It wasn't until the other night that you really let me know that you were onto me -"

She tries to say something, but my hand remains clamped over her mouth.

"I can't hear a word of that," I tell her.

She mumbles again.

Sighing, I lighten the pressure of my hand.

"I thought you were having an affair," she says, her voice trembling as tears flow from her eyes.

I immediately press down on her mouth again.

"An affair?" I reply, feeling the anger starting to rise through my body again. "Are you serious? After everything I've done, after everything I've built, my whole empire, you thought it was all just some kind of grubby little affair?" I try to calm down, but the truth is, I'm infuriated by the suggestion that all my work has just been in the service of an affair. The whole thing sounds so tawdry. Then again, I've been married to three women at once, but that's not an *affair*; that's just an arrangement that makes sense.

She tries to mumble something.

"No," I say firmly, "*you're* going to listen to *me*! For once, someone is going to listen to me and understand that I'm a success! I was not having an affair, you ignorant little piece of shit! I was building a fucking empire! Something to be proud of! How many other men are able to do something like that, huh? Answer me! How many?" I pause for a moment as I try to regather my composure. "You have no idea," I continue. "No idea at all. Your father, Claire, is a genius. I swear to God, I've spent the past two decades creating an empire of people and assets, valuable products to buy and sell. People, Claire. I've been farming people and selling their names, their faces, their identities... Every one of them retails for thousands and thousands of dollars, more money than you could ever fucking imagine! I've got stacks of cash stowed away, but I always pretended to you and your mother that I was some pathetic, hard-working insurance salesmen, and the pair of you believed it!"

She stares at me, and I can see that she's struggling to take this all in.

"Couldn't you guess?" I ask. "When you looked at me, couldn't you have thought, just once, that maybe I was better than that? Did I really look like a downtrodden, put-upon insurance lackey? I mean, Jesus Christ, were the pair of you so blind that you couldn't see my brilliance?"

I wait for her to reply, but of course she *can't* reply, not while I've got my hand over her mouth. All the stupid little bitch can do right now is listen.

"I was insulted, you know," I continue, "that you could think I was just a pathetic little worker bee. I'm the fucking queen of the hive! Not queen, but you know what I mean." I take another deep breath. "I'm tempted to take you out there," I add, "and show you what I created, but I know you wouldn't be able to understand. That's the problem with you, Claire; you get most of your genes from your mother's side of the family, don't you? Dull, dependable, stupid... You could never comprehend the genius of a man like me!"

I watch as her wide-open eyes stare up at me, and after a moment I realize that the tears have stopped flowing. Her expression is stony and calm now, as if she's accepted her fate. I guess the shock of my true nature is probably too much for her.

"You're impressed, aren't you?" I continue with a smile. "Good. Finally, some fucking sense. You should all be impressed by me, but that's the problem; everything I do, my whole empire, has to be kept secret. I can't tell anyone, and do you have any fucking idea how much that hurts? When a man does great things, it's unnatural for him to not shout it from the rooftops. I've had to tuck my greatness away and disguise it, just so that a bunch of idiots wouldn't try to make me stop." Pausing for breath, I realize that I'm starting to get carried away. "You don't understand," I say after a moment. "You never did and you never will. You don't have the brains for it, Claire. It's not your fault that you're stupid and narrow-minded, I should just..."

I press the tip of the blade more firmly against her chest.

"I should just get this over with," I tell her, forcing back the tears. "I'm sorry. I shouldn't have burdened you, not in your final moments. It's not fair, is it? It's not your fault that you could never have been a great person. I just hope that you can take solace in the knowledge that you were the daughter of a brilliant man. That's not so bad, is it? Your life had *some* meaning after all, and I promise: I'll never, ever forget you."

"Please don't hurt me," she whimpers, like a pathetic little bitch. "Please!"

"I've got no choice," I reply firmly, starting to drive the knife deeper into her chest until, suddenly, I'm struck by an even better idea. "Either that," I continue, "or I could take you with me. Would you like to come and see what I've built out there in the middle of fucking nowhere, Claire? You've always dismissed me as just a boring old insurance salesman, but maybe it's time for me to drag you out there and show you the -"

Before I can finish, she manages to grab my head and push me away with enough force to send me tumbling down onto the grass. I try to turn back to her, but there's a sharp, painful flash across my face and I fall back again.

For a moment, I struggle to work out what happened. Reaching up to my face, I feel a sharp, jagged line across my cheek, and seconds later I spot the bloodied knife nearby. I grab the blade and get to my feet, but Claire has already managed to run across the garden and down the side of one of the houses. I hurry after her, but just in time I realize that she's reached the street, where various onlookers have already found her. I can hear voices shouting for help, and screams, and sirens getting closer.

I have to get out of here.

Turning, I run across the lawn and grab my briefcase, before climbing over the nearby fence and hurrying across another garden. The pain on my face is getting worse and worse, but I can't stop to fix myself yet. I just have to keep going, get to a place of safety, and then hope I can work out what to do next. One thing's for certain; with Claire having miraculously managed to slip away, I need to ditch my old identities and come up with a new plan fast. I should have killed the stupid bitch when I had the chance, but I wanted to keep her alive long enough to make her understand that I'm a great man.

In the distance, the house is still burning. Barbara's body is in there, and Claire's should have been too. This is my fault. I need to get my head together, or I'm going to run out of escape routes.

Joanna Mason

"I'm glad you decided to come and speak to us today," Schumacher says, unable to hide the hint of satisfaction in his voice as he stares at me from behind his desk. "I know it can't have been easy, Jo, and I'm sure that Detective Carver will join me in expressing respect for the decision you've made."

"Absolutely," Carver says calmly, sitting on the nearby sofa.

I smile politely, even though inside I'm just about ready to boil over. I've been in the room for less than a minute, and already I've had to hold myself back from grabbing Carver and throttling him. I swear to God, in all my years working as a detective, I've never once had to apologize to a colleague like this, and the worst part is that I walked blindly into Carver's trap. In some ways, this situation is my fault. Worse, the anger is distracting me from getting on with my job.

"Please," Schumacher says, leaning back in his chair. "We're both very keen to hear what you have to say."

I take a deep breath. "Obviously," I say eventually, trying to stick to the little speech I memorized earlier, "I'm very much aware that I said and did some things over the past couple of days that caused Detective Carver some genuine distress. Although I'd like to state again that it was not my intention to upset him, and that I was in fact only joking, I realize now that I stepped over the line, and that my so-called jokes were actually highly insensitive and ill-advised."

Silence.

"I'm very much aware of the debate in this country regarding workplace conditions," I continue, feeling as if this apology is rapidly becoming absurd, "and I might be many things, but I'm not a bully. Nevertheless, I appropriated bullying language in order to make what I believed to be a joke, and while I thought I was being smart and funny, I realize now that this was by no means the case. I was, in fact, being a total ass. I can assure you that I'll moderate my language and behavior in future, and that I'll never again allow myself to cause this kind of emotional distress."

I wait.

Silence.

I stare at Schumacher.

He stares at me.

"So that's how I see it," I add eventually, feeling a little dry-mouthed.

"It's Detective Carver you need to apologize to," Schumacher replies sternly. "Not me."

Sighing, I turn to Carver. "I'm sure that my crass and thoughtless comments caused you genuine distress," I continue, trying to sound polite even though I feel as if my entire body is filled with grinding gears. "My ignorance of this potential distress is by no means an excuse, and is not intended as such. I merely hoped to make clear the reason for my..." I pause as I try to summon up some suitably pathetic words. "The reason for my terrible behavior and my totally uncalled-for use of words," I add, before waiting a moment to see if either of them react.

An uncomfortable silence descends.

I wait.

They wait.

I wait some more.

"Anything else?" Schumacher asks eventually, with a tone of voice that clearly indicates that he's waiting for me to continue.

"I'm sorry for being an idiot," I reply, facing Carver once again, "and I'm sorry if my jokes came across as being abusive or mean in any way. I was trying to prove some kind of asinine point, and it came across all wrong. I hope you can see past that and understand that I never intended to upset you."

Carver stares at me for a moment. "You're sweating," he says eventually.

"Is that a problem?" I ask.

"No," he replies with a smile and extending a hand for me to shake. "I'm happy to accept your apology, Detective Mason. For what it's worth, I don't believe for a second that you were genuinely trying to bully me. I'm quite convinced that this whole situation was basically a misunderstanding caused by some ill-chosen language, and I very much hope that we can continue to work together as partners."

"That sounds great," I reply, struggling to sound sincere.

"Call me Jordan," Carver continues.

I take a deep breath. "Call me... Joanna. Jo. Whatever you want."

"You know," Schumacher says after a moment, "I don't think I've ever heard you say sorry for anything in the past, Jo. In all the years I've known you, and after all the stupid things you've said from time to time, you've never uttered a single apology. Not near me, anyway." He takes a deep breath. "It's a sign of growing maturity, in my opinion. You're becoming a more rounded and acceptable member of our department, and it gives me great pleasure to assure you that all disciplinary action regarding this matter will now be dropped. Provided that Detective Carver agrees."

"Absolutely," Carver replies with a smile that underlines his sense of superiority.

"So how are you two doing, anyway?" Schumacher asks. "I've got the media on at me to give 'em some kind of explanation for those women who showed up. You managed to at least work out why their backs were broken?"

"To immobilize them," I reply.

"They're being handled by a psychiatric team," Carver tells him. "It's going to take a long time to get any answers out of them. For the most part, they're terrified, but some of them also have developmental problems that mean we might never be able to rely on their evidence in court."

"You need a suspect before you can get to court," Schumacher replies.

"We're working on it," Carver continues. "In fact, Detective Mason is pursuing a theory that might just reveal something interesting."

Schumacher turns to me.

"It's just a thought," I tell him. "I mean, there are certain parallels between this case, and the John Benson case that Dawson's working on. I've made a few preliminary inquiries, and I think it's worth pursuing the possibility. For now, anyway." I pause as I realize that this is the first time in years that I've actually sounded professional. A shiver passes through my body as I imagine how pleased Schumacher must be; he probably thinks he's managed to tame me at last thanks to Carver's intervention. I'll let the pair of them feel smug and superior for now, but I'm already planning a way to wipe the grins off their faces. Then again, this brief moment of amity actually feels pretty unusual... and kind of good, in a sickening way.

"I need something to throw to the press," Schumacher continues, "or they're going to start making stuff up. If there's a connection between the two cases, make it stick in the next twenty-four hours." He pauses. "Jo, we need more than your intuition on this one."

"I'll give you more," I tell him firmly. "If there's a link, I can find it, and I don't even think it'll take too long."

"Those girls are gonna look very photogenic once their pictures end up on the front pages," he replies. "If we haven't got anyone in cuffs by that point, people are gonna start turning on us and claiming that we're incompetent. You both know what it's like when the media starts to think it's got a whipping boy. After all the drama over the Sam Gazade execution, I think we'd all be better off if we can get some good news out there for once."

"Then we'll just have to prove the media wrong," Carver replies, before turning to me with a smile. "Won't we, Detective Mason?"

I smile politely.

Five minutes later, having excused myself from the meeting, I hurry into a bathroom stall and quickly lock the door before getting to my knees and vomiting into the toilet bowl. I don't know whether it's the scan or the cancer or the groveling apology I just had to issue, but suddenly my body feels like it's consuming itself. For several minutes, I stay in place, occasionally bringing up a small amount of bile as I struggle to stop sweating; eventually, the bile gives way to a small amount of blood, and I realize that this is precisely the kind of moment when I really need my pills.

Too bad I tossed them away.

Once the nausea has passed, I sit back and wait to feel vaguely human again. This has been, by any standards, a fucked-up day, and I need to find a way to get back to being my usual self. After a moment, I realize that there's really only one method that's likely to work: I need to find Dawson and get him to talk to me. As a wave of fatigue passes over me, I close my eyes and let my head drop a little, and I tell myself that as soon as I've taken a little rest, I'll head out and check every goddamn bar in the city if that's what it takes to track Dawson down and make him talk to me.

John

"Hey," I say, jogging across the road as the man gets to his car. "Hey! I'm sorry, do you have a moment?"

The man stops and stares at me, and I can see that he's already spotted the wound on my face.

"I'm so sorry to bother you," I continue, "but I was just on my way to a business meeting over at Everly Park, and I rather stupidly took a short-cut through kind of a bad neighborhood and, well, as you can see, I guess, I end up getting mugged by this little thug..." I force a friendly smile, but the guy doesn't quite seem to be buying my story so far. "I got mugged," I say again. "He took my wallet, my keys, my cellphone, everything. I don't suppose I could trouble you for a moment and ask to maybe borrow *your* phone? Just to call my office, obviously."

He pauses, before looking down at my briefcase.

"Yeah," I continue with a faint laugh, "they took everything except the briefcase. Crazy, huh? I guess they didn't think it was worth much."

"Huh," he replies cautiously.

"Which is crazy, really," I tell him, "because it's real leather. This is not some cheap, knock-off product." I hold it out for him to see. "You wanna take a look?"

"No," he says with a frown. "I'm sorry, but I don't think I can help you. Good luck, though."

"Can't I just use your phone?" I ask, putting a hand in my pocket.

"I'm sorry -"

"Can I use your car, then?"

"My -"

Before he can finish, I lunge at him and stab him straight in the chest; determined not to make the same mistake I made with Claire, I quickly pull the knife out and stab him several more times, while keeping a hand over his mouth to keep him from calling out for help. I don't like taking this kind of direct action, but sometimes it's necessary. As I feel his body go limp in my arms, I shove him into the car and then glance over my shoulder to make sure that no-one has spotted me.

So far, so good.

Climbing into the car, I push the guy's body over to the passenger seat before reaching across and checking his pulse. This time, I'm certain that the asshole is dead. Pulling the door shut, I fumble through the guy's pockets until I find his keys, and then I start the engine. There's not much time here, and I need to get the hell out of this town. Pulling away with screeching tires, I remind myself not to drive like a maniac; I slow right down and keep well under the speed limit, making my way along the pleasant little suburban street before taking a left at the next junction. In the distance, smoke is rising into the sky, which suggests that the house is still burning.

I can't help but imagine Claire talking to the police, though. That little bitch is going to tell them everything, and they'll be looking for me soon. My only chance is to get the hell out of reach as quickly as possible and hope to God that I don't have any more bad luck.

As I drive along the next street, I spot flashing lights up ahead. My chest tightens for a moment as a couple of police cars come into view, but they quickly flash past on their way to some emergency. I allow myself to relax for a moment as I try to work out how long it'll be before I reach the city limits. It'll certainly take time for Claire to give the cops even the most basic of descriptions, and then they'll need to start planning roadblocks. I've definitely got time to get away, but there's no room for error.

The next few minutes pass with interminable slowness. I keep expecting to see a roadblock up ahead, or to spot a helicopter tracking my every move. Since I had to move fast and I wasn't able to spend much time covering my tracks, it's not impossible that the police might have been able to locate me, although I doubt they're smart enough. I have a small advantage, and I intend to press it home as fast as possible, which means getting to the city limits and then disappearing into the wilderness. Once I'm away from this place, and away from any kind of surveillance, I can reset myself, ditch this old identity, and work out what to do next. After all, I've got a shed full of assets, each of whom has an identity that's basically clean. Sure, I'm a little older than them, but I think I can manage to make things work.

Spotting another flashing light up ahead, I double-check that I'm well below the speed limit before passing the police car, which is waiting at another junction. In my rear-view mirror, I see that the car has pulled out and started to follow me, and for a moment my chest tightens with such force that I'm worried I might be about to have a heart attack. If they pull me over, I'm finished, especially since I've got a dead body in the passenger seat; he's slumped over and not visible from outside the car, but there's no way I can explain myself if I get stopped. Fortunately, at the next intersection, the police car goes a different way, and I realize that I might actually be able to get away.

A few minutes later, I finally hit the interstate. I can barely believe my luck, but then again I guess it's not luck at all: I've been preparing myself for this kind of disaster, and although I hoped the day would never come, at least I have a back-up plan in mind. It would have been wonderful to have had the luxury of working for a few more years and picking one of my three families before finally settling down, but unfortunately those options have been ripped away from me.

By the time I hit the open road, I figure it's time to cash out of the whole operation. I can start again somewhere else, and maybe even get into something respectable. The world doesn't deserve to catch me. I'm far more than 'just' a fucking insurance salesman.

Joanna Mason

I've never counted all the bars in this city before, but there are thousands, and the job of searching them all for one man is extremely time-consuming, not to mention profoundly annoying. I hurry in and out of all the usual haunts, and then I widen my search and try the bars out on the east side, and finally I start poking my head into even the places that I'd previously considered to be completely off-limits. By 11pm, I'm getting tired, and I've started to consider the possibility that Dawson might in fact have gone somewhere else entirely.

And then I find him.

The bar in question is a sleazy place that looks like it should be a strip joint, except that there are no dancers and all the customers seem to have come in tonight for the express purpose of falling asleep. Most of them are slumped in the various booths, while a solitary old guy is shooting pool without anyone to play against. The barman looks bored, but he's not even bothering to clean the dirty glasses that have been piled up in the sink. In other words, this is the kind of place where people come to die, or - failing that - to think about dying.

"Found you," I say with a smile as I reach Dawson's booth.

He turns to me, and although his eyes look a little heavy and tired, I can see that he's surprised.

"You wanna know how?" I ask, sliding onto the seat opposite him as I take a sip from my warm, flat beer. "Admit it, you came here because you didn't want to be found, right?"

"Right," he says with a sigh.

"So how do you think I tracked you down?"

"Telepathy?"

I shake my head.

"The famous Jo Mason intuition?"

I pause, and for a moment it's tempting to go for glory. "No," I admit eventually. "Pure hard work. Back-breaking, feet-on-the-ground slogging it out, just the way you always prefer. This is the one-hundred-and-twenty-first bar I've checked since 8pm, and I finally caught sight of you." I wait for him to say something. "Impressed?" I ask eventually. "I know *I* am."

"So you managed to work out where I was," he replies, taking a swig of beer. "Well done. Of course, I'd have been happier if you'd also managed to work out that I don't want to be disturbed -" With that, he reaches for his coat.

"Wait!" I say quickly, grabbing his arm. "You can't leave yet. I only just got here. I mean, come on, what kind of guy leaves a woman alone along in a crumby bar like this?"

"The kind of guy who knows that you're the kind of woman who can handle herself," he replies, his speech sounding a little slurred. He's clearly had more than a few beers, and it's somewhat shocking to find Dawson drinking alone; the guy's normally far too straight for this kind of night out.

"Does Elaine know you're here?" I ask.

He shrugs.

"Don't you think she might be worried?" I add.

He shrugs again.

"So you've been off all day," I continue. "For two days, actually. No, longer than that. And it's not just me who's noticed, either. Believe it or not, people are starting to talk about you." I wait for a reply, but once again he seems to be happy just staring at me. "You know you can talk to me, right? I mean, fuck, I had the day from hell today. I had to apologize to Jordan fucking Carver just because he mistakenly believed I said something mean to him."

"You should be more careful," he replies, his voice sounding a little slurred. "One of these days, that kind of thing is really gonna come around and bite you on the ass."

"I know," I reply. "I almost got a taste of that today." Pausing for a moment, I realize that maybe it's time to let Dawson see a different side of my personality. I wish this kind of thing came more naturally, instead of always having to be over-thought, but at least it's better than nothing. "The worst thing," I say eventually, "is that Jordan fucking asshole Carver was right. What I said to him was... completely out of order. I meant it as a joke, but I should have thought about what I was saying first. No excuses. I fucked up."

He takes a deep breath. "Who are you?" he asks finally. "What have you done with the real Joanna Mason?"

"I'm trying to open up here," I reply with a smile.

"Good," he says firmly. "I'm glad you realized you made a mistake. This is a rare moment." He takes another swig of beer. "I owe Mezki fifty dollars," he adds.

"Why?"

"He said you'd eventually apologize for something before the year 2020, and I said you wouldn't." He pauses. "Damn it, Jo, why couldn't you have waited before you tried something stupid like growing as a person? I didn't think you had it in you."

"I didn't know you were making bets about me," I reply, before looking down at my beer. "I'm not a fucking cartoon character," I mutter.

"What?"

"Nothing," I reply, realizing that I'm dangerously close to a moment of self-pity. "So why the hell are you in this place, anyway? It's not like Michael Dawson to drown his sorrows after work. Shouldn't you be rushing home to your good lady wife, to snuggle up with her and run your hand over her barely-protruding bump?"

"Not tonight," he says quietly.

"You had an argument?"

He shakes his head.

"You starting to realize that having a child with a demon bitch might not be a good idea?"

"Don't call her that," he replies, with a hint of irritation in his voice.

I open my mouth to argue with him, but at the last moment I realize that maybe this is one of those times I should apply my new-found wisdom and shut the fuck up. "It's still odd to find you out late like this," I continue. "You know, if you want to talk about anything, I can listen."

"You?" he replies with a smile.

"Me what?"

"You're offering yourself for a deep conversation?"

"I can do deep," I reply, feeling a little perturbed by his reaction. "You know I can talk about deep stuff. Just 'cause I *don't*, doesn't mean I *can't*."

"Sure," he replies, taking another swig of beer before checking his watch. "You're right about one thing, though. I *should* be getting home. Elaine'll be okay with me staying out late, but not all night -"

"And not with me," I point out.

"She doesn't hate you," he replies as he starts to get slowly, unsteadily to his feet. "Well, I don't know," he adds. "Maybe. It's complicated, she -"

Before he can finish, he catches his foot on the table leg and tumbles out of the booth, landing flat on the floor and sending his half-full glass spilling across the floor until it smashes against the side of the bar. It's pretty much the most ungainly, most drunkenly hilarious pratfall I've ever seen, especially from someone like Dawson, and all I can do is stare at him for a moment before starting to grin.

"Get him out of here," the barman calls out gruffly. "The guy's wasted."

It takes a few minutes to get Dawson back up onto his feet, and then a little while longer to escort him out the door and onto the sidewalk. It's a cold night and the city is filling up with parties and traffic, light and noise. I slip under Dawson's arm and try to keep him upright as we make our way from the bar, although it's hard to get him to walk in a straight line. I carefully prop him against a wall while I flag down a cab, and finally I'm able to bundle him into the back seat before climbing in after him.

***

The drive to the suburbs takes almost half an hour, and Dawson sleeps most of the way. I'm wide awake and wired, though, and all I can do is stare out at the lights of the city and think about the fact that one day they're going to be burning and I'll be dead in my grave. For the first time in ages, a few tears reach my eyes, but I manage to sniff them back by the time the cab reaches Dawson's street. Pulling some cash from my pocket, I try to remind myself that it's better to accept death than to cling desperately to hope. The test program at the hospital is most likely going to be a waste of time, even if I get accepted.

I should just pull out and try to come to terms with the way things are going.

"There you go," I say as Dawson and I reach his door. Still supporting him, I ring the bell, and moments later I hear someone hurrying to the door. I brace myself, ready for my first face-to-face confrontation with Elaine for a couple of years. I hope she's really showing her age, and I'd absolutely love it if she's angry.

"Hi," she says, opening the door and staring at us with a shocked look on her face. Unfortunately, she looks pretty damn good, even as I transfer Dawson's weight to her and she eases him down onto a chair in the hallway.

"I found him out and about," I say after a moment. "Sitting in some cheap bar, nursing a beer. Before you start leaping to conclusions, I didn't get him drunk. He was like this when I found him."

"Sure," she replies wearily. "I believe you." She pauses. "Did he... say anything?"

"Nothing interesting," I tell her. "Just the usual crap."

"Thanks for bringing him back," she replies. "Do you have a ride back?"

"I can walk to the intersection and catch a bus," I tell her. "I could kinda do with the night air." I look past her for a moment and see that Dawson is fast asleep on the chair. "This isn't like him," I add eventually. "Don't take this the wrong way, but I've known him a hell of a long time, and I've *never* seen him like this."

"I'm sure you haven't," she replies a little awkwardly. "I should get him to bed, though."

"Totally," I reply, taking a step back. "Just make sure to rub it in tomorrow when he asks how the hell he got home. Make him really suffer, okay?" I turn to walk away.

"Joanna."

Stopping, I look back at her.

"Are you sure he didn't mention anything..." She pauses, as if she's reluctant to say the next words. "Anything about me?"

"Like what?"

She pauses again. "Did he tell you about the baby?"

I nod. "Congratulations."

She stares at me for a moment. "We lost it," she says suddenly.

I open my mouth to reply, but no words come out.

"We're going to try again," she continues, "but I miscarried. It's not a huge issue, really, but..." Her voice trails off for a moment. "We'd just started to get used to the idea. That's all. I think he's taken it pretty hard."

"He didn't say anything to me about a miscarriage," I reply, feeling a wave of sadness pass through my chest. Dawson and I have always told each other everything. Sure, I've kept the truth about my cancer from him this time, but that doesn't give him the right to withhold stuff from me in return.

"Well," Elaine replies, "I guess he wouldn't, would he? Goodnight, Joanna." She starts to push the door shut.

"Wait," I call out.

She pauses.

"Why wouldn't he tell me?" I continue. "Why did you just assume that?"

"Because it's something that really hurt him," she replies, "and because he probably realized you'd just make a joke about it."

"I wouldn't," I reply, feeling as if my blood is running cold.

"Yeah," she says. "You would. We both know that."

She pushes the door shut, and I'm left standing alone on the sidewalk. I can hear the sound of Elaine struggling to get Dawson off the chair and up to bed, and for a moment I can't help but think about the fact that she's right. Up until tonight, at least, I'd totally have ended up making jokes about their miscarriage; however, after the events of the past few days, I think that maybe - just maybe - I've started to realize that I need to hold back from time to time. I think there's just a chance that I *wouldn't* have made a joke.

I hope so. I'd hate to think that I'm such a bad person, my best friend can't even tell me what's going on in his life.

As I walk along the dark street, I can't help thinking about Elaine's words. I gave the bitch a chance to take the moral high ground, and she grabbed it with both hands. Hearing my cellphone start to ring, I reach into my pocket and see that Jordan Carver's trying to get hold of me. Sighing, I figure I might as well answer.

"You seen the news?" he asks.

"No, is -"

"We've got a situation," he replies, interrupting me. "I think your John Benson guy just struck again."

John

"Fuck!" I shout, kicking the side of the car. "Fucking bitch! Fucking asshole!"

I'm miles out of town and it's almost midnight. Having parked by the side of the road, I've taken a moment to get out and try to calm my anger. All I can think about, however, is Claire, and the fact that right now she's probably blabbing to everyone about the things I told her. How could I have been so stupid? What the hell is wrong with me?

"Whore!" I scream, kicking the side of the car so hard that I hurt my foot. Hopping away, I soon topple over and land hard in a nearby bush. I swear to God, if that little bitch ruins my empire, I'll make sure she pays.

I will fucking destroy her.

Epilogue

Five years ago

"Daddy, do you have to go?"

Stopping at the door, he turns to see that Claire has come through from the kitchen. She looks thoughtful and concerned, and the fact that she has one thumb in her mouth only adds to the impression of childish innocence.

"Someone has to put food on the table, sweetie," he replies. "All you have to do is stay home and focus on your schoolwork, okay? You also need to get your strength up for the operation in a few weeks. Meanwhile, I'll be out there selling insurance to people all over the tri-state area, and in a few weeks I'll come home and we can have some fun. How does that sound?"

"Do you go away because you don't like us?" she asks.

Sighing, her father realizes that his hopes of a quick getaway have been dashed.

"Claire, it's nothing like that," he says, hoping to get this little confrontation over and done with as quickly as possible. "It's *because* I love you that I'm going on this long trek, silly. I want to earn money to buy food, and toys and clothes and all the things a little girl deserves. If I didn't love you, would I bust my back like this?"

No reply. Claire simply stares at him.

"Stop worrying," he continues. "I'm good at my job, sweetie, so there's really no reason to be concerned. I'll just go and sell insurance to some people, and then I'll get the commission, and then I'll come home and we can have fun. I wish I could be home all day, every day, but the world simply doesn't work like that. Families have to be brave while someone goes out to earn a pay-check, you know?"

"Sally's father doesn't have to go away the way you do," Claire replies.

"And what does Sally's father do?"

"He's a garbage collector."

"Exactly," he replies. "Would you like me to be a garbage collector, Claire? Would you like me to work so hard all day that I'm exhausted in the evening? Would you like me to come home stinking of rotten fish and meat and whatever else people are throwing out?"

"No," Claire mutters.

"Exactly. My job is very good, but unfortunately it takes me away from home sometimes. It won't be forever, though. One day I'm going to come home and stay. Does that sound good?"

"Annabelle's father's an airline pilot," she replies, "and Kelly's father works for a bank in New York. Why don't you do something like that?"

"What's wrong?" he asks, with a hint of irritation in his voice. "Is your old Dad not good enough for you?"

Claire doesn't reply.

"See you in a few weeks, kiddo," he adds, before heading out the door.

It's a hot day, certainly not the kind of weather to endure while cooped up in a warm little car. As he throws his briefcase into the trunk, John can't help but feel sorry for all the poor assholes who are *really* out there working hard and slogging their guts out for a slice of commission. He's never been the kind of person who can work under someone else, and he knew from an early age that he'd have to be his own boss. Of course, he initially assumed that he'd pick up a legitimate, respectable profession, but things didn't quite work out that way and when his big idea came, it turned out to be morally suspect; still, he'd managed to get over those concerns, and he no longer had any moral worries at all.

He'd even become adept at juggling his three different families.

He was good at it.

He liked doing it.

He enjoyed the sensation of being better than everyone else.

As he got into the driver's seat and pulled the door shut, he couldn't help but smile at the fact that while he appeared to be an ordinary family man, at heart he was a ruthless businessman who cared nothing for the suffering of others. He liked the incongruity: he had three families, each of which considered him to be theirs and theirs alone, and yet he was playing them off against one another, making fools of them and taking his time as he tried to decide which family he'd choose when the moment came to kick back and enjoy the fruits of his labors.

Just as he was about to start the engine, however, he happened to glance back at the house, and that was when he saw her. Claire was standing at the window, watching him with cold, intense eyes. Although she was young, she seemed to have knowledge and wisdom beyond her years, and he couldn't help but wonder if in some way she might have been able to pick up on more than he'd realized. Their eyes met for a moment, and yet she didn't flinch, didn't even try to look away; her eyes simply bored into him, and he was convinced that there was a hint of suspicion in her gaze.

"Fuck off," he muttered as he eased the car out of the driveway. He told himself that she was just a stupid kid, and that there was no way she could know anything about him. She was dumb and naive, and he'd been too careful to keep his secrets safe from his various families. There was no way she could know, and no way she could ever find out. He knew that, barring hideous bad luck, he was far too smart to ever get caught.

Part Seven

A Face in the Crowd

Prologue

Thirty-five years ago

He's coming.

    I can hear him.

    I *hate* him.

    The way he walks down the stairs, the way he smiles as he enters the room, the way he ties his dressing gown so that his bare chest is still visible, with all those curly black hairs bursting out like bristly worms... I swear to God, there's nothing about my father that I don't hate with a passion, and I wish he'd just disappear from my life completely.

    "Morning, kiddo," he says, heading through to the kitchen, where my mother is making breakfast.

    I don't remember why I hate him, but there's never been a time when his presence was welcome. There's just something about him that fills me with hatred, and I desperately want to just make him go away. My mother seems to like him, but I can't help wondering if maybe she's just pretending; after all, she seems so nice, and I don't understand how she can possibly put up with his fake bullshit.

"You want eggs?" my mother calls through to me.

"Yes please," I reply politely.

"You want them fried?" my father asks, leaning through to grin at me with that disgusting smile of his. "Or do you want to have them boiled and runny, like a little boy?"

"Fried is fine," I mutter, bristling at yet another attempt to make me feel like an idiot.

As he heads back into the kitchen, I turn and look out the window. One day I'm going to get the hell out of this place and leave everything behind. I won't take anything; hell, I won't even keep my name. I'll strike out on my own, and as far as anyone from my old life is concerned, I'll simply have faded from view. They'll never be able to find me or stop me. I'll just be gone forever.

It's the only kind of freedom that I've ever wanted. I can be better than this.

Joanna Mason

"You don't understand!" she screams. "He's crazy!"

To say that this place is chaos would be an understatement. It's 2am and despite the fact that I'm exhausted and slightly drunk, I've come back to the office following Carver's phone call. Whatever's actually happening right now, there's no damn way I'm going to go back to my apartment and sleep, giving Carver time to pull ahead of me and maybe grab all the glory. It's as if the case has suddenly blown wide open, and although I'm not in the right frame of mind to deal with any of this stuff right now, I figure there'll be time to sleep later.

"Please try to calm down," Carver says as I enter the room. He's crouching next to a terrified-looking teenage girl, whose leg is being attended to by a paramedic, but Carver has fixed the girl with a determined stare. "I need you to tell me exactly what happened, Claire," he continues. "Don't leave anything out. We don't have much time here."

"He's insane!" the girl shouts, with tears streaming down her face. "He tried to kill me!"

"What's going on?" I ask as I reach Mezki, who's sitting at his desk on the other side of the room.

"Claire Sutter," he replies, keeping his voice low. "Local cops picked her up a few hours ago. She says she barely escaped with her life this afternoon after her father killed her mother and then set the house on fire. Does that kind of set-up seem familiar?" He passes me a printout that shows a familiar face. "This is her father, John Sutter. Remind you of anyone?"

"John Benson," I mutter, staring at the image.

"So this guy has now burned down two houses in a week, and tried to kill both the families. I mean, it's clearly the same person, right?"

I nod, still looking at the printout. John Sutter and John Benson are most definitely the same person, and they also both happen to have the same face as the man who terrified the girls we found. Whatever's happening here, it's pretty clear that this guy is in something of a panic, trying to cover his tracks; it's also clear that he must have been living at least two entirely separate lives, both of which he decided to destroy.

"Burner families," I say quietly.

"Huh?"

"People buy burner phones that they can use and then get rid of," I continue. "Burner debit cards, burner email accounts, burner laptops... This guy had burner families, even burner lives. He used them, and now he's decided to destroy them. He must have thought they were going to cause problems. Clinical, huh?"

"Please!" the girl shouts from the other side of the room. "You have to stop him!"

"That kid's gonna be scarred for life," Mezki mutters, before checking his watch. "I should get going. Color me cynical, but I'm expecting a roasted corpse or two in the next thirty minutes. They're always my least favorite. The skin kind of crinkles when you touch them. I'm not gonna be able to eat grilled food for a week." With that, he gets up and slips past me, heading out into the corridor.

"Claire," Carver says firmly as I make my way through the gathered crowd, "you need to focus for a moment. If we're going to find your father -"

"He's not my father," she spits. "Not anymore! Don't say that word!"

"I need to get her to the hospital," says a paramedic as she examines Claire's damaged leg.

"Not yet!" Carver says firmly. "Claire, if we're going to find him, we need your help. A cellphone number, a car, something that'll allow us to trace him."

"None of that's going to work," I say as I reach them.

Carver turns to me.

"This guy uses stuff and then ditches it," I continue. "If you think you can get his cellphone number and track him down like that, or wait until he logs into his email from somewhere, you're wrong. He created entire fake families and I'm pretty sure he kept them completely separate. He's not gonna do anything stupid that'll let you find him."

"We need to get her to hospital," the paramedic says. "This wound needs cleaning, and I can't do it here. The bullet only grazed her, but there's a risk of infection."

"Is she going to be okay?" I ask.

"She's been very lucky," the paramedic continues as she starts packing her equipment away. "There should be no major nerve damage, but I have to take her right now."

"I'm going to come and see you in the morning," Carver tells Claire, reaching out and holding her hands for a moment. "What I need is for you to rest. I imagine the doctors will give you something to help you sleep, and then tomorrow we can begin to piece this all together, but right now you have to trust me when I tell you that there's no way in hell your father is going to get near you."

"What about my Mom?" she asks through the tears.

"I don't have any answers for you on that," Carver replies.

"Because he killed her," she says, her voice trembling. "Just like he tried to kill me. I wish he'd succeeded. There's no point living now."

As the paramedic leads Claire away, it's hard not to feel for the girl. Her mother's dead, her father's on the run, and her family home is just a burned-out shell. She's probably going to find, in the next couple of days, that the Sutter surname was a complete fiction, made up by her father to provide cover for his new life. She's going to feel as if she's not real, and I can't even begin to imagine the trauma she'll face as she tries to live with all of these new truths.

"You were right," Carver says after a moment.

"Of course I was," I reply. "About what? Something specific, or everything in general?"

He takes the printout from my hand. "This John Sutter guy, or John Benson or whatever his name is... We need to find him fast. He's burning through families like they're going out of fashion. Where's Michael Dawson? I need to -"

"He won't be any use tonight," I reply, interrupting him. "Dawson's kinda tied up."

"Then untie him."

"By tied up, I mean blind drunk. Right now, he's probably flat on his back, snoring so loud that his long-suffering wife has to use ear-plugs."

Carver sighs.

"It's okay," I continue. "I know his password, so we can get to all his files."

"He's drunk?" Carver asks, before leaning closer to me. "Seriously? Are you drunk too?"

"One beer," I reply. "Not even that. I had to abandon it when Dawson got thrown out of the bar."

"Thrown out?" He pauses. "What the hell kind of operation have you people got running here?"

"Dawson has problems," I say with a faint smile. "What can I say? Some people just can't handle their drink. But *I'm* here, and I haven't slept for almost forty-eight hours, so I should be right in the zone soon. Just try not to be alarmed if I get a twitch in my left eye. Happens sometimes, nothing to worry about."

"Why haven't you been sleeping?" he asks.

"I've been looking at maps," I tell him. "A friend said I should try to get a hobby, so I figured, why not try cartography? Maps are pretty cool, right?"

"Whatever," he replies, holding up the image of John Sutter. "If you're in the zone, as you call it, and if your famous intuition is as good as I've heard, then tell me where the fuck to find this guy. For all we know, he could be out there torching another family home and burning another wife and daughter. And then another, and another, and another."

Staring at the photo, I realize that Carver's right. This Sutter guy, or Benson, or whatever his real name might be, is a psychopath, and sooner or later he's going to kill again. Fortunately, I'm pretty sure we don't have to worry about any more burning houses tonight. Something tells me that the guy's panicking, which means that he's probably going to try to shore up his business, or maybe even cash out. Hell, that's what I'd do if I was a maniac with multiple identities and a tendency to kill everyone who cared about me. There's something clinical and efficient about this bastard.

"He's out of the city," I say after a moment.

"What makes you say that?"

"Those girls we found," I continue, "were *just* the girls. There has to be at least one more place where he's storing the men. If he's doing what I think he's doing, anyway. The girls escaped, but that was just bad luck. Somewhere, probably within a few hours' drive, there's another place where he keeps the men."

"You still think this is some kind of identity farm?"

"If I had a bunch of people chained up, that's what I'd do with them," I reply. "I'd sell their identities. Useful for a guy who wants to disappear, huh?"

"Then we need to -"

"The last place wasn't on any maps," I continue. "This other place probably isn't either. You can go over every map and every planning application in the state, and I doubt you'll find it. It'll be like looking for a needle in a haystack, but I promise you, that's where he's going." I pause for a moment as I try to imagine what I'd do if I was in the guy's position. "He probably has a stash of cash," I add, "and more fake identities. If he doesn't have another wife and child out there, he will soon. He'll disappear from trace and change his appearance, and then he'll settle into a new life and we'll never catch him. It's now or never."

I take a deep breath as I try to work out how to find this guy. Unfortunately, my mind seems to have reached a dead-end, and I'm not sure I can come up with anything in time. Then again, I guess I could always hit the maps again.

"Give me something to go on," Carver says after a moment. "Where do we start looking?"

Still staring at the photo, I try to work out how the guy might slip up. No-one's perfect; everyone makes mistakes, and this guy has to have done something wrong that'll allow us to track him down. Somewhere out there, there's a trail, or a clue, or something that'll point us in the right direction. Right now, however, I can't work it out.

"Sir," another detective calls out from across the room, "there's a call for you!"

"I'm kinda busy right now," Carver replies.

"It's a woman named Susan Pierce," the detective continues. "She says she just saw a photo of John Benson and John Sutter on the news, and... Well, she thinks he might be her husband too."

John

"Come on," I mutter, waiting for Leonard to pick up the damn phone as I drive through the night. "Answer, you pig-fucking asshole. What the hell else have you got to do with your time?"

Up ahead, I can just about make out a single light from the office at our facility. I've always told Leonard to keep the lights off at night, so that no-one can spot the place from a distance, but of course the idiot has chosen to ignore my orders yet again. Speeding up, I aim straight for the metal gate that blocks the entrance, and as I drop the phone onto the passenger seat, I figure that rather than stopping and opening the gate, I might as well just smash my way through. It's not like there's any need to keep the place secure, not now that the whole damn operation is crashing down.

"Fucking bastards!" I shout as I accelerate and aim straight for the gate.

As soon as I hit the metal, the car jolts and instead of ripping the gate open, I end up getting part of it snagged around the front of the vehicle. I immediately hit the brakes as the car bounces across the rough yard with a large section of the gate trailing behind and beneath, and after a moment I hear a loud popping sound as one of the tires bursts. The car almost flips before settling down with a heavy bump.

"What the fuck was that?" I shout, scrambling out of the car and looking down to see that some kind of metal spike is embedded in the tire. I turn to look at the office, just as a figure emerges carrying a shotgun. For a fraction of a second, I'm ready to scream at him, before I realize that he's aiming the shotgun directly at me. "Leonard -" I start to say, before ducking behind the car just as a shot rings out, blowing the car window apart in a hail of glass.

He fires again, this time hitting the side of the car.

"It's me!" I scream, cowering behind the door. "Leonard, it's me! It's John! For God's sake, put that thing down!"

"What the fuck are you doing here?" he shouts.

Getting to my feet, I hurry around the car before grabbing the shotgun from Leonard's hands and throwing it to the ground. I'm damn near ready to teach this asshole a lesson, but fortunately I'm able to restrain myself.

"What is *that*?" I shout, pointing down at the spikes embedded in the car's tires.

"It's a defense system," he replies, his panicked face barely visible in the moonlight. "You told me years ago to set something up in case anyone ever tried to break through the gate, so I installed a kind of modified cattle grid to, you know, slow people down and... stuff like that."

"Jesus Christ," I mutter, kicking the side of the car before turning to walk over to the office. "Jesus fucking Christ, Leonard, it's like you just don't think!"

"You told me to do it!" he complains.

"Well, you did it wrong!" I shout.

"What the hell's going on here?" he asks, hurrying after me. "Are we in trouble?"

"Why didn't you answer your phone?" I reply, turning to him. "I tried to call you!"

"I was asleep!"

"And you didn't hear it ringing?"

"I had it turned off. I didn't know you were gonna try to call!"

"Of course you didn't know I was going to call!" I scream. "That's the whole point of a cellphone! You don't have to book a fucking appointment to get in touch with someone! What kind of moron are you?"

"What's going on?" he replies, clearly worried. "John, are we in trouble? Are they onto us?"

"Onto us?" I reply. "No, of course they're not fucking onto us. They're onto *me*, but I can fix that soon enough, I just..." Taking a deep breath, I can't help but once again imagine Claire sitting in some police station somewhere, singing like a canary. Then again, I guess it doesn't matter so much, and it might even be of benefit if she leads them on a wild goose chase for a while. I can just get a new identity, make a few changes, take some cash, and start again somewhere far away. The only danger is that I might panic, but as long as I keep my shit together, everything's going to be okay.

I just need to calm down.

Just as I start to feel as if I've got the situation under control, however, I remember the tracking device on my old car. If Claire has the logs from that damn thing, she might be able to help them find this place.

"John," Leonard continues after a moment, "do we need to close things down? Is it time to get the bags from the safe and just call it a day?"

"Of course not," I spit, before realizing that he might be right. "Maybe. I don't fucking know, okay? I need time to think. This has all come as something of a surprise, and I need to take a moment and come up with a new plan." I pause as thoughts flood into my mind. "It was always set up like this," I add eventually. "From the very beginning, I designed this entire operation to be disposable. I hoped the day would never come, but I knew it probably would. Then again, it would definitely be a shame to cut and run too soon. The situation might be salvageable, but we need time, and time is the one thing that's running out."

"Man," he replies, "maybe... I don't know, I think this is a sign."

"A sign?" I reply, staring at him. "A sign from who? About what?"

"You know, a sign from God or something -"

"God?" I shout, unable to believe the bullshit I'm hearing. "Are you fucking serious? We spend twenty-five years running a fucking identity farm, selling and killing people for money, keeping whole barns full of men and women with broken backs so they can't get away, and now you think that God, in his infinite wisdom, has decided to pipe up and help us decide when enough is enough?"

"Fuck this," he replies, pushing past me and heading toward the office.

"No!" I shout, grabbing the shotgun and aiming it at the back of his head. I pull the trigger, but the only sound is an empty click. As he turns to look at me, I realize that he fired two shots earlier, so the damn thing must be empty now.

"You fucking asshole," he says, before turning and running to the office.

"Come back!" I call after him. "I didn't mean it!"

Realizing that he undoubtedly has more weapons in there, I race after him. I can't afford to let him get to another gun, but fortunately I'm a little faster than him and as he gets through the door I'm able to grab him by the waist and drag him down onto the floor. He tries to fight me off, but I raise the unloaded shotgun and then slam the butt down several times against his face; I finally feel the side of his skull crack, and although he's still alive, I climb off and head over to the window. Peering out at the yard, I take a moment to catch my breath and regather my composure.

Behind me, Leonard writhes in agony, clutching his head and trying to speak.

"Hang on," I mutter. "I'll come and finish you in a moment."

He lets out a scream.

"If it's any consolation," I say finally, turning on the lights before looking down at his bloodied face, "I was going to kill you anyway. The only question was how I'd do it, and whether I'd spare you the pain of knowing what was coming."

He tries to shout at me, but it appears that I might have broken his jaw.

"I couldn't let you ride off with half the money, could I?" I continue, starting to calm down after the exertion of the past few minutes. "I mean, Jesus Christ, Leonard, how naive *are* you? I was the brains behind this whole operation, wasn't I? It was my idea, my set-up, my organization." I pause for a moment as those words sink in. "I was the brains," I whisper. "I built an empire based on a great idea, and yet I was never able to boast of my achievements. Instead, I had to fucking scurry through the shadows and keep my brilliance hidden, telling people I was some kind of pathetic insurance salesman. What kind of a sick world do we live in, where a man can achieve such greatness but he can't appreciate the applause of the masses?"

As he tries to get up, Leonard lets out a scream of pain. There's blood flowing from his mouth, and he looks as if he should just give up and die as soon as possible.

Stepping past him, I head to the cabinet where all the paperwork has been filed. I hate the idea of destroying all the records from this place, but at the same time, I know that one day someone's bound to stumble upon the facility, and I can't risk anything falling into the wrong hands. I've burned so many places and people in recent days, and now isn't the time to lose heart: I need to start one final fire, and then I can drive away and never look back.

Opening the safe, I pull out the bags of cash that Leonard and I have been building up over the years. There's easily fifty million dollars here, which is more than enough for me to start a new life somewhere else, somewhere out of the way. Hell, if I can find a way to get the money into a legitimate new business, I might finally be able to build an empire that I can dare show to the world. Then, and only then, I might actually get the praise that I so richly deserve, while this moldering pit of filth can be left to rot.

I can be respectable.

I can be legitimate.

I can be a real family man, and maybe finally I can relax.

But first, I need to finish Leonard off and torch the couple of hundred men who are currently chained in the shed.

Joanna Mason

"How's the leg?" I ask, taking a seat next to Claire's hospital bed.

She stares at me with suspicion in her eyes, and it's clear that she doesn't trust me at all. On the way over here, I was able to access Claire's social networking profiles and get an idea of her background; I saw photos of her hanging out with friends and playing sports, and she generally came across as a very ordinary girl; now she's sitting in a hospital gown, with heavy padding around one leg, and her eyes are red with tears.

"Where's the other guy?" she replies eventually.

"Detective Carver is following another lead," I tell her, choosing each word carefully, "and I'm -"

"Have you found him yet?"

"Your father?"

"Don't call him that," she spits. "I don't want to think that there's any of him in me."

"We're working on it," I say after a moment, "but -"

"But he's out there," she continues, becoming visibly more agitated as she looks over at the door.

"He could just show up here and come into the room and finish what he started. You don't know what he's like. He's smart and he can trick his way in! His face is bland as fuck, he's one of those guys who just sinks into the background! He doesn't look like a serial killer! He'll find a way to get to me!"

"No," I say firmly. "We have so many police stationed in this hospital right now, there's absolutely no way he can get anywhere near you. Anyway, I doubt he'd even try. He's probably long gone by now, Claire. I'm sure he's trying to escape, but that's something we're not going to let happen, okay? I need some information from you, but we're going to catch him before -"

Pausing, I realize that I should try to keep things as vague as possible.

She stares at me. "Before what?"

"Never mind," I reply, opening my notebook. A bunch of folded map print-outs tumble out, and it takes me a moment to stuff them back in.

"What are those?" Claire asks.

"Just a hobby," I reply.

"So did you pull my Mom's body out of the wreckage yet?"

"I'm not sure if -"

"Do I need to identify her?" she continues, with tears in her eyes. "Do I need to, like, walk into a room where they'll take a sheet off her face and ask me if it's her or not?"

"I don't think that'll be necessary," I reply.

"They'll use dental records?"

I nod.

"So her teeth won't have been destroyed?" She pauses. "It's weird to think of her all burned up like that, and then someone opens her mouth and checks her teeth. Will they still be white?"

I try to think of something to say, but everything just feels so pointless. It's not often that I'm affected by a case like this, but Claire Sutter has really got to me.

"Is it true that he had another family?" she asks eventually. "I heard some of the nurses talking, and they said he had this whole other family with, like, another wife and other kids. I saw on the news about this house that was burned down the other day, and the guy looked a lot like my Dad..." She pauses, as if the word 'Dad' tastes like poison. "He looked like *him*," she adds, correcting herself. "I joked about it at the time, but now..." Tears are starting to trickle down her cheeks, and I can see that she's in danger of cracking up. "He's a murderer, isn't he?" she asks. "He killed my Mom, and he killed those people, and he tried to kill me..."

"This is why we need to catch him," I reply.

"What if you don't?" she asks. "What if he gets away?"

"We're going to do our best to make sure that he doesn't have that chance."

"But what if he does?" she continues. "What if he's smarter and luckier than you, and he manages to slip away so that you never manage to find him?

What if he just blends in with everyone else, like some kind of blank face in the crowd?"

"We have to work very hard to make sure he *doesn't* get away," I reply after a moment. "That's why I'm here -"

"You're not very good at this," she says. "At being reassuring, I mean. No offense, but you suck."

I pause.

"Sorry," she adds. "That other guy was better." She wipes the tears away. "I feel like everyone's waiting for me to turn into some kind of wreck," she continues after a moment, "but I have to stay strong, right? At least until you've caught him. I can turn into a sobbing mess later, but right now I need to stay calm." She pauses. "I was thinking," she adds, "that maybe you could use me as bait."

"I don't think we're going to need to do anything like that," I tell her.

"I can do it," she continues. "If it means that you catch that asshole, I can totally do it. I'll break down and become a wreck later, but right now, I want to catch him. I want to see his face as he's cuffed and led away, and then I want to be there when he's fucking executed, so you have to let me be, like, some kind of bait. He wants me dead, right, so why don't we offer him the chance?"

"It doesn't work like that," I reply.

"Why not?"

"Because I don't think he'd come back and try to kill you."

"Of course he would."

I shake my head.

"You think he can't even be bothered to try? Am I so unimportant to him that he can't even be bothered to finish me off?"

"I think he's probably focused on trying to get away," I continue. "From the little we've learned of your father, we've built up an approximation of his character, and I personally believe that his actions are motivated by survival. He knows that you're with us now, and he knows you'll tell us what you can, so there's no real benefit, from his point of view, even if he manages to get to you." I pause for a moment. "In fact," I add, "he might try to use the situation to his advantage."

"But he hates me," she replies, her bottom lip trembling as more tears trickle down her face.

"No," I tell her, "I don't think he does. I think he's just a very clinical man who's able to focus on his own needs."

"Then why are you sitting here with me?" she continues. "Why aren't you out there looking for him?"

"I think he's left the city," I reply. "I think he's gone to a place that we're never going to find if we just start looking randomly, and I also think we don't have long if we're going to catch him. That's why I want to ask you if there's anything he's ever said or done that made you suspicious, or anything that you can think of that might help us. Even if it's a tiny detail that seems totally insignificant, it might fit with something else we've got. I know you must be tired, but I have to ask you to think back to anything he might have said."

She stares at me.

"Anything at all," I continue.

Her trembling lips seem poised to say something, but at first she seems to be a little hesitant. "Leonard," she says eventually.

"Leonard?"

"I heard him arguing with someone on the phone a couple of times," she says cautiously. "Someone named Leonard. The first time was about five years ago, and then I heard him again recently, using the same name when he was talking in his office. He sounded angry, like he was pissed off at something that this Leonard guy was telling him. He was really ranting."

"What about the name Albert?" I ask. "Did you ever hear that name being used?"

"I don't know."

"Or Manuel?"

"Maybe," she replies. "I'm not sure about those two, but definitely Leonard. I don't know who he is or anything like that, but I think this guy Leonard is involved in it somehow. He seemed to be, like, the main guy my Dad was talking to on the phone all the time." She pauses. "Does that help?"

"It might do," I reply, closing the notebook. It's clear that Claire, for all her keenness to assist in the investigation, knows very little about her father's hidden life. If my suspicions are correct, she's soon going to have to deal with the horror of learning the truth, and if we capture the guy alive, she'll also have to endure years of media coverage as the trial gets underway. There's no way she's going to be able to hide from all of this.

"I thought he was having an affair," she says after a moment.

"You did?"

She smiles weakly. "I knew he was up to something, but I thought he'd just got another woman. That was, like, the worst thing I could think of, and I hated him for it. I wanted to expose him for it and get my Mom to leave him. I never really liked him, so I thought we could get away and be happy someplace else."

I try to think of something to say, but words seem to be failing me right now.

"I hope he dies," she says eventually. "Can you do me a favor? Promise me that when you catch him, you won't arrest him. Pretend he attacked you or something, and just kill him right there and then." She fixes me with a determined stare. "Please," she whispers, as if she wants to make sure that no-one overhears us. "I want him to die."

"I can't promise you that," I tell her.

"But you *could* do it, couldn't you?" she continues. "If you catch him when there's no-one else around, and no cameras, you could just put a bullet in his head and end it."

We sit in silence for a moment as I try to find an appropriate moment to leave.

"I'll do it," she says eventually, staring into space. "If I ever see him, I'll kill him. If you're smart, you'll do the same. Just blow his brains out and make sure he can never hurt anyone else ever again. Some people just don't deserve to take another breath."

John

"Come on," I mutter, as I root through Leonard's desk drawers. "Where the fuck did you leave them?"

It's almost 4am and I've spent the past half hour looking for the master keys to the main shed. Having checked Leonard's pockets and even rolled him over in an attempt to see if they were hanging off his belt, I've ended up taking the whole goddamn office apart as I try to find the damn things, but there's still no sign of them.

"Fuck!" I shout, slamming the last drawer shut. "Fucking cock-sucking asshole!"

I take a deep breath.

My whole body is trembling. If I don't calm down soon, I'm liable to start making mistakes, and that's when the risk will start to rise.

And then I realize that although the keys weren't in the drawer, there was something else that I should have double-checked.

Opening the drawer slowly, I stare at the ragged manual that appears to be a guide to a tracking device. Gently taking the manual and flicking through it, I quickly realize that it's for the exact same type of device that I found on the underside of my car. It wasn't Claire who planted that thing; it was Leonard. Staring at the manual with white hot fury in my veins, I start to understand that I had no need to kill Barbara, or to try to kill Claire. I could have let them live. Claire only thought that I was having an affair. There was no need to go this far.

"Great," I whisper, getting to my feet and walking over to the spot where Leonard is groaning on the floor, with blood still seeping from his damaged features. I stare down at him for a moment, before taking a step and then kicking him in the face so hard that several of his teeth fly across the room.

Joanna Mason

"Nothing?" I reply, shocked by the news. "Are you fucking kidding me?"

"Nothing for now," Carver replies, his voice sounding a little scrambled over the line. "John Sutter's car was found abandoned outside the house. There were some items in the trunk that make us think he was planning to make a getaway, but for some reason he abandoned the car and left on foot. We think he might have made his way through neighboring gardens, so we're checking to see if any of the residents have cameras that could have picked something up."

"He was chasing Claire," I point out, looking over my shoulder and watching as a nurse enters the girl's room. "By the time she escaped, it was too late for him to go back for the car, so he had to try something else."

"So he can't have got far."

"Unless he jacked another ride," I continue, turning back to look out the window for a moment. The lights of the city are bright, but in the distance there's a vast band of darkness; even in the twenty-first century, there are plenty of places for someone to hide. "You need to check for anyone missing in the area," I continue, "anyone at all, especially if their car's also disappeared. This guy wouldn't risk public transport, but he'd also want to get the hell out of town. Unless he's got an accomplice in the area who could pick him up at short notice, I think he'd probably try to force someone to give up their car."

"We're running facial recognition programs on various databases," he continues. "This guy can only change his appearance so many times. Once we've got a few results, we'll go check every single possibility until we've ruled them all out. Or not, as the case may be. We've also checked out the claims made by Susan Pierce, and I'm fairly confident that her husband John Pierce is the same guy as John Sutter and John Benson, so we've now got three completely separate identities that this asshole was using. God knows how many more there might be. I've got some guys at the Pierce house now, waiting to trace him if he tries to contact her."

"He won't."

"You don't know that."

"I know he's smart," I reply. "Calling one of his other wives would be insanely dumb right now."

"Sometimes smart people do dumb things," he points out.

"Maybe," I mutter, "but we can't rely on it. I pause for a moment as I try to work out a common theme in this guy's activities. "He sure likes the name John," I say eventually.

"It's probably his real name," Carver replies. "I figure a guy with lots of different identities is going to try to simplify things as much as possible, so he probably wants to avoid the confusion of being known by lots of different first names. As for his real surname, we're still working on that. If we can cross-reference the visuals and maybe get some additional hits, it's possible that we can make an educated guess and zero in on this guy's real identity."

"Good luck," I mutter. "He's probably left it far behind."

"I'll find it eventually," Carver replies. "Don't worry about that. I'll get this guy and haul him in, and I'll fucking have his real name if I have to squeeze it out of his goddamn throat."

"I think a lot of people would be very relieved if you did just that," I point out.

"Trust me," he continues. "Once I get this asshole in an interrogation room, I can break him. I've dealt with some tough sons of bitches over the years, and I've managed to get through to all of them eventually. This guy probably thinks he's the smartest fucker in the room, but give me a day or two with him and I'll have him vomiting the truth onto his own shoes. There's no-one in the world who can withstand a face-to-face confrontation with Jordan Carver."

"I'll call you later," I reply, turning back to look over at Claire's room, I see that the sedatives have finally kicked in and she's out cold. "I have a few leads to chase up," I add. "Some ideas, that kind of thing."

"Care to share them with me?"

"Not really."

"I'm the senior -"

I cut the call and switch my phone off before he has a chance to call back.

"You're the senior asshole," I mutter, heading along the corridor. Jordan Carver's doing all the right things, and it's useful to have his input as back-up. However, this isn't the time for plodding, procedural detective work; I need to come up with something, and time is definitely running out. If we don't find this guy soon, he's going to disappear into the crowd and we'll probably never have another chance. Reaching into my pocket, I pull out some of the crumpled maps I've been examining. All I need is one lucky break, one moment of inspiration, and I think I know just how to kick-start the process.

Jordan Carver would never approve.

John

"Sun's coming up," I mutter as I drag Leonard's still-bleeding corpse across the yard. "You see that? Take a good look, 'cause it's the last sunrise you'll ever get to watch. I guess it's pretty beautiful, if you like that kind of thing."

It's almost 7am and having spent the past few hours trying to work out my best course of action, I've come up with a plan that I think will ensure I can get the hell out of this place and start again somewhere else. My original aim was to get to Susan's house, but it's clear that I can't take that risk; she's probably suspicious by now, and I wouldn't even be surprised if she's talked to the police. Hell, they're probably sitting at her home right now, waiting for the phone to ring so that they can track my location.

No fucking chance.

I won't give those dumb, smug assholes the satisfaction. I'd rather die than let them catch me.

Reaching the steps that lead to the barn door, I drag Leonard up with such force that he lets out a pained groan. Leaving him on the deck for a moment, I head over to the door and pull out the keys that I finally found hidden behind the safe. God knows why Leonard hid them there, but then again he was clearly more suspicious than I'd realized; after all, the asshole had placed a tracking device under my car. I wouldn't be surprised if he'd been planning to rip me off, in which case I have no reason to feel bad about what I'm about to do. We were going to double-cross one another, and it's not my fault that I happened to be smarter and more careful.

"I always had my suspicions about you, Leonard," I continue as I struggle with the padlock. "Hell, I was surprised you stuck around for so long. You never really had the stomach for this kind of thing, though, did you? That was always the biggest challenge for me. I just couldn't find anyone else who really understood the moral side of things."

Although he tries to reply, Leonard can only manage a faint gurgle.

"The empire," I mutter, as the rusty padlock springs loose and I finally manage to get the door open. The stench from inside is overwhelming, and it's clear that the hundred or so men in the place haven't been cleaned for a while. Reaching around the corner, I flick a switch, and seconds later some small lights flicker into life along the walkway that runs down the length of the building. I can already hear the assets groaning as I turn and grab Leonard's body and start hauling him into the shed. If I had a spare hand, I'd cover my mouth and nose, but as things stand I guess I'll just have to put up with the stench. Still, it's shocking to realize how low the human body can fall when it's left in a place like this. It's as if these sons of bitches have no sense of dignity whatsoever.

"No -" Leonard whispers as I dump him on the narrow walkway.

Ignoring him, I look out across the shed and marvel for a moment at all the hunched, naked figures. These are my assets: they were just babies when I acquired them, in the days when I started out by paying drug-addict mothers a pittance in order to buy their newborns; once I brought them here, they were chained up and kept alive, and then they were occasionally cleaned so that they could be taken into town and given a check-up by a dentist or a doctor. Once their existence had been established, their backs were broken, they were chained up for good measure, and we began to wait for customers to come along. All I needed to do was to ensure that each and every one of the assets had some kind of presence in official systems; they all have social security numbers and credit histories, which means that their identities are valuable and worth selling. It's hard to put a precise figure on their value, but there's easily a hundred million dollars of human stock in this barn.

And now it's all going to be wasted.

"What good is an empire," I say after a moment, "if it has to be kept in the dark? What good is a great man, if he can't step out of the shadows and accept the plaudits that are due to him?"

Looking down at Leonard, I see that he's slowly trying to crawl away. He won't make it, of course, but it's amusing to see him making the effort. "One day," I continue, walking after him and keeping pace as he heads for the door, "I'll be revered as a great businessman. I'll reinvest all the money from this operation into something laudable and legitimate, and no-one will ever know that I started out doing something like this. But I promise you, Leonard, that when they come to write my story, there'll be no mention of you. Not even a footnote. Do you know why?"

He cries out in pain as I step on his hand.

"Because you're not like me," I add. "You were always just a hired assistant, paid to keep watch on things and born to be forgotten, just like the idiots we kept chained in this barn. You did a decent enough job most of the time, but now I feel that I must let you go." I crunch down harder on his hand, and seconds later I feel his bones cracking and snapping. He tries to scream, but I simply kick him in the side and send him tumbling down off the walkway and into the main area of the barn, where the assets are tied up.

I can't help but smile. After all, it's no more than he deserves.

One by one, the nearest assets start to notice Leonard. They approach him, dragging themselves through the dirt, and some are on long enough chains to reach him. They seem suspicious at first, almost animal-like in their aversion to a possible threat, but I watch in delighted horror as they begin to cautiously paw at him, and although he can't get up and pull himself free, the poor old fool has enough about him to call out for help. Slowly, however, the assets start to pin him down; one grabs a leg and tries to pull him closer, while another does the same with an arm. I don't know if they're acting out of some primordial desire to kill, or if they're starving and will eat anything, or even if they recognize him as one of the architects of their misery, but whatever the explanation, they soon begin to tear at him. Although I usually hate to witness violence first-hand, I can't help but watch and enjoy the experience as Leonard tries desperately to get free. Soon, the beasts have begun to dig their teeth into his belly, and blood starts to flow onto the filth-encrusted concrete floor.

"Goodbye," I whisper with a smile, as I watch one of the assets reach into Leonard's chest cavity and snap several of his ribs away.

Not wanting to witness any more of this squalor, I turn and head to the door. After flicking the lights off, I make my way outside and push the door shut, before walking over to the storehouse. There's enough sunlight now to be able to see pretty well, so I don't even need a torch as I search for the gasoline canisters I stored here a few years ago. Once I've found them, I take them back to the main door and unscrew the lids in order to make sure that there's enough left to get the job done. Satisfied that I'm prepared for the next phase of my plan, I head to the office and open the filing cabinet. Pulling out the catalogs, I take them to the desk and sit down. It's going to take me a while to find an identity that I can steal, since the assets are all so much younger than me, but I'm convinced that I can find something that'll be useful.

In the distance, Leonard lets out a cry of pain.

I flick through page after page, discounting scores of faces until finally I come across one that looks as if it might just be good enough. Slipping the photograph out of its plastic cover, I take it over to the mirror in the corner. It's not a great likeness, but this particular asset has a similar facial shape to me, and similar hair, plus we share the same color eyes and more or less the same height. It'll take some work, but I think I can pass for him. Turning the photograph around, I check the details written on the back.

"Brian Cantard," I whisper, a little disappointed by the ugliness of the name. "Brian *Cantard*." I stare at myself in the mirror and practice saying the name over and over, hoping to get used to it. "Brian Cantard," I mutter, before tilting my head a little in order to get a better view. "Brian Cantard," I say again, and finally I realize that I can definitely do this. Within a few hours, I can change my appearance enough to pass for this Brian Cantard individual, and then I can take Leonard's old truck and hit the road. I have no idea where I'll go, but with the cash at my disposal, my choices are more or less unlimited. Of course, I can't just take that money and shove it into a bank account; I'll have to be much more careful, and I'll have to start from the bottom again, but I can begin to build a new life, and no-one will ever be able to link me to my old identities.

John Noone is dead.

John Benson is dead.

John Sutter is dead.

John Pierce is dead.

Brian Cantard, however, is about to have a whole new lease of life.

Any man can build an empire, but I think I might just be the first person in human history who manages to build two.

In the shed, in the distance, Leonard is still screaming.

Joanna Mason

"You sure about that?" the barman asks.

I nod, preferring to avoid conversation as I stare at the screen of my laptop. I've come to this out-of-the-way dive in order to get away from dumb questions, so I sure as hell don't appreciate having my every decision queried. After a moment, realizing that I'm being watched, I glance over at the barman and see that he's eying me with suspicion.

"You don't want my money?" I ask.

"It's 8am," he replies. "Are you sure you wanna be -"

"Yeah," I say firmly. "I'm sure."

He smiles politely, but I know what he's thinking.

"It's the only thing that works," I tell him, although I instantly realize that it was a dumb thing to say. I sound like one of those chronic alcoholics you see standing outside a liquor store, coming up with all kinds of excuses to explain their behavior, except that in my case it really *is* the only thing that works: I'd normally go and shoot the breeze with Dawson and come up with ideas while he talked, but he's probably sleeping off his heavy night and I figure my next best option is to just sit here, drink a few whiskeys, and hope that inspiration strikes me when I'm least expecting it.

If I fuck this up, Jordan Carver's going to think he's beaten me. That alone should be enough motivation for me to come up with something.

"Maybe this should be your last one," the barman says, sliding a shot over to me.

"Do I seem drunk?" I ask.

"No, but -"

"I can hold my drink," I tell him, before taking a sip. "If I start swaying or falling over, feel free to kick me out. You might find this hard to believe, but while I'm sitting here, I'm actually working. I'm trying to get something done, and if this is the best way to do it, then what the hell, why not give it a go?" I pause for a moment as I stare at the homepage of the local planning authority. "It's not like I'm gonna need my liver for much longer anyway," I mutter darkly. "Might as well use and abuse it while I can still get something out of it."

Trying to ignore the barman, I scroll down the homepage, looking for something that might help. I'm convinced that this guy we're looking for has got some kind of set-up away from the city, but it can't be *too* far away since his three families were all in the same state; the problem is, the burned-out facility we found when the girls escaped was a building that didn't appear on any maps, so the most likely reality is that we're looking for another place that was erected without permission, in which case we're searching for a needle in a haystack. Sure, we can probably find it eventually, but by that point it'll be a burned shell, the guy will be gone, and any people being held captive will probably be long since dead.

There has to be a way to find this guy.

I just need my head to start working properly again.

"Hey!" a voice calls out from behind me. "Sunshine! Over here!"

Sighing, I turn to see that a drunk guy is waving at me from his position slouched in the corner of a cubicle. My first instinct is to ignore him, but at the last moment it occurs to me that maybe this asshole could be useful. After all, a spot of righteous indignation might be just the spark I need to get my inspiration back up and running, so I close the lid of my laptop, grab my whiskey and head over to join the guy.

"That doesn't normally work," he says, clearly unable to believe that I've actually responded to his drunken heckles.

"So you're a serial killer," I reply. "In theory, anyway. Just imagine that you've been holding people hostage in a big building somewhere out in the middle of nowhere, and killing them from time to time, and you've got various false families dotted around the place. You're a real asshole. You probably managed to rationalize your behavior a long time ago. You told yourself that you're..." I pause as I try to put myself in the right frame of mind. "You told yourself that you're smarter than everyone around you," I continue, in a moment of clarity, "and so you figure you might as well cull anyone who gets in your way. It's harsh, but it works for you."

He sits up straight.

"You've killed your family," I add. "Most of them, anyway. Your daughter got away, and now you realize that the cops are onto you. Time's running out, but you've got an escape route planned. You probably had one set up from the start, and now you're going to put it into action. You'll take a whole new identity, one of the ones you were gonna sell, and you'll disappear into the crowd. It's actually a decent plan and you know that it'll work, but you also know that you need to stay calm and do things methodically rather than rushing."

"Lady," the guy replies, "I just came in for a drink -"

"It's a hypothetical situation," I continue with a smile. "Imagine you ended up having to kill your families and head somewhere safe. Quick, tell me the first thing that comes into your head: where the hell would you go?"

He stares at me.

"Come on," I add. "This is important. It might actually help. Just tell me what you'd do or where you'd go, or... anything. Even if you say something totally dumb, it might help me to think of a better answer. If you can't say something smart, just say whatever comes into your head. Believe me, I can tell from looking at you that you're not exactly a genius, so just do your best and I'll take it from there."

"Are you for real?" he asks.

"Deadly," I reply. "Come on. My usual sounding-board isn't available, but I still need to talk to someone. Try to imagine that you're a complete psychopath. Can you do that?"

He opens his mouth to reply, but no words come out.

"I can," I continue. "I can imagine that *I'm* a psychopath. Hell, maybe I am? Maybe that's..." I pause as it occurs to me that I might be onto something: maybe my so-called 'inspiration' is actually a way of accessing my inner psycho and thinking like the people I'm trying to catch. I guess that's probably something I should think about when I get a free moment. "So if you're on the run," I add, "and you've got a place out in the middle of nowhere, you'd go there, right? I mean, it makes sense. You'd be crazy not to, and anyway, you might have associates. You'd need to warn them and make sure they were going to leave too." I pause as the pieces start to come together. "Or you'd kill them. That's probably what you'd do. After all, you killed your families, so why not the guys you work with? A total scorched-earth policy."

He pauses. "I guess..."

"But how do you time it all?" I continue. "Imagine you're panicking. Would you lay low, or would you try to run for cover?"

"I don't know -"

"Try!"

He takes a deep breath. "Jesus, woman, you're sobering me up pretty fast here."

"Sorry," I reply, "but try to think. What would you do?"

"I'd lay low," he says after a moment, "and I'd... I guess I'd wait until the heat was off before I made my move, and then I'd go find somewhere new to hang out. Somewhere no-one could find me."

"And what about your daughter?" I ask. "The one you tried to kill... Would you bother trying to finish her off?"

"Not unless she knows something," he replies. "I guess... Plus, it's his daughter..."

"Take emotion out of it," I continue. "Ignore the fact that she's family. Would you bother?"

"Probably not. I'd just, like, not wanna do anything that might attract attention, if you know what I mean."

"That's what I thought."

"But seriously, lady," he continues, "this is way beyond anything I know about, okay?"

"Relax," I tell him. "I'm a detective -"

"Fuck!" he shouts, getting to his feet. "I don't know anything about anything, okay? I just came here for a quiet drink, and now you're making all these accusations and shit, it's totally not on. I'm just a normal guy, okay? Don't go acting like I've done something, 'cause I haven't."

"Calm down," I reply, "I'm just -"

"I don't know anything about it. I don't even *like* gambling! I haven't been anywhere near that place! This is entrapment!"

With that, he stumbles to the door, clearly filled with panic, and I'm left to frown as I try to work out what the hell he was rambling on about. I guess he thought I was after him for something specific, but I really can't be bothered dealing with the kind of lowlife scum that hangs around in this kind of place. Sure, I join them occasionally, but only because it helps me think.

"He was a good customer," the barman mutters. "Did you really need to chase him out?"

"Yeah," I reply, heading back over to the bar. "I did." Pausing for a moment, I can't help but feel that this John Benson or John Sutter guy is in the grip of full-blown panic. It's pretty damn clear that his little world is falling apart, so I doubt he's thinking clearly. Just like the guy in the bar a few moments ago, the guy I'm hunting is probably jumpy and ready to run at a moment's notice. If that's the case, hopefully it won't be too hard to push him into making a mistake sooner rather than later, and hopefully he'll be a little more cautious than usual.

Feeling a shooting pain in my belly, I wince for a moment. I could really use some of those pills that Dr. Gibbs prescribed a while back, but they'd just cloud my head even more. I have to stay clear-minded, and I have to focus. If inspiration won't strike, I think there might be one other way to find this asshole before it's too late.

"You want another one?" the barman asks.

Ignoring him, I grab my laptop and head to the door. It's time to go spend some more time on my new hobby.

Part Eight

The Man Who Disappeared

John

It's time.

Standing in the office, I stare at my reflection and - I swear to God - I barely recognize the man staring back at me. I've spent the past few hours working on my appearance: I fixed my hair, I found a pair of glasses that alter the look of my face, and I fitted contact lenses to change my eye color from brown to green. Sure, I can still see my old face peering out from beneath the disguise, but I'm certain I can pass for Brian Cantard in public.

A new name.

A new face.

A new life.

I can't help but smile.

Grabbing the bags of money, I start hauling them out to Leonard's old truck. Now that my plan is set, I feel much more settled. There's no way the police can track me down in time, and even if they one day stumble upon this place, all they'll find will be some bones and a set of burned ruins. I've spent the whole night here, avoiding all contact with the outside world, safe in the knowledge that I can't be found; now I just need to find somewhere else to keep low for a few weeks, until the search for my old identities dies down a little. Once the roadblocks have been lifted. I can just slip away in the crowd.

There's still one final job to do, however, and I honestly can't tell whether I'm dreading it or looking forward to it.

Grabbing the gasoline can, I head to the shed. Although there's a part of me that knows this is wrong, and that the poor unfortunate souls in the shed are going to die in horrific agony, there's another part of me that recognizes the importance of ensuring that I get out of this mess. It would be a crime against humanity for a great man such as myself to end up getting caught by this city's pig-ignorant police force. There's no reason why the strong *shouldn't* profit at the expense of the weak.

It's just human nature.

Once I'm inside the shed, I don't bother to turn on the lights. I can just about make out a dark, smudged patch on the ground near the walkway, which I assume is all that's left of Leonard. It wouldn't surprise me if these animals tore him apart and then ate whatever parts of him they could digest; sure enough, several bones have been scattered nearby, and I just hope that the bastard suffered as he died. Leonard was never much use, and that tracking device he put under my car was a bad move on his part. If he deserved to live, then he would have been smarter, but idiots like Leonard are ten-a-penny and I'm not going to waste any time mourning him.

"Let's get this over with," I mutter, unscrewing the lid of the gasoline can and starting to pour its contents over the heads of the assets down below the walkway. They start to moan as they desperately attempt to get free of their chains, but of course they've got no chance. I make my way slowly along the walkway, taking care to ensure that the gasoline covers each and every one of them, and then when I get to the far end I turn around and do the same again. After all, I gain no pleasure from their pain, so I figure it's better to ensure that they die as quickly as possible. By the time I get back to the door, the whole place stinks and I pour the last of the fluid against the wall.

Done.

I step out of the barn and leave the door hanging open as I reach into my pockets and pull out a box of matches. In a strange way, I actually feel a little sorry about this situation. After all, this facility represents decades' worth of work, and now it's going to be destroyed in just a few minutes. I can't deny that there's a part of me that wants to preserve the whole place as a testament to my brilliance, and to maybe even invite people to come and take a look. Hell, in an ideal world it might even be preserved as a museum, but this isn't an ideal world, not remotely. Soon there'll be nothing left here but ruins, and my empire will be gone. Still, with millions of dollars in the truck and a new identity, I've got a damn good chance to start again somewhere far away.

I light the match.

From inside the barn, there's the sound of moans and wails. The effect is contagious, and it's as if they know what's about to happen to them. That's impossible, of course; these brutes can't possibly have any understanding of gasoline, so they're probably just mindlessly shouting their rage at the roof. Somewhere among their number, the real Brian Cantard is waiting to die alongside his fellow captives, with no idea that he and he alone will live on past this day, albeit with someone else assuming his identity.

"Thank you, Brian," I mutter, reaching through to drop the match. "You've been very helpful."

And that's when I hear it.

Turning, I look across the yard, convinced that somewhere in the distance there's a faint rumble. I scan the horizon, but I don't see anything, and I try to tell myself that it's just an airliner passing high overheard. Suddenly, however, I spot movement far away, and I realize that a helicopter is approaching. My chest immediately tightens as I realize that there are also several dark vehicles racing this way, and this time there can be no question as to their purpose: I have no idea how, but the police have managed to locate the facility, and they're coming for me right now. I guess Claire must have somehow helped them after all.

I don't know whether to laugh or cry.

Still holding the match, poised to drop it and ignite the assets, I turn and look over at the truck. There's no way I can outrun a police helicopter, especially not in that old thing, and I don't have the necessary firepower to neutralize the threat. Momentarily unable to think, I stand in silence, watching the cars getting closer and closer until they screech to a halt just before the wrecked gate. Police officers swarm out and take position, and I'm soon being targeted by a dozen or more weapons.

"Stop what you're doing and put your hands above your head!" shouts a voice, and moments later I spot a tall, determined-looking black guy heading toward the gate. He's clearly in charge, and I've already taken an instant dislike to him. He probably thinks he's got this situation all under control, but I have a feeling he's going to change his mind pretty damn soon.

I stare at him for a moment as I try to decide how to respond.

"Stop what you're doing," he shouts again, aiming a gun at me, "and put your hands above your goddamn head!"

Turning, I look at the burning match and realize that I could just drop it right now and then either run or hurry into the building. The possibility of death suddenly seems strangely enticing, and I can't help but think that maybe I could be satisfied with posthumous glory. After a moment, however, I realize that I'm fooling myself. I want to live, and I want to know that these fools have recognized my brilliance. It's not enough that *I* know how great this empire has been; I need to know that the world understands too.

"Insurance salesman, my ass," I whisper.

"This is your final warning!" the black guy shouts, aiming a gun at me as he gets closer. "Put your hands above your head now! I will *not* repeat myself again!"

"That would necessitate dropping the match," I reply, as the flame burns closer and closer to my fingers. "I think there are some people in the barn who wouldn't be very happy with that idea. They've taken a little shower in gasoline, and it wouldn't take much to set them off. Can you have that on your conscience? All those deaths? So many men, screaming as they burn? You'd have nightmares for weeks."

I smile as I see the look of concern in the guy's eyes. He clearly knows that I mean business, and I imagine he has a rather deeply-ingrained aversion to mass murder. He'll do anything within his power to ensure that I don't set fire to this place and kill the assets, which means that although escape is clearly out of the question, I still have a great deal of power if I can use his humanity against him. Unfortunately, the match is already half-burned, which means I need to get on with this as quickly as possible.

I never asked for a showdown, but if it has to happen, I'm damn well going to rise to the occasion. I've spent too long keeping my ego folded up in the shadows; it's time to let the damn thing out. My heart is racing, and I feel that maybe I've been waiting for this moment my whole life.

"I have certain demands," I say eventually, feeling the heat of the flame becoming more uncomfortable as the match burns shorter and shorter, "and you don't have very long to decide whether or not you're going to give me exactly what I want."

Joanna Mason

"He'll do it," I whisper, keeping a little way back as Carver continues to aim his gun at the suspect. "Don't push him too far. He'll do it if he thinks it's his only option."

"We can negotiate," Carver shouts, "but first you have to put the match out!"

"And why would I do that?" the suspect shouts back at us. "You've got your weapons trained on me. As soon as this match goes out, you'll take me down. I'm not an idiot; I know how this works, so I'd suggest that we hurry up. I doubt there's more than thirty seconds left."

"He's got a point," I whisper.

"My name is Jordan Carver," Carver calls out to him. "I want to help you, but I need you to meet me halfway. Can you start by telling me *your* name?"

No reply.

"What's so difficult about telling me your name?" Carver asks. "It's a simple thing. Everyone has a name, right?"

"Brian Cantard!" the guy shouts suddenly.

"Brian?"

"Bullshit," I whisper to Carver. "That was way too easy."

"As of this afternoon, anyway," the guy replies with a smile. "Before that, I was John Benson, and John Pierce, and John Sutter, and John this and John that and all the in-betweens." He pauses. "I hope that isn't too confusing for you. I can give you a long list, if you like. I've been quite a few people over the years, and none of you assholes ever even noticed."

"I'd like to know your real name," Carver replies.

"I just gave you a whole *bunch* of names," the guy replies. "Pick one and use it. I don't care; names are just temporary things, like identities and feelings. They can be dropped whenever they become inconvenient."

"The way you dropped your families?" Carver asks.

"They were just props. I needed to blend in with society, so I got myself a few wives and children. I'd have chosen one eventually, once I'd retired. I wasn't too far away from that point, you know. If you assholes had just stayed at your usual level of incompetence for a little longer, no-one else would have died and I'd have settled into a nice, comfortable retirement. There would have been no more deaths."

"Apart from the people in that warehouse behind you," Carver points out.

"They're not people," the guy replies with a half-smile. "They're just products to be sold to the highest bidder."

"There's no way out of here," Carver continues. "If you think you can somehow swing this situation to your advantage, you're wrong. We've got this place completely surrounded. You still have a chance to do the right thing here and let those people live. I don't think you really want to kill anyone else, do you?"

"How did you find me?" the suspect asks. "I'm sorry to change the subject, but I'm genuinely curious. I went to great lengths to keep this place off the map, so I'm confused. Did someone tip you off?"

"Care to answer that one?" Carver whispers to me.

"I don't think he'd like the answer," I reply, keeping my voice down.

"Stop whispering at each other!" the guy shouts. "This match is starting to get too short to hold! I want you all to get the hell out of here, and I want..." He pauses, and it's as if he knows that he can't get away. "Hell, do you know what?" he continues. "There's nothing you can give me. I know you won't honor any agreement we make, so I might as well just torch this whole place. Believe me, you'll be grateful in the long-run. The people in this barn, they're basically just animals. They're no use to anyone, not anymore, so why bother spending time and money trying to help them out? They're better off dead."

"That's not a decision for you to make!" Carver shouts. "Step away from the door and put the match out!"

"Time's ticking," the guy replies. "This is starting to hurt! Hell, at this rate, I might drop the match by accident!"

"We can talk," Carver continues, "but not until you've put that match down. Do you understand?"

"He'll do it," I whisper. "You need to drop him before he gets a chance."

"If I shoot him," Carver whispers back at me, "the match will fall anyway."

"It'll probably go out in the process," I point out. "Even if it's still burning when it hits the ground, it might not land in the gasoline. At least there's a chance." Removing my gun from its holster, I take aim at the guy.

"Do *not* fire," Carver hisses at me.

"He hasn't even made any demands yet," I point out. "He's just stalling. He's enjoying this! Can't you see it in his eyes? He wants to feel important, and I guess killing does the job."

"Time's up!" the guy shouts, and a fraction of a second later he drops the match.

Everything seems to freeze for a moment as the little burning piece of wood falls to the ground. The flame is still visible as it lands, but it's quickly extinguished by the impact and everyone seems to be waiting to see if the gasoline ignites. I keep my eyes on the guy and see that he's just staring at us, as if the fate of the building doesn't even matter to him. Finally, however, I spot a flicker of emotion in his eyes, and I realize that I was right: he *was* hoping to ignite the gasoline when he dropped the match just now, although I imagine he'll claim otherwise later.

"It's okay," Carver whispers.

"It's not gonna burn," I reply. "I think it -"

Before I can finish, Carver fires once, hitting the guy in the shoulder and sending him tumbling back against the wall of the barn before dropping down to the ground.

"I guess you're right," Carver adds after a moment.

As we hurry across the yard and up the steps, I realize that there's a sound coming from inside the barn. Carver goes to check on the suspect, who has already started trying to get to his feet, while I head to the door and peer into the barn's dark interior. There's a powerful smell of gasoline, along with the stench of human excrement. It's pitch-black inside but as I step forward I realize I can see lots of human forms in the gloom, most of them huddled on the ground with just their painfully thin, bare backs visible. As I make my way along the walkway, I can honestly say that I've never seen such a horrific scene; I always thought I'd become immune to the sight of human suffering, but this is something else entirely and eventually I stop and simply stare down at the hunched, naked figures.

After a moment, one of them looks up at me, staring with terrified, wide eyes.

I open my mouth to tell him that everything's going to be okay, but no words leave my lips. The truth is, I know that I can't make any promises, and even if I could, they wouldn't understand me. These men are more like animals, and it looks as if they've been treated as nothing more than property. As the smell becomes overpowering, I turn and hurry out of the barn, just in time to find that the suspect is being led away.

"Wait!" the guy says, turning to look over at me. "You have to tell me. How the hell did you find this place? It was that bitch, wasn't it? It was Claire!"

"No," I reply, thinking back to Claire's attempt to persuade me to shoot the guy if I got the chance. I'm glad I wasn't put in a situation where I had to contemplate that option, because I'm not sure what I would have done. "No, it wasn't Claire."

"Then how?" he asks. "You at least owe me an explanation."

"No," I tell him after a moment. "No-one owes you anything. We found you, and that's all that matters."

He stares at me, and I can see that he's desperate to know how we tracked him down. As police officers lead him away, Jordan Carver comes over to join me.

"So are you still sticking to your story about how you found this place?" he asks after a moment. "More of your famous intuition?"

"Absolutely," I reply, trying not to let him realize that I'm exhausted. "How else could I have done it?" I pause for a moment, amused by the look of irritation in his eyes. "What's wrong?" I add. "Annoyed?"

"Inspiration is one thing," he says firmly, "but finding this place is another. Are you claiming to be some kind of fucking clairvoyant, Detective Mason?"

"I'm not claiming anything," I tell him. "We found the place, didn't we?"

Instead of answering me, he follows the rest of the officers into the barn. Rather than joining them, I step down into the yard and watch as the suspect is led into the back of an ambulance. We still don't know anything about the guy; hell, we don't even know his real name, and I swear to God, I want to unravel his entire life story. I want to know what kind of person could do something like this, and how a mind could become so twisted. Finding the barn was just the first step; getting to the truth about this psychopath is next on the list.

Feeling something wet on my upper lip, I press a finger against my left nostril and see that there's a spot of blood. Worried that I might faint again, I hurry back to my car.

John

There's a way out. There has to be. There's *always* a way out.

As the paramedic examines my shoulder, I'm vaguely aware of a distant pain; still, it's not enough to make me cry out or ask her to stop. Sometimes, pain is good; hell, sometimes pain is the most vital thing in the world. Right now, for example, the throbbing pain in my shoulder is louder than my heartbeat, and I feel strangely calm as a result. I'm content to stay here, flat on my back and staring at the ceiling, while my shoulder is padded ready for the journey to the hospital. My right wrist is handcuffed to the bed, but it's not as if I'm planning to go anywhere. I need to think carefully about my next move. There'll be time for action later.

"Okay," says a police officer, climbing into the back of the ambulance and taking a seat next to the trolley, "I'm gonna need a name."

"Cantard," I reply, not even bothering to look at him.

"I'm gonna need your real name," he replies calmly.

"Cantard," I say again. "Brian."

"Right," he mutters, writing something on a clipboard. "And what was your name before that?"

"I had several," I continue. "They were concurrent, so I can't really put them in any kind of order."

"Okay," he says with a sigh, "why don't you just give me your original name, huh? The one you were born with? The one on your birth certificate."

I pause for a moment. "I'm sorry," I say eventually, "I don't think I recall that one."

"You don't recall your birth name?"

"Sorry."

"What about your parents' names? Can you tell me those?"

Another pause. "I'm sorry, but no, I can't."

"Because you don't know them, or because you're refusing to cooperate?"

I can't help but let a faint smile cross my lips. "Yes," I say calmly.

"Yes? Yes what?"

"Just write what you want."

"Okay," he continues, clearing his throat. "Let's start this again. Have you ever officially changed your name as a matter of public record?"

"No."

"So your original birth name is still valid."

"Not to me."

"In a legal sense," he replies. "Let's just end this charade right now, okay? You're gonna cough it up eventually, so let's do it now and just get it over with so we can move on."

"No."

"You think you can keep it hidden forever?"

"Yes."

"You can't. We can check your fingerprints, your DNA, your dental records -"

"You won't find anything," I reply, interrupting him. "I was always very careful. Before all of this started, I mean. It was so long ago, and I can assure you that nothing remains of my original identity. I can't stop you wasting your time, but I promise you, you'll never find the answers you're looking for." Finally, I turn and look at him, and I'm shocked to see that he's younger than his slightly gruff voice had suggested. "My original name is gone," I tell him, "just like my original life."

"It was that bad, huh?"

I feel a flicker of emotion run through my body, but only for a fraction of a second. "I suppose you could say that," I tell him.

"You have to be known by some name in order for the legal process to go ahead," the cop replies, sounding a little tetchy. "You can't keep changing it, either. If you're really not gonna offer up your real name for the time being, we'll have to go with one of the names you've been known to use in the past." He checks one of the sheets of paper on his clipboard. "How about John Sutter?"

"John Sutter is dead," I reply quickly. "He died when his house burned down."

"But *you're* John Sutter," he points out.

"I was for a while," I continue. "The original John Sutter was..." I pause as I realize that perhaps I shouldn't give away too many of my trade secrets. "You'll never unravel it all," I add after a moment. "Do you want to know why? The truth is, I'm too smart for you. You're all assuming that I made a mistake somewhere, and that you'll be able to start getting to the bottom of who I really am and where I really come from, but you don't have a chance. I didn't make any mistakes."

"That's confident talk," he replies drolly, "coming from a guy who just got shot and arrested."

"You don't know what you're talking about," I mutter, annoyed by the fact that he's daring to contradict me.

"Fine," he mutters. "You know what? The guys down at the station can deal with your bullshit. I was just trying to save some time, but you'll crack eventually. Just for the record, though, you don't look particularly smart to me right now. You look just like all the other criminals we catch, day in and day out."

I take a deep breath, trying to stay calm. This moron is overstepping the line, and I'm tempted to leap up and pin him against the wall. Then again, I'd just be wasting my energy: idiots never truly learn, and we smarter members of society have no need to spend our time trying to educate and rehabilitate less fortunate intellects. What this world needs is a cull of all the idiots.

"Let's get going," the cop says as he sets the clipboard aside.

"We're taking you to hospital to get this wound looked at," the paramedic says as she pulls the rear door shut. "It should be a fairly simple procedure to get the bullet out. You shouldn't have any lasting damage."

She keeps talking, but I zone her out as the ambulance starts up. These idiots have nothing to say to me, and I'd rather be left in peace so that I can come up with a new plan. In a way, I'm quite glad that the full extent of my business empire is going to be exposed. Sure, there'll be those who think that I'm just some kind of common criminal, but I don't care about the opinions of idiots. What matters to me is the knowledge that I'll go down in history as someone who actually made something out of his life. After all, how many other men have ever even *held* bags containing fifty million dollars' worth of cash?

I waited all my life for my true nature, my full ego, to finally get a chance to come out. Now that it's here, I have to say, I'm rather enjoying it.

Joanna Mason

"You look exhausted," Carver says as he joins me in the observation area. "When was the last time you slept?"

"No idea," I mutter, watching through the one-way mirror as the suspect sits alone in the interrogation room. For the past couple of hours, Carver has been trying to get answers out of him, but the asshole hasn't given us anything to work with. I thought that once we caught him, the case would move forward, but now I realize that unless he breaks and gives us his real name, we'll never be able to truly put this one to bed. Granted, it's kind of amusing to watch Carver throw himself up against a brick wall over and over again, but the lack of progress is starting to grate.

"Go on," Carver continues. "I can handle this. I'll tell Schumacher -"

"No," I say firmly, even though I'm exhausted and I feel as if I'm going to crack at any moment. "We have to find out his real name. Until then -"

"I'll do that," he replies, interrupting me. "You already did enough, Jo."

"That's just what you want," I mutter.

"Excuse me?"

"Nothing."

I stare at the suspect, but I'm painfully aware that Carver has his gaze fixed on me. I feel as if, now that the case is reaching its conclusion, our so-called partnership is starting to become even more strained, and Carver is trying to find a way to score a few extra points. Since I'm the one who managed to locate the facility where the guy was holding all those men, Carver's desperate to be seen as the one who manages the interrogation. The truth is, I'm almost too tired to bother fighting him.

"Are you okay?" he asks eventually.

"I'm peachy," I reply, trying to sound calm.

"I mean your health -"

"None of your business."

He pauses. "This is my area of specialty," he says after a moment, turning back to look at the suspect. "I've cracked harder nuts than this guy. Give me twenty-four hours, and I swear to God, I'll have his name, his date of birth and his goddamn life story. I will this asshole writing his autobiography by sundown."

"I admire your confidence," I say quietly, unable to stop staring at the suspect's icy, determined expression. To be honest, I'm pretty sure he's not going to break. Carver and I can spend the rest of our lives trying to get answers out of him, but he's just gonna sit there and act like he's so goddamn superior. The thought of trying to get him to talk to us is daunting, because for perhaps the first time in my career, I genuinely think that there's no way we can succeed. I hate being beaten, but I think that on this occasion, this 'nut' might be too hard to crack after all.

"So why don't you tell me how you really did it?" Carver says after a moment.

I turn to him.

"Don't tell me it was intuition," he continues, with a faint smile. "The rest of these idiots might buy that bullshit, but I know how things work, Jo." He waits for me to say something. "Come on," he adds eventually, "tell me how you figured out where to find that facility out in the middle of nowhere. You found a clue, right? Something you kept to yourself so you could get ahead of us?"

"Like I said -"

"Bullshit!" he replies. "That's bullshit, Jo. You went away for a few hours, and then when you came back you said you'd found it, but I'm not buying the idea that you had some kind of moment of inspiration, okay? You don't have magical powers, so there has to be a method to the way you worked it out."

I stare at him for a moment, and finally I realize that this question is driving him insane. "It's really killing you, isn't it?" I say with a smile. "It's really pissing you off that you don't understand how I did it."

"I don't believe in intuition," he says firmly. "Not like this, anyway. You can't just pull concrete facts out of your ass."

"*I* can," I tell him, enjoying his frustration. "You want to know how I did it? I did what I always do: I just focused real hard on all the facts, and I waited for the answer to pop into my head, and then finally everything just came together and I knew, I mean I really *knew*, the coordinates. After that, I just needed to have total confidence that I was right, and then I had to persuade you and the others to believe me, and the rest was history. We got there just in time. Another few minutes, and he'd probably have been gone forever." I pause for a moment, and finally I can't resist adding a little flourish. "Sometimes, I actually find myself wondering if it's not just a *little* supernatural..."

"Bullshit," he replies firmly.

"I'm serious," I continue. "I just let all the information circulate in my head, and then eventually the answer just pops out. It's like I have a second brain in there, doing all the hard work in the background and -"

"Bullshit!" he says again, this time with more frustration. I've got him right where I want him.

I can't help but smile. "I'm sorry your brain doesn't work that way," I tell him, "but I really think you should be more grateful. I mean, if I *hadn't* had the location just flash into my head like that, you'd still be running around searching for this guy. Hell, he'd be long gone by now. Face it, without my intuition, he wouldn't be in custody right now, so whether you like it or not, and whether you believe it or not, it's real, and you'd better get used to it, 'cause if you stick around, you're gonna need me to save your ass again from time to time."

He stares at me, and I can tell that he's seething with barely-repressed anger.

"You know what?" I continue, turning toward the door. "We're partners, right? So why don't I use my intuition to come up with the guy's name?"

"No fucking way," he replies, putting a hand on my arm. "You're a bullshit merchant, Mason, and that guy's name is gonna be revealed by good, solid, methodical police work."

"So you don't want my help?" I ask, turning back to him and carefully hiding the fact that he's walking right into my trap. Carver has a flaming ego, and it feels good to use it against him.

"Hell, no," he replies. "I'm going back in there, and if it takes me all night and all of tomorrow, I'll get his real name." He pauses. "In fact, I'm gonna call Schumacher tonight and make damn sure that he knows not to let you in with the prisoner. You'll only fuck things up, anyway. Hell, if you spend five minutes with that guy, he'll clam up and never give us what we need!"

"You know," I continue, "if you turn my help down now, there's no going back. I won't come and save your ass later. Everyone'll know that I found the guy, and that you fucked up the interrogation."

"You'll see," he says firmly. "You might have your so-called intuition, Mason, but I have certain skills that are gonna make you realize that we're not even in the same fucking league." He heads to the door, before turning back to me. "And you can wipe that fucking smirk off your face!"

Once he's gone back into the interrogation room, I watch through the one-way mirror for a few more minutes before heading out into the corridor and making my way toward the elevators. I know Jordan Carver doesn't have a hope in hell of getting the guy's real name, but it amuses me to think of him trying. By tomorrow morning, he'll have damn near lost his mind, and by that point he'll have told Schumacher to keep me away from the prisoner. Sure, it'll piss me off if we never learn the guy's real name, but then again, I can take solace in the fact that Carver's reputation is gonna take a nosedive.

No-one can really win in life, but you can pick up little victories along the way.

John

"I've got all the time in the world," he says, sitting calmly on the other side of the desk. "I can sit here all day and all night, and then I can come back again tomorrow, and the next day, and the day after that. Makes no difference to me. For you, though, I think it'd be a hell of a lot easier if you just accepted the inevitable and gave me a name."

"I've given you plenty of names," I tell him.

"You know what I mean."

I can't help but smile. This guy has been attempting to break through to me for hours now, and I think he's actually managed to delude himself into believing that he's getting somewhere. He probably thinks I'll snap and give him what he wants, and I suppose that kind of approach would probably work with most people, but not with me. It's not entirely his fault; I doubt he's ever met anyone like me, but he'll learn soon enough. There's no way in hell I'm ever going to give him my real name.

I got rid of my old, 'real' life a long time ago.

We sit in silence for a moment.

"You think you're all that, don't you?" he continues eventually. "You think you've got everything covered."

I lean forward and take a look at his name-tag. "Detective Carver," I say after a moment, leaning back in my chair, "I think you misunderstand the situation. Granted, I intended to drive off into the sunset and start a new life, and I must admit, I'm a little annoyed that you caught me at the last minute. Still, I can see a positive to the current situation. I'm sure you've been through the files in my office, or at least you've started to organize them. Surely you can see by now that I built up quite an impressive empire over the years. That's really what I am, you know. I'm an entrepreneur. I saw a gap in the market, and I -"

"Tell me your name," he says firmly.

I smile.

"What's wrong?" he continues. "Are you ashamed of something? If I find out your name, am I gonna be able to trace it back and learn the truth about you?" He fixes me with a determined stare. "Maybe I could even learn what makes you tick. I'm thinking something pretty bad must have happened to you as a child to make you turn out like this. What's wrong? Did Mom or Dad hurt you? Did they neglect you? Did someone put their hand somewhere they shouldn't?"

"Wouldn't you like to know?" I reply. "The problem with the modern world, Detective Carver, is that there's nowhere left to run. Throughout human history, there has always been a chance for men to abandon their old lives and strike out into the unknown. Sure, most of them probably died pretty quickly, but at least they had the opportunity to start a new life. In the twenty-first century, that basic human right is denied to us. Credit reports, criminal records, social networking... We have no choice but to drag our pasts with us everywhere we go, with no possibility of ever getting free. That's a pretty significant psychological burden, don't you think?" I wait for him to reply, but it appears that I've finally made him think. "I offered a way out for people who wanted to start again," I add. "It's a shame that I had to do it by raising and killing those people, but I think that in this case the end justifies the means."

"Tell me your real name," he replies.

"You don't get it, do you?"

"Tell me your name!"

I can't help but laugh.

"You think this is funny?" he asks.

"Kind of," I reply. "If only you could get past your need to feel morally superior to me, Detective Carver, you'd realize that I'm right. You're focusing on my name, but that's completely immaterial; in fact, if I gave you the information you're after, I'd be undermining my own beliefs." I pause for a moment, amused by the look of irritation on his face. "Please try to understand," I continue, "that if -"

"Tell me your name," he says again, this time getting to his feet as if he thinks it might help to tower above me.

"No," I reply calmly.

"Like I said," he continues, "I've got all the time in the world to stay here until you realize that you need to cooperate."

I shake my head.

"Tell me your name!" he says yet again, this time raising his voice almost to the level of a shout.

"You can try all the techniques in your little book," I reply calmly, "but none of them will work. I'm taking a moral stance here, Detective Carver. You wear your name proudly on a little tag, and I keep mine hidden away deep in the darkest recesses of my mind. We're opposites, really, aren't we? In a way. I mean, can't you see things from my point of view? Don't you even have, for example, an embarrassing middle name? Something you'd rather keep back from the world?"

"Go to hell," he replies, "you smug little bastard."

"You look tired," I tell him. "Maybe we should pick this up tomorrow."

Sitting down, he leans back in his chair, folds his arms and stares at me.

"You think this is going to work?" I ask, raising an amused eyebrow.

No reply.

"Fine," I continue with a sigh, "if you want to waste your time and mine, we can have a staring contest." I wait for him to say something, but he clearly thinks the silent treatment will work. Sighing again, I simply meet his gaze and await his next move. It's a little tiring to be constantly badgered like this, and I believe it might take quite some time for him to finally give up; still, I guess time is the one thing I have in abundance now that I've been caught. These idiots might have managed to track me down, but they'll never, ever learn my real name.

It'll be amusing to watch Detective Carver try, though.

"Tell me your name," he says again, getting to his feet. I swear to God, he can't decide what to do next; he keeps switching from one strategy to another. "Just tell me," he adds. "Get it over with."

I smile.

"Tell me your name!" he shouts, slamming his fist against the table. "Tell me your goddamn fucking name!"

Joanna Mason

"Hang on!" I call out as I get out of bed. Making my way across the darkened room, with sunlight peeking through the closed drapes, I somehow contrive to trip over my own shoes and land with a thud on the floor. Sighing, I get to my feet, slip into my old clothes from yesterday and make my way to the front door.

Peering through the peephole, I see that Dawson is standing out in the corridor.

"I was wondering when you'd be in touch," I say, forcing a smile as I open the door. "Long time, no see, stranger."

"So how did you do it?" he asks.

"How did I do what?" I reply, still feeling as if I'm not quite awake. "I've done so many brilliant things lately, it's hard to -"

"How did you find that place out in the middle of nowhere?"

I shrug. "Intuition."

"No," he replies. "That's what you told Jordan Carver and Schumacher and all the other guys, but I'm not buying it. I know how your famous intuition works, Jo. You take in a load of information, you process it somewhere in your subconscious mind, and then suddenly you spew out the answer, but that's not what happened this time. You didn't have any information to process. All you had was hundreds of square miles of land, and the vague hunch that there might be something hidden out there."

I open my mouth to reply to him, but I'm not quite sure what to say.

"So how did you do it?" he asks again, this time with a faint smile.

"Come in," I mutter, turning and making my way through to the front room, where all my papers and files from the past couple of days are strewn across every surface. "Sorry about the mess," I add, rubbing my eyes, "but you've been here before. You know how things get sometimes."

"Thanks for getting me home the other night," he says as he comes through to join me, picking his way through the piles of folders on the floor. "I'm sorry you had to see me like that."

"You were pretty wasted," I point out.

"Yeah, well..." He pauses. "Whatever. But come on, Jo. Help me out. This whole thing is driving me crazy, and I *know* you didn't use intuition alone to find that facility."

I stare at him for a moment. "You remember the other night when you were drunk?" I say eventually. "You remember how I found you in that rundown little bar, even though you'd deliberately gone somewhere out-of-the-way because you wanted to be left alone?"

"Don't think that wasn't intensely annoying," he replies.

"I went to hundreds of bars before I found you," I continue. "It was the only way. Fuck, my feet were aching by the end of it, and I almost gave up several times, but somehow I pushed on and eventually I spotted you slumped in a booth." I wait for him to say something, but he doesn't seem to be getting the link. Smiling, I indicate the papers on my desk. "You were right," I add. "Sometimes good old-fashioned leg-work is the best approach."

He walks over to the desk and picks up some of the print-outs.

"Official planning records for every structure out there in the wilderness," I tell him. "If anyone built so much as a chicken shed, it's in those files."

"But the place where that guy was holding the people... That wasn't in the records."

"Exactly," I continue, opening the lid of my laptop to show him the mapping app I've been using. "If intuition played a part in this, it was only that it made me realize that this guy had tried to hide his business away from prying eyes. So I used one of those online aerial photo sites to check for anything that wasn't listed in the planning documents."

He stares at the screen for a moment. "No," he says eventually, turning to me. "No way, Jo. The area you would have had to cover... You'd have had to sit and look at page after page for -"

"Three days, twenty hours and nineteen minutes," I reply, interrupting him. "With no sleep, barely any food, and just a few pee breaks. Plus a few trips out, but I printed off maps and took them with me. No rest for the wicked, huh?"

He pauses. "You're telling me that you checked the entire area manually?"

"There was some luck involved," I add. "I was barely a third of the way through when I spotted a little smudge in the middle of nowhere. I zoomed in, and there it was. A fairly large building that didn't appear on any official documentation."

"That's insane," he replies. "I mean, any normal person would've lost their mind."

Nodding, I can't help but feel a little proud of myself. "In case you haven't noticed," I add with a yawn, "it's kinda taken it out of me. I think I have a lot of sleeping to do. Jordan Carver can handle the processing of that jerk."

"Jordan Carver's not doing too well," Dawson replies. "He's been interrogating him for days now, and he still can't get his real name."

"He never will," I reply.

"Schumacher's tried to pull him out, but Carver..." He pauses. "I think he's going a little strange. Sometimes you can even hear him down there, shouting and screaming at the guy, but he's not getting anywhere. I think Schumacher's thinking of putting him on forced leave for a week or two, just so his sanity doesn't crumble."

"I offered to help," I point out with a shameless grin, "but I think Detective Carver was very keen to perform the interrogation without my help. Anyway, he's on a hiding to nothing. The guy won't give his name up, and even if he did, what's the point? It's not what matters. What matters is..." I pause for a moment as I try to work out what, in this whole mess, really *does* matter. "Those men and women are going to need a lot of help," I say eventually. "They probably won't ever recover fully from the way they were brought up."

"At least they're alive," Dawson points out. "While they're alive, there's hope, right? If not for all of them, then at least for some. It'll take a while, but they might be able to lead normal lives."

"It's false hope, though," I point out. "You've seen what they're like. That asshole kept them chained up like animals. There's no coming back from that."

He smiles, but it's a sad smile, worn down over the years. "There's always hope, Jo," he says after a moment. "It's a lot harder to live when you don't even have hope."

"Did you come here for anything specific?" I ask, hoping to change the subject. "I mean, now that I've given away my trade secrets, I kinda need to get back to sleep. I was having a lovely dream about unicorns and ponies and all that shit before you came banging on my door."

"I guess I'll see you around, then," he replies.

I nod, before following him back out to the hallway.

"So how are things going?" I ask. "How's Elaine?"

"She's good," he replies.

"And..." I pause, waiting for him to tell me about the baby, but instead a kind of uncomfortable silence descends; I have no idea whether or not he knows that Elaine told me. "I mean," I continue after a moment, "is everything going okay? You know, with the..." I take a deep breath, hoping that he might get the hint. "Last time, you told me she was pregnant, so -"

"Right," he replies, looking distinctly awkward. "Yeah. Everything's... You know, ticking along. There's no rush."

"You thought about names?" I ask, suddenly feeling as if I'm about to cry.

"Not really," he mutters. "Names aren't that important, not at this stage. We've just got to keep on pushing forward and..." He pauses. "We're just hoping for the best, overall," he adds finally.

With that, he turns and heads toward the elevators, leaving me to push the door shut and stand alone in my apartment. Dawson has now had two opportunities to tell me that Elaine lost the baby, and instead he's kept the news to himself. I guess the bitch was right: Dawson thinks I'd make jokes about it, so he'd rather not talk to me about anything that involves real emotions. I can kind of understand why he's reached that conclusion, although I can't help but wonder if there's some way that I can make him see that I've changed. Then again, I don't know if I really *have* changed.

Trying to ignore the dull ache in my chest, I turn and head back toward the bedroom. Tomorrow morning, I've got my first meeting with the doctor who's running the experimental treatment program, so I guess I need to get some rest. After all, maybe there's still a chance that I'll have a miraculous recovery. Like Dawson said, everyone needs hope, although sometimes I think I was better off when I was absolutely certain that I was going to die.

Sometimes, hope is just cruel.

Epilogue

Thirty-five years ago

"Hey! Get the fuck back here!"

Stopping at the intersection, I glance over my shoulder and see that he's still chasing after me. I turn and run, almost getting hit by a car before reaching the other side of the road. It's late, and people are starting to flood out of a nearby movie theater; the crowd slows me for a moment and I have to push past them, all the while glancing over my shoulder to make sure that my father hasn't caught up with me. In this sea of people, it's impossible to really pick anyone out, but I'm convinced that he must be somewhere nearby.

I've come this far.

I can't let him catch me now.

Ducking beneath the crowd, I get onto my hands and knees and crawl past all the legs of oblivious theater patrons. I'm really starting to panic now, and I'm convinced that at any moment I'll feel a hand grab the back of my shirt and haul me back to reality. Still, I know I have to take this chance, because I can't risk being forced to go home. Now that he knows I want to get away, my father's going to be a thousand times harsher with me, and I knew when I left the house tonight that I was crossing a line. I just have to -

Suddenly I feel a foot slamming into my side, and I drop down onto my chest. The crowd parts and I'm grabbed from behind, hauled up onto my feet before being turned around so that I come face to face with him.

"Where are you going?" my father asks, his voice filled with restrained, white-hot fury. "Didn't you hear me calling you, John?"

I stare at him, unable to summon any words. I'd hoped that I'd never, ever have to see him again, and now he's got me in his grasp. It took so long to summon up the courage to get away from him, and I don't think I can do it again. This is it. I tried to escape, and I failed. For the rest of my life, I'm going to have to live in his shadow.

"Come on," he continues, holding me by the arm and pulling me through the crowd. "We need to talk about this."

I try to keep up, but as I stumble on a crooked paving slab, one of my shoes comes off. I try to stop and grab it, but my father pulls me along.

"Wait!" I call out.

"What the fuck is it now?" he shouts, yanking me over to him.

"My shoe!"

Sighing, he lets go of me for a moment and hurries back to my lost shoe, before turning and kicking it at me. I put a hand up to shield my face, and the shoe bounces harmlessly off my chest and lands on the sidewalk. Instinctively, I step back into it, and seconds later my father grabs my arm and continues to pull me along.

"Try to keep your fucking shoes on," he says firmly. "It shouldn't be that hard, or did you never learn to tie your goddamn laces?"

I want to reply to him, to tell him to go to hell, but I'm already starting to cry and I know that whenever I try to stand up for myself, I end up sounding like an idiot. It's better if I just keep my thoughts to myself and wait for him to lose this temper. After all, although I've never seen him become truly violent, I've always been worried that there's an extra edge to him, and I'm terrified that one day he'll go beyond the point of no return.

"So why don't you tell me what this is all about?" he asks as he marches me across the road. "Huh? Where do you think you're going?"

I open my mouth to reply, but the truth is, I don't know what to say. All the explanations I came up with earlier now seem so foolish, and I know he'd just rip my ideas apart. Ten minutes ago, I thought I was on the brink of escaping from my old life, and now I realize that I was just binding myself closer than ever. I hoped, for a brief moment, that I was smart and capable, and now it's clear that I'm just a dumb fantasist who gets these crazy ideas and then gets carried away.

"You really make it hard sometimes," he continues as we get closer to his car. "I try so hard with you, John, but it's as if you really don't care. I blame your mother, of course. She's kept you in a kind of bubble, and you've got no idea about how the real world works. Sometimes I really worry about how you're going to get through life."

"I'm sorry," I whimper, with tears in my eyes.

"Being sorry isn't enough," he replies, pushing me against the side of the car before walking around and pulling his keys from his pockets. "We're going to have to sort you out, boy. It's not too late. You're still young, and we can fix the way you see things."

As he gets into the car, I take a deep breath and try to prepare myself for the drive home. I'm well aware that I've probably made a rod for my own back, and I've got no doubt that my father is going to punish me when we get back to the house. Of course, I could always turn and run, and maybe I'd be luckier this time, but I guess I just have to accept that for now, I'm not going to be able to get away. One day, though, I'll escape from my father, and I'll leave everything behind so that I can start a new life.

I'll disappear completely and I won't let anyone ever find me again. In fact, I can already feel a new person bubbling away in my heart; someone smarter and stronger and more intelligent, someone who's ready to make his mark on the world.

ALSO AVAILABLE

The Night Girl

When she starts her new job as a night shift assistant, Juliet Collier has no idea that she's about to meet a mysterious entity that lurks in an abandoned part of the building.

Soon, Juliet finds herself granted a gift that means she can kill indiscriminately, and apparently without consequences. Meanwhile, eleven years earlier, a young Juliet makes a terrible mistake that sets her on a dark course.

This is the story of a girl whose decisions lead her to a devastating end-point, as she struggles to reconcile the voices in her head with the reality in front of her eyes.

ALSO AVAILABLE

Devil's Briar

In the remote wilderness of Colorado, Bill and Paula Mitchell discover an entire lost town. Devil's Briar was abandoned many years ago, and has fallen into disrepair. But it soon becomes clear that the town contains some special and highly unusual qualities, and that elements of the past are seeping through into the present.

As she tries to get to the bottom of the mystery, Paula finds herself drawn deeper and deeper into the bizarre time loop that keeps the entire town trapped in eternity. Soon it becomes clear that nothing in Devil's Briar will ever be the same again, and that two time periods are merging with horrific consequences.

ALSO AVAILABLE

Broken Blue

Returning home for her father's funeral, Elly Bradshaw soon finds herself drawn into the dangerous world of billionaire Mark Douglas.

Although she finds Mark irresistible, Elly learns he hides a dark secret. She's quickly pulled deep into a dark sexual game that threatens to change the way she views the world forever. Meanwhile, back in the late nineteenth century, another set of players are caught up in the same game.

Tortured by his role as Mr. Blue, Edward Lockhart sets out to end the game forever. His failure, however, results in the arrival of Jonathan Pope onto the scene. Cynical and only interested in a payday, Pope begins to investigate the shadowy trio of players who keep the game alive.

ABOUT THE AUTHOR

Amy Cross writes horror, paranormal and fantasy novels, although she sometimes stumbles into other genres.

She has been writing all her life, but only started publishing her work in 2011. Since then, she has sold more than 200,000 copies of books such as Asylum, Dark Season and The Girl Who Never Came Back. She lives in the UK.

Printed in Great Britain
by Amazon